D1742115

PRAISE FOR UNBROKEN KINGDOM

Unbroken Kingdom oozes adventure and excitement, and Lorie Gurnett's masterful storytelling, the nonstop action, and the many holding-your-breath moments keep you turning the pages in this engrossing tale. You will be blown away by the author's creativity in developing imaginative, unique, and quirky creatures with magical powers, one of whom made me laugh out loud with his sarcastic sense of humor. However, beyond the excitement of this stunning fantasy and classic battle between good and evil are deeper threads running throughout the novel, which are based on Biblical truths. They highlight the complexity of human relationships, show us that fear and self-doubt can rob us of our true purpose in life, but courage and determination in the face of those fears can strengthen and refine us to be who we were created to be. We learn that forgiveness is freeing, there is hope for healing despite past hurts or trauma, we are stronger together, and love and righteousness are the ultimate armor. *Unbroken Kingdom* is a tour de force that you will not want to miss.

— SANDRA E. DUCLOS, PH.D., CLINICAL PSYCHOLOGIST, AUTHOR: *WAITING FOR LUIGI*

You have no idea how much I needed this in my life-right now I am at a crossroads and I was not even aware. This book sparks so much life into my very daily life- this is an incredible and powerful book that has brought me to my knees in prayer! This is a God-given book. Holy as He is Holy. Thank you. Thank you for being His vessel.

— HEATHER CONGO, FORMER FIREFIGHTER AND HOMESCHOOLING MOM

Lorie Gurnett's second book in the *Treasure Kingdom* series continues the saga of faith and fantasy in her signature style as it uses Biblical references to support the gospel message through storytelling. If you are a believer who loves the idea of incorporating spiritual truths into daily life, and if you love the power of story, Lorie's books provide hope and inspiration for you. Her characters are worth rooting for, and her messages lead to victory every time.

— NANETTE O'NEAL, AUTHOR: *A DOORWAY BACK TO FOREVER* SERIES

The first book, *Treasure Kingdom*, is a wonderful read … it has a fantastic purpose that every reader can find as they explore the story and relate it to their life. The second book has the same purpose– even more so. My only regret is that the story didn't end—now I must wait for the next book to come out!

—JOHN W. SCHLITT, LEAD SINGER OF PETRA

Fear can hold you in bondage, disorient you, and rob you of focus. Throughout this story of courage, determination, and battles within Lorie shows her readers there is hope in the shattered life of abuse by overcoming forgiveness and refining who you are. There is courage to be found as you face your fears, and this book will truly inspire you to do so.

— Niccie Kliegl, Owner of Fulfill Your Legacy Author, Speaker, and Talk Show Host of *Living the Sweet Spot*

Lorie spins another gripping fantasy adventure that confronts real-life challenges and pain. She brings us memorable heroes who excel and fail, much like every committed believer in the battles of life. She employs Scripture throughout as the keys to unlock secrets and the Sword to win victories. Her characters remind us that we don't need to be held captive by our weaknesses and mistakes; we can overcome by putting our trust in God and obeying Him. You'll be blessed, challenged, and entertained by *Unbroken Kingdom*.

— Sandra Fram, Author: *Wings in the Storm*

Woven around Biblical truths, Lorie shows her readers there is hope in the shattered life of abuse through forgiveness and by refining who you are. There is courage to be found as you face your fears.

— Kary Oberbrunner, CEO of Igniting Souls, Author: *Your Secret Name, Day Job to Dream Job, Elixir Project*, and *Unhackable*

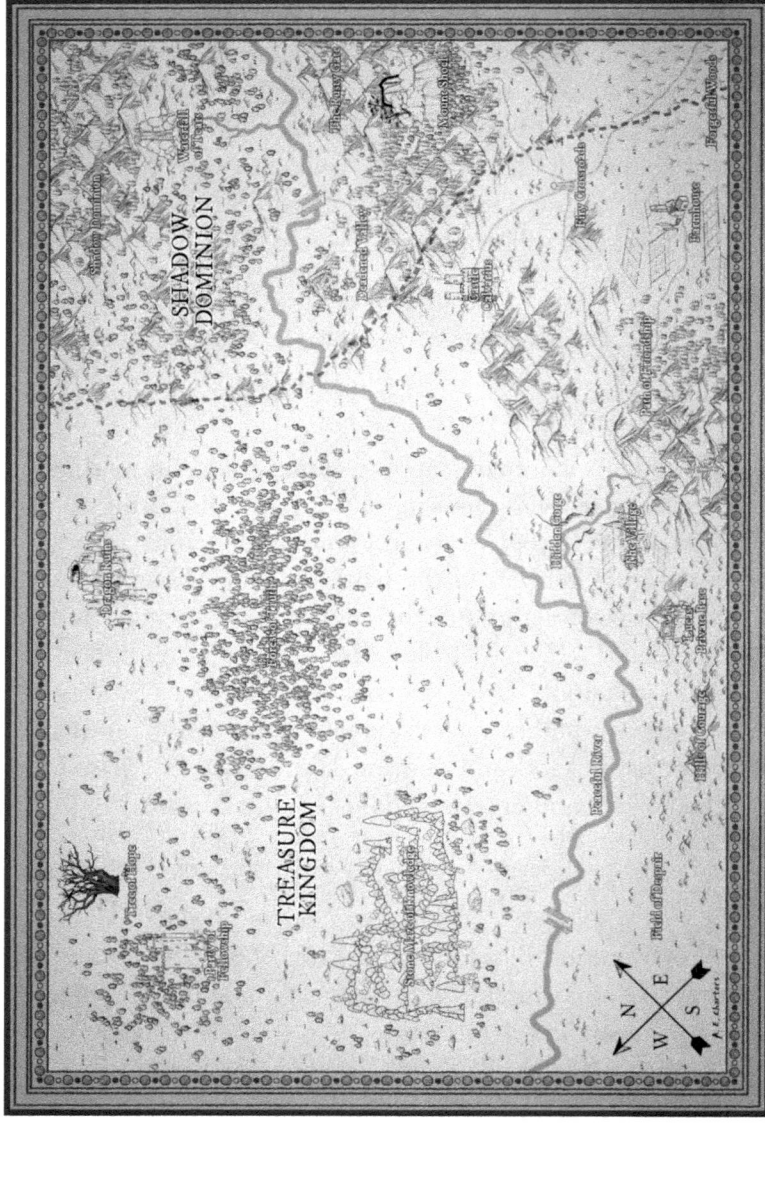

UNBROKEN KINGDOM

LORIE GURNETT

Unbroken Kingdom

AUTHOR ELITE AWARDS
First Prize Winner

LORIE GURNETT

"STAND WHERE IT HAS ALREADY BEEN BURNT."

Unbroken Kingdom © 2021 Lorie Gurnett

Printed in the United States of America

Published by Author Academy Elite

PO Box 43, Powell, OH 43035

www.authoracademyelite.com

All rights reserved. This book contains material protected under International and Federal Copyright Laws and Treaties. Any unauthorized reprint or use of this material is prohibited. No part of this book may be reproduced or transmitted in any form or by any means, electronic or mechanical, including photocopying, recording, or by any information storage and retrieval system, without express written permission from the author.

LCCN: 2021902268

Paperback ISBN: 978-1-64746-714-2

Hardcover ISBN: 978-1-64746-715-9

Ebook ISBN: 978-1-64746-716-6

Available in paperback, hardcover, e-book, and audiobook coming soon

All Scripture quotations, unless otherwise indicated, are taken from the Holy Bible, New International Version, ESV. Copyright 1973, 1978, 1984 by Biblical, Inc. TM. All rights reserved worldwide.

Book Cover Designed by: Jervelyn Bonifacio

I dedicated this book to my mom, Doris Moir:
you always believed in me even when I didn't.
Your prayers and support helped me to
stay focused and to trust God for the outcome.

To my mother in-law, Irene Gurnett:
Your strength of character and servant heart
remind me daily how important the human heart is
and that everyone is worth fighting for.

To my Husband Merv, my daughter, Aurora, and my son, Logan:
Never stop living and pursuing your dreams.
You will be surprised what God will choose to do through you.

ACKNOWLEDGMENTS

Thank you to Mervyn and Logan Gurnett for your silly one liner's, quirky sense of humour, and creative view on life. You truly made the creation of the silly new character of Chester and made him come alive. Thank you to Andrew Chambers for your inspiring messages of hope: you helped define the meaning of standing where it has already been burnt so life flames of discouragement, trauma, fear, and self-hatred will not harm you. You brought meaning to finding one's courage as you face your fears. Thank you, Dan Sudfield, for faithfully speaking God's truth every Sunday: you inspired me greatly through the study of Philippians.

Thank you to all my beta readers who helped with the flow, content, editing, and story plot in the creation of this novel: Cordie Moir, Heather Congo, Sandra Fram, Stacey Armstrong, Sandra E Duclos, April Gurnett, Monika Polefka-Proulx, and Rena Groot. Thank you for the endorsements: John W. Schlitt, Nanette O'Neal, Niccie Kliegl, and Kary Oberbrunner. Thank you to all my artists: Kimberly Maloy, Rosella Ormshaw, Veronica Zhenya, Zahidul_Joy, and thanks to Ae_Charters for creating my map for me. Thank you,

Author Academy Elite, for supporting, training, encouraging, and believing in me and the message God has placed on my heart tc share. Everyone can find their courage as they face their fears. As scary as life challenges may be, there is hope and truth to be found both within yourself and in the courage to keep moving forward. Never give up on yourself or your dreams.

CONTENTS

PROLOGUE

*L*ife seemed so dark when death hung before them. Grief might win the battle unless they learned their true strength within and became an immovable force. Senora and Josiah risked it all as they found the greatest treasure and learned its value. Sam, the Red Dragon, and the Tall Bearded Man guided them through their adventure. They were reminded that friendship was a bond, but family was unbreakable and to never give up. The battle raged, and they were forced to choose sides. In a kingdom where good and evil are unrecognizable, who stood for truth, and who was only seeking power and control?

As they fought to free Princess Delores, Queen Scarlett, Katerina, and Crystal from Lucas's bondage, they learned the true strength they held within. Their hope grew even when darkness surrounded them like a veil.

PART 1: THE RECKONING

1

DECEPTION ARISES

*R*obert paced the floor and stared impatiently at the clock as time seemed to crawl toward the end of his shift. He turned to busy himself with straightening some product on the gas station shelf. Robert stared out the front window at children playing street hockey and vehicles driving by, longing for his chance for freedom. Robert's mind spun over the wave of emotions weighing him down. The bell rang as someone pulled up to the gas station. Robert ran out to greet them. "Need a fill?" Robert asked as he reached for the gas nozzle.

Senora turned her head and smiled. "Hey, Bobbie, I didn't know you were working today. I just need twenty dollars in the tank today. Just enough to last until payday. How are you doing? I haven't seen you in a while."

"Nora? Yeah, well…" Robert stammered as he started to put gas in Senora's vehicle. He nervously ran his fingers through his wavy hair. "I have been picking up extra shifts."

"Oh, it isn't to avoid someone, is it?" Senora busied herself with digging into her backpack.

"Avoiding someone? What do you mean?"

"Isn't your dad coming up on parole next month? Have

you gone to visit him?" Senora searched Robert's blank expression.

He pulled the gas nozzle out and returned it to the pump. "Ok, that'll be twenty dollars." He nervously ran his fingers through his hair and shifted his weight.

Senora handed him a twenty-dollar bill and an envelope.

"What's this?"

"An invitation. I want you and your mom to attend my graduation."

"Huh. It's that time already?"

"It would mean the world to me."

"I don't know. Will Jo be there?"

"Of course, silly. Jo is attending with his new fiancée."

"That sly guy. He actually found someone to put up with him?"

"Now, now. It takes a special person to do that."

"Special huh?"

"Be nice! He would love to introduce you to her."

"So, you like her?"

"She's quite nice. They're only able to come down for the week."

"Why only a week?"

"Sylvia has a short break from nursing school."

"A nurse? That explains a lot."

"Oh, stop teasing. Jo took some time off work so they could attend. I don't see them much. Please say you'll come."

Robert shifted his feet. "I'll have to see if I can get the time off. I'll let you know. Oh, Nora, thanks."

"For what?"

"For the invitation and for thinking of me." Robert forced himself to make eye contact.

"Of course. You're like family to me. You've taken on Trevor's role in my life. Especially since Jo went off to college. Thank you."

"For what?" Robert wiped some sweat off the back of his neck with a paper towel.

"Looking out for me." Senora started up her car and drove away. Robert watched her until she drove out of sight. He frowned when he saw Mark pull up in his clunky, old truck.

"What're you doing? Just standing around? My dad doesn't pay you to stand in the sun." Mark barked at him.

"Hey, Mark. I just finished gassin' someone up." Robert said, "Are you here to take over?"

"Whatever. I guess so. You should stop being lazy," Mark said as Robert followed him into the gas station.

"What? Lazy? I've been working steadily all day. Yeah, it's been slow, but I've kept busy." Robert flexed his muscles and pursed his lips into a thin line.

"Yeah, right. Look how dusty this place is."

"Dusty! You do realize it's May? Everything's dusty in May."

"That's no excuse," Mark replied with a sly smirk, almost daring Robert to say something.

Robert hung his head in defeat and slumped his shoulders. "Fine, Mark."

"You may go. See you tomorrow." Robert clenched his fists as he marched out of the gas station. He turned to the side of the building, out of sight, his rage ready to blow a gasket and punched the stucco wall several times. Each punch sent several small rocks cutting and embedding themselves into his knuckles. Taking a deep breath, he climbed into his truck and failed at cleaning his hand with a napkin he pulled from his glovebox. He pulled out of the parking lot and headed for the local diner.

As he entered The Diner, he could see Senora sitting with some friends in a booth. He tried to sneak past her without being seen. Senora jumped in front of him and stared. "What happened to your hand?"

7

"Oh, stop your fussin'," Robert snapped and pulled away from her. "I can take care of myself." He turned and stormed into the men's bathroom, leaving Senora worried and puzzled. She slumped back in her seat, her face showered with frustration.

"Why do you bother with that nut case?" Gloria asked as she twirled her finger around a strand of red curly hair. She reached for a French fry and carefully took a bite, trying to avoid getting it caught in her braces.

"You take that back. He's not a nut case."

"Whatever you say. All I know is he's always ready for a fight, and he never lets anyone close. Why do you even bother with him?"

"There's more to him than you know. I know him better than any of you. I'd do anything to help him. I only wish I knew how." Senora stared at the bathroom door, looking for the right words to reach Robert once he came back out.

Robert stomped toward the bathroom sink and turned on the water. He rubbed and pulled the embedded stones from his hand. "Stupid Robert, you did it again. You need to get your anger under control." Looking up at his reflection he thought, *I hardly recognize myself anymore. So much has changed over the last two years. I know Nora means well; I would die to protect her. She's like the little sister I never had. I'd fight for her for Trevor's sake.* He slammed his fist on the counter, instantly regretting it as more pain rushed up his arm. He pulled out handfuls of paper towels from the dispenser, wrapped his hand with them, and took a deep breath. *At least pain reminds me I'm still alive.* He winced and turned toward the door. Pulling the door open he sighed. *Well, here it comes. Time to face Nora.* He pulled the door open as Senora jumped to her feet.

"Bobbie, can we talk?" Senora asked as she approached him cautiously.

"I guess so," Robert replied as Senora motioned to a nearby empty booth.

"Don't mind her. She has her own issues." Senora waved her friend off.

"Gotta love fiery redheads," Robert responded, attempting a chuckle.

Senora rested her elbows on the table and stared at Robert. "So, you going to tell me what happened?" she asked as she stared at Robert's hand.

"You know, the usual. Mark being Mark and me being me."

The waitress approached. "What can I getcha, or do you want menus?"

"I'll just have an iced tea," Robert said.

"Ok, one iced tea, what about you? Or are you just taking your order from the other table?" The waitress asked as she turned to Senora.

"I have my peppermint tea, but can I have a refill on my hot water?" Senora asked, sending a pleasant smile her way. The waitress just winked and walked away.

"I don't want to take time away from your friends," Robert said.

"Nonsense. I can see them all day at school. What's really going on? Is it your dad?"

"Why do you keep bringing that loser up?" Robert yelled and instantly regretted the idea as he looked around The Diner. All eyes shot in their direction.

"As you were. Nothing to see here. You all have your own lives to worry about," the waitress announced as she handed Robert his iced tea and Senora a fresh kettle of hot water.

"Thank you," Senora whispered as everyone returned to their conversations. The waitress smiled and mouthed the words *you're welcome*.

"Sorry for yelling. You know the pain and chaos that man brings. He destroyed my life and yours," Robert grumbled.

"Yes, but he has been in prison for his crimes."

"Not all his crimes. Mom never came forward about

Trevor's death. He's only doing time for armed robbery. He deserves as much pain as he caused. I hate him."

"Haven't you ever heard that bad company corrupts good character? When you allow angry and negative thoughts to surround you, you will start to view everything as bad." Senora reached for Robert's hand.

Robert flinched away and stared at his glass of iced tea. "Why do you bother with me?"

"I see great potential in you. I believe in you just as Trevor did. The most important things is to learn from your mistakes, and not dwell on them."

"I know, what you say does hold great weight, but pain reminds me I'm still alive, that I still feel, even when I don't want to. How did you get to be so smart?"

Senora stared off as she remembered her friends, Sam and Delores, but Robert wasn't ready to hear about them—and she wasn't ready to tell him. She sighed and simply sipped at her tea.

"What're you in such deep thought about?"

"Oh, just pondering your question. I guess I've been growing in my faith and in what I've been learning at school."

"Ok, keep your secrets." Senora was distracted as Gloria approached them.

"Sorry to interrupt, but I'm going home. See you at rehearsal tomorrow, Nora?" Gloria asked.

"Yeah, I'll be there. I hope you have a good day." Senora replied.

"What rehearsal?" Robert asked.

"Oh, grad rehearsal. We're going over our speeches and practicing the routine of the order we enter for the ceremony," Senora said.

"Oh, fun." Robert rolled his eyes. Senora playfully punched Robert's shoulder.

"Whatever," Gloria replied as she bit her lip and left The Diner.

"She really doesn't like me, does she?" Robert asked.

"I think she's just nervous about grad and the decisions that are before her."

"I get that. At least she has decisions."

"Do you regret not attending college?"

Robert stared at the closed door as he pondered Senora's question.

He turned and stared intently at Senora so hard she squirmed uncomfortably. "Sorry to make you nervous, but that's a heavy question. One I'm not willin to answer at this time."

Senora fiddled with her teacup and gasped as she let out her breath. "I understand. Facing the unknown, myself, I feel the fear and turmoil boiling beneath the surface. But I also understand where my peace comes from. You know we live in a strange and dark world yet as believers in the Lord Jesus Christ we know about the true light."[1]

"What're you talking about? What's the true light?"

"In the midst of a crooked and twisted generation, among whom you shine as lights in the world.[2] So, no matter how dark life gets, God's light will shine through you, surrounding you with that peace. As children of God we have something to be joyful about. Not only has God saved us out of the world we've been brought into this fellowship called the church."[3]

"The church? What has the church ever done for me? I'm an outcast, a reject. I see them looking down their noses at me. They don't want to get their hands dirty. They only tolerate me."

"Not everyone's like that. I admit there're a few, but that just makes them more like you than you realize."

"What? How does that make them like me?"

"You see, ignoring you they don't have to face their own issues. They trap themselves in the comparison game, so they don't have to own up to their mistakes."

Robert leaned back and folded his arms in front of his chest. "Sounds like you're making excuses for them."

"You have to understand: as humans we are not perfect and we do make mistakes. When you dwell on those mistakes, we tend to fail ourselves. A lot of people try to shift blame and point fingers to take the focus off their own failures. We've been saved out of the world through blood of Christ but we've been saved and united into His body; therefore, we're brought into fellowship. This fellowship's something to rejoice about and to relish and not to ever take for granted."[4]

"Take for granted? That's an understatement if I ever heard one. I look at your church and all I see is division, nit-picking, strife, and heartache. Where's the fellowship in that?"

"We can be joyful because our citizenship is in heaven.[5] So even though we're in this world and face many discouragements, we don't belong here. God has a plan for each of us, Bobbie. Trust God for that plan. Don't allow where other people are in their walk with Christ to hinder the direction God's leading you."

Robert finished off the last of his iced tea and threw a five-dollar bill on the table. As he stood to leave, Senora reached for his arm. "Please take the time to think about the importance of unity and fellowship. It is not always easy to go it alone."

"You say a lot, but you don't speak for everyone. I know God loves me, and has forgiven me, but I'm not ready to face their glares." Robert turned to leave. Senora stood and nodded goodbye to the waitress and quickly shuffled after Robert. Robert climbed into his truck when she exited. She ran to the driver's side window.

"I'm sorry if I touched a sore spot. I care about you." Senora said.

"I know, just give me time." Robert sighed as he started up the truck engine.

"Wait, have you thought about coming to my grad?"

"I'll talk to Mom about it."

"I hope you'll come. After grad I'm parking my car, so if you do come can I get a ride to The Diner? We're meeting for supper afterward."

"I can do that. I'll keep you posted. I've got to go." Robert pulled out of the parking lot. Senora stared at the back of his truck until he was out of sight. She subconsciously fiddled with her eagle pendant as her thoughts turned to Sam and Delores.

———

*T*he Red Dragon circled the castle's perimeter. Slowly she landed in the courtyard, quickly transformed back into her human form, and turned to face her friend. "Princess Delores," she said, as the two ladies embraced in a gentle hug.

"Any news on your patrol this morning?" Delores asked. Sam stared off toward the western border of Treasure Kingdom. "What is it?"

"I don't know, but there is a heaviness in the air this morning. Something is pulling at my heart. Almost like darkness is screaming for freedom." A dull roar of thunder ripped off in the west.

"Strange, Lucas is still in bondage. These last two years have been full of peace and unity." Delores shrugged off Sam's warnings, turned and pulled out a scarf and her sword, casually cleaning it.

"I just feel the floodgates are going to overflow. Darkness can only stay in bondage for so long. Where's Queen Scarlett?" The two ladies jumped as another clap of thunder sounded off in the distance, a little closer and louder than the first.

"She's in communion."

"Communion? Communion with who?" Sam looked over her shoulder at the throne room window.

"You know who. The Silver Dragon."

"How can she trust that monster?" Sam questioned and as anger glared in her eyes, she crossed her arms and stomped her foot.

"Steady your anger. Let me ask you this: When you're one with another, while the other is within, they almost replace your subconscious. How can you silence their voice?" Delores asked.

"That's what worries me. The Silver Dragon's united with Lucas and they both thrive on deception. How do you know the Silver Dragon's not corrupting Queen Scarlett again?"

"Hold your tongue. Queen Scarlett's aware of the former deception; she's guarded in her conversations."

"But how do you know? You can't hear their conversations since these communions happen within Queen Scarlett's mind." Sam stared up toward the throne room window. Delores placed her hand on Sam's shoulder.

"We have to trust the Saviour's protection and the queen's rule."

"I know, but I also carry great warning within my soul."

———※———

Queen Scarlett sat calmly on her throne with her eyes closed, "Hear me, Silver Dragon," she whispered. Scarlett found herself standing face to face with the Silver dragon in a white room.

"What is it now?" The Silver Dragon circled around Scarlett as smoke rose from the dragon's nostrils.

"We have a depth of fellowship within my soul," Scarlett reminded her and she straightened her posture and stared confidently in the dragon's eyes.

"You sure delight in reminding me we're now one, don't

you? I feel your hands at my throat." The dragon sends two rippling blasts of flames on either side of Scarlett.

"Remember it was Lucas who betrayed you by giving me the elixir," Scarlett reminded her as she stepped closer and grabbed her finger in the middle of the dragon's nose. "I no longer see you as a threat. I see you as a friend. We were both deceived and now we have to learn to unite together as one."

The dragon shifted and body slammed Scarlett to one side. "Friend? Is this like keeping your friends close and your enemies closer?"

Scarlett braced herself and wrestled the dragon's tail. "No, it's not like that at all. I have been praying for you."

The dragon violently shook her tail as Scarlett slide to the very end. "I don't want your prayers."

Scarlett let go and stood firm. She brushed her clothes smooth. "I ask that you grow and learn."

"Learn? What could you teach me?" The dragon thrust her tail into Scarlett's chest, knocking the wind out of her.

Scarlett rested her hands on her knees regaining her composure. "You can't hurt me in here without hurting yourself."

The dragon staggered and let out a huge gasp for air.

Scarlett stood firm once more and stepped closer to the dragon again. "You're on the way between conversion to completion."[6]

"Completion of what? My destruction?" The dragon let's out an ear-deafening roar and then swayed. Scarlett swayed and covered her ears.

Through the ringing in her ears, Scarlett refused to back down. "We all need God's help in order to make it."

The dragon pawed at her own ears to fight of this unfamiliar ringing. "Make what?"

"You see, there's still hope. There's still light. I believe that God has not given up on you. We all have our own struggles and sin. Nobody's perfect on their own we are all flawed. No matter how hard they fight for it. We all need prayer. We all need to be on a progression as we go from conversion to completion. I press on toward the goal for the prize of the upward call of God in Christ Jesus.[7] You see it was not a mistake that you and I were united in this way."

The dragon wrapped her tail around Scarlett's leg and hung her upside down. "I think Lucas would speak otherwise on this matter." The Silver Dragon's words weighed heavily upon Scarlett as the dragon dropped her with a thud.

Scarlett pushed the dragon to one side as she stood. "You need to sever that bond. You deserve to be free too." She clenched her fists, preparing for another fight if necessary.

"You don't know what you are asking me to do." The dragon shook the ground as she lay to one side.

"He'll listen to you." Scarlett placed her hand on the dragon's shoulder.

"Don't be so sure of yourself. You've had Lucas in chains for two years now. He has had a long time to plan and plot." The dragon looked as Scarlett with a smirk as a tear escaped from her eye.

"But you're his Silver Enchantress. You've been connected for decades." The dragon leaped into the air and flew in a figure eight formation before landing in front of Scarlett.

"Exactly, decades. What makes you think that two years of being within you would change my mind after decades of love bondage with Lucas?" The dragon pinned Scarlett with her front paws. Scarlett pricked the dragon's paws as they both cried out in pain.

"You and I both know that truth is stronger than lies. You have seen firsthand the power of truth." Scarlett kicked her feet and jumped up into a standing position.

The dragon lowered her head in defeat. "I'll speak with him. Just be prepared for what you might unleash." The Dragon spoke each word with great conviction.

———⟨⟨⟨⟩⟩⟩———

*R*obert pulled up to his old house on the edge of town. He took a deep breath before entering. His mom met him at the door. "How was work today?" she asked.

"One word. Mark," Robert growled.

"You shouldn't allow him to get to you." He glared at her and walked to the fridge. "You know, not everyone's bad."

Slamming the fridge door, Robert stared intently at her, almost daring her to continue. "I know life hasn't been easy for us. It was kind of Mark's dad to give you a job at the gas station."

"Why do you feel the need to defend everyone's actions? I mean, you're not Jesus. You can't save everyone," Robert snapped at her.

Looking down at his clenched fists, she reached for his hand. "What happened?"

Pulling away, Robert quickly grumbled, "Don't."

Shying away, she slowly looked up at him. "I'm going to see him on the weekend."

Robert stepped forward and punched a hole in the wall beside her head.

"Hit me, if it makes you feel better," she demanded.

His face fell and he turned away. "Why do you keep letting him back into your life? You know, I'm not him."

"I didn't say you were." She reached for his shoulder but he flinched away.

"Whatever. Before you bring that loser back up in conversation, I saw Nora today."

A smile formed on her face at the mention of Senora's name. She folded her arms in front of her and leaned against the wall. "How is she doin'? I haven't seen her since-"

"Don't-don't go there. She's invited us to her graduation next month." Robert tossed the envelope on the table and retreated into his room. She followed him to his bedroom door holding the envelope.

She waved the envelope in Robert's face, challenging him. "Do you want to go? I mean, I would like to see Tanya again."

Robert softened and slumped his shoulders. "It might be nice. Nora also invited us to The Diner after the ceremony for supper."

Standing defensive, the envelope slipped from her fingers, floating to the floor. "You know I'm not welcome there."

Robert punched the wall and glared. "No, he's not welcome there."

She raised her hands in front of her and backed away. "I'll go to the ceremony with you, but not supper. I can find my own way home from there."

He dropped his hands to his side and paced the hallway. "See that's what I'm talkin about. He has made you a prisoner even from your friends. How can you allow that?"

"I love him, just as I love you. He has changed," she pleaded as he tried to stop him from pacing. She turned him to face her.

"Leave me alone," Robert interrupted her again. He pushed away from her grasp, turned, and slammed the door in her face. "I'll tell Nora we're coming."

"Fine," she whispered as she shuffled back to the kitchen table and fell into a chair, weeping into her hands.

2
DIVIDE AND CONFLICT

$\mathcal{A}$ subtle, rhythmic tapping broke through the silence footsteps matched the rhythmic tapping as Scarlett approached the jail cell door. The jail keys rattled as she slowly opened the door with a creak. Scarlett looked up with a flash of her dragon-like silver eyes. "Hello, my love," Scarlett said.

"My Silver Enchantress, you're back," Lucas announced.

"Lucas, you betrayed me."

"Betrayed you? I would never. What makes you think this?"

"Scarlett has shown me. Light is stronger than darkness. We used to thrive on lies, deception, and fear. Life and death didn't matter because we had power and each other."

"Life and death don't matter when power and fear rule. You believed that with me once. What makes this any different?" Lucas smirked and stared at the floor resting his hand on his knee.

"Life does matter. It has value. Fear is fleeting. Death is not the final destination anymore."

Lucas stood and rattled his chains. "Lies! You and I are one."

"I will always love you, but I can't follow you any longer."

A darkness rose within him. Blankly, he looked at her. "What are you saying?"

Scarlett leaned close to Lucas and kissed his cheek. "Goodbye, my love."

Chains rattled as Lucas crossed his arms and smirked. Scarlett's eyes slowly changed from silver to blue as the Silver Dragon retreated back within Scarlett.

"My Silver Enchantress." He leaned again the cell wall and crossed his legs.

"She doesn't want to talk to you anymore." Scarlett glared over at Lucas and her voice grew louder with each word she spoke, as she backed toward the door.

"You, you corrupted her." Lucas spat his words.

"No, I helped her to understand the truth."

Lucas ran at Scarlett in an attempt to choke her, but his hands sprang back against the wall. He stumbled backward.

"Goodbye, Lucas." Scarlett turned to walk away. "Enjoy your solitude."

"You will regret this."

Scarlett looked over her shoulder and smiled, "It looks like you're the one who has regrets. You lose."

As the door closed behind Scarlett, Lucas smiled back. "We'll see who has lost."

———

*S*carlett entered the throne room and walked toward the large window overlooking the valley below. As she took in the view of endless wheat fields to the right, she saw they were boarded by the hilly country-side of canola fields backing onto rockier terrain. She shivered as she thought of what lay beyond those mountains. She pondered the conversation that had taken place between the Silver Dragon and Lucas. She closed her eyes and there before her stood the Silver Dragon. Standing three times taller than Scarlett, silver feather-like whiskers dangled from her chin. A thin shell-like head with sparks of lightning jumped from ear to ear. She four turtle-like legs supporting her long snake-like body with her long sleek tail swaying back and forth in a cat-like manor preparing to pounce. "You have done it," Scarlett said.

"You have no idea what I have done," the Silver Dragon warned.

Scarlett hugged herself as she twirled excitedly. "What do you mean? You've broken free from his lies."

"He's the signet of perfection, full of wisdom and perfect in beauty."[1] The dragon lay down comfortable as she chuckled at Scarlett's giddiness.

Scarlett stopped twirling and placed her hands on her hips. "That is how he presented himself to you."

"You don't understand. You don't know the wrath that's coming. He's stronger than you think. He only appears to be defeated. He's biding his time. He's known by many other names, and he has a backing greater than you can imagine. He was a murderer from the beginning, and does not stand in the truth, because there is no truth in him."[2] Fire gives him power, the more his lies and deceit spread the stronger he becomes. When he lies, he speaks out of his own character, for he is a liar and the father of lies."[3]

Scarlett clenched her fists in a boxer stance and stomped her foot. "We know the truth and can guard ourselves against any lie."

The dragon hung her head and shuddered sadly. "The god of this world has blinded the minds of the unbeliever, to keep them from seeing the light of the gospel of the glory of Christ."[4]

Scarlett playfully punched the air before her. "The darkness is forced to flee from the light. You've seen this."

The dragon slammed her tail on the ground, knocking Scarlett off balance. "He even disguises himself as an angel of light. So, it is no surprise if those who follow him also disguise themselves as servants of righteousness. Their end will correspond to their deeds."[5]

Standing firmly, Scarlett shook her head in disgust. "What do you mean to disguise themselves?"

Tears began to ripple like wave down the dragon's cheeks. Without moving her head, she looked up with both sadness and fear in her eyes. "He knows our fears, and he knows our past. He can convince others of their unworthiness and deceive them into following his plan. So, no matter how prepared you think you are, he was born to deceive, lie, and manipulate."

Scarlett's hands fell, her shoulder slumped, and she stared at her feet. "You mean like he manipulated me? If that is true, is anyone safe? How can one guard and prepare for something like that?"

The dragon stood and pounded her legs on the ground. "Be sober-minded; be watchful. He prowls around like a roaring lion, seeking someone to devour. Resist him, firm in your faith, knowing that the same kinds of suffering are being experienced by your children, friends, and family."[6]

Looking up and folding her arms, Scarlett looked straight in the dragon's eyes. "How can I trust anyone?"

The dragon pranced around Scarlet forming figure eights. "His deception wants to divide us. You must trust in the truth. Just as Nora and Jo spoke truth into you, they defeated his lies that held you in bondage so many years ago. Put on the whole armour of God, that you may be able to stand against his schemes."

Scarlet reached out and climbed on the dragons back as it continued in its figure eight pattern.

"For we do not wrestle against flesh and blood, but against the rulers, against the authorities, against the cosmic powers over this present darkness, against the spiritual forces of evil in the heavenly realms. Therefore, take up the whole armour of

God, that you may be able to withstand in the evil day, and having done all, to stand firm."[7]

Scarlett rested her stomach on the dragon's back. "I remember the battle for my mind and soul. I'm grateful for Nora and Jo, wherever they are. I sure could use their wisdom and truth now."

The dragon stopped so abruptly that Scarlett slid up to its neck. "Don't be deceived. It wasn't their truth. They were mere messengers speaking the truth."

Scarlett sat up and slid off the dragon's back and ran to face the dragon again. "What do you suggest we do?"

The dragon pounded the ground again with her paws. "Prepare. Fill your mind and heart with truth. So, you can recognize a lie when it comes."

Scarlett opened her eyes as the Silver Dragon's eyes faded back into blue once more. "Guards," Scarlett yelled. Four guards enter the throne room and bowed before Queen Scarlett.

"You called, my queen?" one guard replied.

"Summon my daughters. I need to convene with them," Scarlett ordered.

"Yes, my queen." One guard stood to get Katerina and Crystal. Scarlett looked at the other three guards kneeling before her.

"Rise," Scarlett ordered. The three guards stood at ease. "I want you to double the guard tonight, especially around the prisoner. I have a feeling this'll not be a quiet night."

"Yes, my queen." The guards nodded and turned to leave the throne room when Katerina and Crystal entered.

"You called Mother?" Katerina asked, bowing.

"Yes, I want you two to be strong. Guard your hearts and minds. Don't be deceived." Scarlett warned.

"What do you mean?" Crystal asked.

"You're young, but I know you're both strong. Just be ready." Scarlett warned.

"Ready? Ready for what?" Katerina questioned.

"I can't explain now. But in time you'll understand. Fill your mind with truth, and the truth will set you free." Scarlett paced between the girls in a figure-eight pattern. She paused in front of each girl and embraced them slightly, then held them at arm's length and nodded. "Just guard your thoughts. Do not allow yourselves to fall to deceit."

The two girls bowed their heads and turned to leave. "Yes, Mother."

Scarlett turned to look out over the valley again. Her eyes turned silver as she closed them. "You're only delaying the inevitable," the Silver Dragon affirmed.

"No, he's already defeated. Lucas will not win." Scarlett declared.

"I warn you again, don't underestimate him. We've been connected for centuries of time. We were in union before his fall. He fought for ultimate power, with me by his side. We would silence anything that threatened our end goal. You've shown me the power of the Saviour in a different light. I see now how undefeated He really is. Lucas has no choice but to strive for his ultimate rule. I no longer have that bond with him. My love for him no longer keeps him in bondage; I no longer hold him back. He'll no longer be distracted by what he saw as his driving force. He now will see me as his downfall. He'll harden his heart. Be prepared. You'll experience his full wrath. Bittersweet as it may be. As prepared as you think you are, you aren't," the Silver Dragon said.

"You'll see." Scarlett pondered.

"No, you will see," the Silver Dragon affirmed as she turned to look over the valley. "There'll be blood spilled. Guard yourself. The time is coming."

—◦◦◦—

ap, tap, tap. "Oh, will you stop that infernal tapping?" the guard said from outside Lucas' cell.

Tap, tap, tap, "What's the matter? I've nothing else to do."

"Do you want me to give you something to do?" the guard growled under his breath.

The chains rattled as Lucas stood to his feet. He leaned toward the door. "I know your fears."

"Enough already! You've already lost. Now silence." the guard grumbled.

"Darkness is coming the wrath will feast, you can't hide from it." Lucas warned.

The guard turned to face Lucas when Crystal walked up to him. "Man your post," Crystal ordered.

"Lady Crystal, what're you doing up at this late hour?" the guard asked.

"I couldn't sleep. Is the prisoner still secure?"

"Yes, my lady."

Tap, tap, tap, clang, clang, clang.

The guard pulled out his sword and banged it vigorously again the cell door. "Oh, will you just stop?"

BOOM! The prison door exploded into splinters, knocking the guard and Crystal off their feet. Lucas emerged through the smoke and dropped the chains that had bound him for two years. He turned, smirked at the guard, and picked up Crystal.

Katerina startled awake as the guard's alarm and spotlights illuminated the courtyard. "Lucas!" she yelled as she jumped out of bed, then reached for her bow and a handful of arrows. As she stepped out into the hallway, a group of guards met her as they rushed down the hall. "What's happening?"

"I'm not sure yet, my lady. I'm on my way to the prison to investigate." one guard replied as he rushed forward. Katerina quickly fell into pursuit.

"I'm coming too." Screams of injured guards reached her ears and the stench of sulfuric acid stung her nose as they crossed the courtyard and descended the stairs toward the prison cell. The alarm blared in her ears as smoke thickened with each step. When Katerina reached the first set of guards, she helped one to his feet. "What happened here?" she questioned. In confusion, the guard only pointed down the hallway. Katerina ran with more guards to discover what caused the explosion. As they rounded the last corner before the cell room, Katerina saw Lucas descending the hallway. The guards started firing, but Katerina ordered them to stop when she saw her sister in Lucas' hands.

"Lucas, let her go. You've nowhere to run." Katerina declared.

Lucas smiled at her. "You forget, child, as darkness can hide, blackness deceives, deception will rise, and fear conceive." The hallway filled with smoke. Katerina ran into the black smoke without regard for her own safety in the direction she thought her sister and Lucas might be. After some smoke cleared, she found herself alone. But Lucas's voice called from a distance. "I know your fears. Remember, I hid you and your sister away for years."

Katerina armed her bow and turned in a circle. "Stop hiding in the shadows you coward! Face me head-on, and you will see who's stronger."

"Oh, I know you're strong. I also know your fear of being alone. You can have Crystal back, but you need to do something for me first."

"I'm listening."

"It's just a small journey. I want all threats diminished."

"I'll not hurt my family."

"No, no, I can deal with your family. If you want Crystal back, eliminate Nora!"

"Nora? I haven't seen or heard from her in two years. What does she have to do with anything?"

The guards ran up to Katerina as she shot her arrow forward. "Face me!" The rest of the smoke dissipated right as the guards joined her. In a flash, Lucas and Crystal vanished. "Inform my mother at once. Lucas has escaped."

"What about Crystal?" A guard asked.

"Don't mention her. I'll get her back. She needs to focus on battle plans. Lucas won't go down easily," Katerina warned as she swung her bow over her shoulder.

The guards marched to the throne room to inform Queen Scarlett of Lucas' escape.

Katerina, the twelve-year-old raven-haired beauty, stormed off. She looked down at her fist. As she slowly opened her hand, a small, red glow emitted from her palm. A flash of anger washed over her face; she quickly closed her fist tight, readjusted her bow, and headed for the front gate.

3

GRADUATION DAY

Senora wiggled in her chair and bit her fingernails, as her mom put the finishing touches to her hair. "I can't believe this day has finally arrived. My baby's graduating," her mom said as she wiped a tear from her eye, "It seemed like just yesterday Jo was graduating. You two need to stop growing up so fast."

"Oh, Mom, I'll come to visit as often as I can. You know that." Senora smiled at her mom, stood, and turned to face her. "How do I look?"

"You look absolutely stunning," her Dad replied as he leaned on the doorframe of her room.

"Awe, thanks, Dad." Senora ran to wrap her arms around her dad in a big hug.

"My baby girl, all grown up. I'm not sure if I'm ready for all these changes," her dad responded.

"Oh, don't you start too. Change is just a new adventure."

"Not sure where you learned that one. Definitely not from me. That's for sure. Oh, Jo just called. He's waiting for Sylvia to finish her exam, and they'll be on their way. Said they may be a little late, so they'll meet us at the ceremony."

Senora frowned a little but quickly shook the sadness off.

"This is an exciting day. I'll not allow lateness to bring me down. Bobbie and his mom will meet us there too. Is it all right if they sit with you?"

"Of course. Sarah's my friend too. I'll be happy to see her again. She seems to be either busy at home or at the prison visiting Tony. I feel I never get to see her anymore. I'm so proud of you for thinking of inviting them," her mom replied.

"Thanks, Mom. Bobbie has been looking out for me these past few years. He has really grown up."

"Everyone has matured so much over the years." Her dad looked at his watch. "You know, if you don't want to be late yourself, we should get a move on."

"Yes, Dad. I'm ready. Let me just put my grad cap on."

"You can go bring the car up, and we'll be out soon." Her mom nodded at her husband. He nodded back and headed down the stairs and out the front door.

As the three parked the car in front of Montgomery High School, Senora jumped out of the car and ran to meet Alex, her shy and quiet grad partner. "I was beginning to think you were going to skip your own grad, and I would have to walk down to the stage by myself," Alex whispered as Senora joined him in the line. "Cutting it kinda close, aren't you?"

"At least I made it before we started walking. Right?" Senora winked.

"Barely," Alex responded as the group started moving toward the stage. They each walked up the stage stairs, found their placement seat, and turned to face the crowd.

"Welcome, everyone to Montgomery High 2022 Ceremonies," the principal declared as the grad class hooted and cheered. As everyone sat down Senora's mind began to wander. Her thoughts drifted over the many different memories that made her who she was.

She shifted her feet and smoothed out her grad gown. While the principal continued his address to the crowd, Senora panned the sea of faces, some beaming with pride and others full of tears. Her eyes fell on her parents. Her mom was resting her head on her dad's shoulder. Dad's arm was around her, gently stroking her right shoulder. Her eyes moved over to see Josiah with his arm around Sylvia, his fiancée, a smiling blonde-haired beauty. Robert and his mom sat next to Josiah.

He has changed so much over these past two years, Senora thought. *Then again, I have changed a lot too.* She remembered her adventures with her friend Sam in Treasure Kingdom. She and Jo learned so much about themselves and each other. In her mind, she saw flashes of Robert crumpled in a heap on his basement floor, the gray revolver dangling from his fingertips. The wave of pain, sorrow, angry, grief, and hopelessness danced in his dark eyes. He was ready to kill himself. The weight of Trevor's death weighed heavily upon him. *Thank you, God, for making him realize his value in you and how to receive your forgiveness.*

I miss Trevor so much; I wish he could have been here to cheer me on. I'm glad Bobbie was able to attend. Today would feel a lot darker without both of them. Bobbie and Trevor were always a good team. With Jo in tow, you never knew what Trevor would come up with next. She recalled a lighter time when the paperboy had made fun of her, mocking her clumsiness. This was her first year at school when everything was new. Grade one was hard enough without the paperboy teasing her on a daily basis. This made her more self-conscious and clumsier.

Two days in particular brought a smile to her face. Stumbling off the bus and landing with a thud, she cringed as she heard one of the bus windows open. "Way to go! Little Klutzy strikes again," Bancroft, the paperboy, announced to his friends. As the bus rolled away his laughter trailed off with it. Trevor turned to help her up and glared at the bus, turning out of sight.

"Hey, what was that all about?" Trevor asked. Senora brushed off her pants and shyly smiled.

Oh, just Banni being Bancroft." Senora sighed. "I have

homework to do. Talk to you later." Little Senora ran up the porch steps and disappeared into the house.

Robert clenched his fists, and his jaw tightened. "He had no right to laugh at your sister, Trevor."

"Hey there, Bobbie. Calm down. I've an idea to deter him. You two in?" Trevor asked mischievously.

Josiah and Robert smirked and nodded. Two eight-year-olds and a ten-year-old leaned close to come up with a plan.

The next day, Senora arrived home from another long day at school, and as usual she quickly went inside to do homework. Trevor met Robert and Josiah on the porch late that afternoon.

"Now, I know the paperboy delivers his paper to us today," Trevor declared. "Let's shake him up a bit." Trevor handed Josiah and Robert a rifle air gun. "It only shoots air, but boy it can make a loud bang." Trevor's eyes twinkled.

"Oh, Trevor, you always come up with the best plans," Josiah said through laughter. The three boys waited in anticipation of Bancroft's arrival.

Soon, the paperboy came riding his bike up to their house.

"Bobbie? Trevor? Jo? What'sup with y'all?" Bancroft asked with panic in his eyes.

Trevor stood holding the air rifle. "I hear you've been givin' Nora a hard time, Banni." He clicked the rifle. Bancroft swallowed hard. Robert and Josiah stood and clicked their rifles. Trevor pointed his rifle toward Bancroft. "Choose your next words wisely."

"What do you want me to say?" Bancroft questioned.

"Are you goin to leave Nora alone?" Robert asked as he aimed his rifle.

"My sister deserves respect," Josiah proclaimed as he raised his rifle.

"It was all in fun. She knows that." Bancroft whispered under his breath.

BANG! Robert fired a round. Bancroft flinched, turned on

his bike, and started to ride away as fast as his little nine-year-old legs could carry him.

BANG! Josiah fired his air rifle.

Senora ran out to the back porch at the sound. She saw three boys firing their air guns as Bancroft peddled his bike away. Papers flew in every direction. "Bobbie, Jo, Trevor, what're you doing?"

BANG! "I missed!" Trevor yelled as he took a few steps forward and aimed again. BANG!

"Dang, I missed too," Robert said.

"Let me try." Josiah aimed. BANG!

"Stop it right now!" Senora stomped her foot to grab their attention.

Bancroft reached the end of the long gravel driveway. "You're all crazy!" he yelled.

BANG! "I missed again," Trevor said as he stifled a laugh. Bancroft jumped and rode out of sight. Senora ran up to the three boys and placed her hand on Trevor's back.

"Trevor, stop! What're you doin?" Senora asked. The three boys lowered their air rifles and laughed uncontrollably. "What's so funny?"

"Oh, did you see the look on his face?" Trevor laughed.

"Yeah, I think he lost most of his papers." Josiah chuckled.

"I think he almost peed himself." Robert declared.

"You scared me. I doubt we'll be getting' a paper anytime soon. He could report you," Senora warned.

"For what?" Trevor laughed so hard he nearly fell on the ground.

"Ummm, for shooting at him," Senora replied.

Robert coughed to clear his throat. He turned and looked at Senora while trying to control his laughter. He held up the air rifle, "look." Senora walked closer, BANG, a small cloud of dust gathered in a small dust cloud at their feet.

She held her arms in front of her. "Oh, you didn't." She

grabbed the air rifle and shot at the ground. BANG! She started laughing. "It looks so real."

"Yes, but it only shoots air," Trevor affirmed.

"You're so sneaky," Senora said as she tossed the air rifle back to Robert. She disappeared into the house.

"Hey, I'll do anything to protect my little sister." Trevor winked.

Senora was pulled from her thoughts as she focused back on the principal's words. "As you end your time with us, may you look ahead to brighter futures. Thank you. Now help me welcome our valedictorian this year, Miss Senora Fredrickson."

The crowd clapped as Senora stood and walked to the podium.

"Thank you, Principal Stroble," Senora said.

She fixed her eyes on Josiah and took a deep breath.

"Good afternoon Montgomery High. I would like to thank my parents, my brother Jo, Bobbie Armstrong, and the teachers. You've all touched our hearts in some special way. You've encouraged us to never give up…"

Her gaze panned to Robert, "to fight for what we believe in," she looked at her parents, "to hold our loved ones close," her gaze surveyed the crowd once more.

"Thank you for believing in us." She locked eyes in admiration with her science teacher and thought, *All those many hours of tutoring really got me through,* "Without you, I could not represent this grad class and share these words. There're many different moments in our lives, moments of great laughter and adventure, and moments of great sorrow and many tears. But each new moment brought a lesson. It's our choice on how we'll receive those lessons. We've all made mistakes and hopefully learned from them."

The crowd nodded. Senora's gaze reached the back of the room. Right beyond the crowd stood a young girl dressed in black with her hood pulled down over her eyes.

"We have been on a journey of self-discovery, and some would say we've arrived. But our journey's only beginning." Senora squinted her eyes. *There is something familiar about this girl.*

She looked down to regain her thoughts. Her gaze slowly rose back to the crowd, continuing. At the end of her speech, she sat down. The crowd stood and clapped. Her eyes searched the back of the room once again. She caught a glimpse of the mysterious girl walking away from the crowd.

———⟨∅∅⟩———

T‌he grad class stood and threw their caps in the air to celebrate their accomplishment.

Senora met Josiah, Sylvia, her mom and dad, and Robert at the back of the room. Each hugged and congratulated her. As she pulled away from Josiah she saw that mysterious girl standing off in the distance. *Why does she look so familiar?* she wondered.

"Holding memories close today?" Josiah pointed at the eagle pendant necklace Senora wore.

"Memories and friends," Senora replied as she subconsciously reached to touch the pendant.

Josiah nodded and smiled. "I'm proud of you."

"We're all proud of you. Have you made any plans for the summer or for the fall school term yet?" Sylvia asked. Senora looked toward the young girl again; Senora noticed a hint of a red glow as the girl turned around a corner. *What was that?* she wondered.

"Are you lost in thought?" Sylvia chuckled.

"What? Sorry. What was your question?" She tried to refocus on the conversation around her, self-subconsciously fiddling with the eagle pendant again. Her thoughts returned to this mysterious girl.

"Oh, never mind. You've too much happening in your

mind right now to think past today. I understand. You've time to make a decision once today's finished." Sylvia hugged her.

"Nora, are you coming?" Robert asked as she slowly pulled away from Sylvia. She followed Robert to his truck and looked over her shoulder, calling back to the rest of her family, "We will meet you at The Diner in fifteen minutes. Ok?"

"You bet," her dad replied.

Robert and Senora climbed into Robert's car and drove away. As she looked out the window, she saw that girl again. "Hey, you seem lost in thought," Robert said. "Is something bothering you?"

"I'm not sure. I just thought I saw someone I used to know."

Robert pulled the truck up to The Diner and they both entered. They joined Josiah and Sylvia who were sitting at the long table in the back. Josiah sipped his coffee, and Sylvia chatted away about the new things she had learned in nursing school. Soon, her mom and dad arrived, and the waitress took their orders.

Senora tried hard to concentrate on the conversation, but her thoughts kept wandering back to that mysterious girl. The waitress returned to the table with a folded piece of paper in her hand, then handed it to Senora. "What's this?"

The waitress looked toward the door as the same mysterious girl walked out. "Umm, she asked me to give you this."

"Who's that?" Robert asked.

"I'm not sure," Senora said and unfolded the paper.

Nora,

I need your help. Meet me in

your barn tonight!

K

"Who's K? Josiah asked.

"Not sure," Senora replied as she placed the note in her pants pocket. The waitress returned with two extra-large pizzas.

"Enjoy," she proclaimed cheerfully.

"Oh, I will!" Robert rubbed his hands together excitedly.

———⊰๏๏⊱———

Senora sat calmly on the bench swing on their back porch pondering all the events of the day, listening to the ocean waves lapping against the shore in the background. Josiah came out and sat down beside her. "Hey, you've got that look in your eye," Josiah stated.

"What look?" Senora asked.

"You know, the one that says you're preparing for another adventure."

"Well, I just graduated. I might go for a horse ride tomorrow along the shore. I've a lot on my mind."

"Ok, I get it. I went through that same thing two years ago. If you ever want to talk." Josiah stood to go back inside.

"Trevor would have loved today."

"Yeah, he would have. I miss him too." Josiah sighed as he pulled the door closed behind him. Senora hugged her knees to her chest and turned her attention to the barn. *I am so thankful Dad built that barn last year; riding calms my nerves so much. It sure helps me not miss Trevor so much.* She saw a small dark figure standing by the side of the barn and reached in her pocket to pull the note out.

"Meet me in your barn tonight," Senora read. She stood and slowly walked toward the figure. "Are you the one who sent me this note?"

The figure shifted and moved toward the back of the barn, out of sight of the house. Senora ran to catch up.

—◦◦◦—

*R*obert drove up to his house and entered. His mom greeted him from the kitchen table. "Hey, Bobbie. It was a lovely ceremony this afternoon, wasn't it?"

"Yeah, it was really nice," Robert replied.

"How was supper?"

"Wonderful. It was great to be able to celebrate Nora's accomplishment. You should have joined us." Robert approached the table.

"I was tired after the ceremony, so I needed to rest."

"I understand." Robert sat down next to his mom when he noticed an envelope in her hand.

"What's that?"

"A letter."

"Oh? From who?"

"Your dad." She slowly looked up at Robert.

He instantly clenched his fists and stood.

"He's not worthy of that title." Robert pursed his lips into a thin line.

"You should give him a chance." His mom stood and tried to shove the envelope into Robert's hand.

He flinched away and scowled at her. "That man'll never change."

His mom took a step closer to him and raised her hands, pleading. "He would like to see you."

"I doubt that. All he speaks is lies. The only reason you think he changed is because he's sober. He's only sober because he's in jail." Robert's words grew louder as he backed away from his mom.

"Robbie, there's more to it than that." She tried to force the envelope into his hands again.

This time, he grabbed the envelope from her, crumpled it, and threw it at her feet. "He's not worthy of forgiveness. He's only trash and doesn't know how to love."

She kneeled down and picked up the envelope. "I'm going to visit him next Saturday. Will you come with me?"

"No." Robert stormed toward the door.

"Bobbie, at least read the letter." She ran to Robert and shoved the envelope in his shirt pocket as he stormed out.

"I've got to go."

"But you just got back." She fell to her knees, covered her face with her hands, and wept in the open doorway.

"Yeah, well, I need some air." He ran to his truck and squealed the tires as he drove away.

He tore the envelope from his shirt pocket and threw it on the floor of the passenger side as he sped away. *How could she allow that man back into her life? Next time, he just might kill her, like he did Trevor. No, I'll not allow him to tear us down again.*

Speeding down the gravel road, Robert headed toward Senora and Josiah's place.

That man only brings chaos and pain. He only cares about himself. God, I'll never forgive him. He doesn't deserve it. Robert turned down the driveway to Josiah's place. *Maybe Josiah can help.*

—◦◦◦—

*A*s Senora ran around the back of the barn, she almost ran over the small figure. The person turned to face Senora and slowly removed her hood. "Kat? Is that you?" Senora said with surprise.

"Nora," Katerina called.

Senora leaned over and hugged Katerina.

"What are you doing here? How did you get here?"

Katerina raised her hand to stop her from talking. "Nora, slow down with the questions. I need your help."

Senora stepped closer and embraced Katerina in a big hug. Katerina quickly pulled away from the embrace and held Senora at arm's length. "Of course. Anything. What is it?"

Katerina wiggled from Senora's hold and started pacing,

creating distance between the two of them. "Do you remember what Sam told you?"

She thought for a moment as she leaned on the barn wall. "You mean that friendship is a bond, but family is unbreakable?"

Katerina snapped her fingers, nodded, and turned abruptly to stare at her. "Yes, do you remember what happened to Crystal and me when you met us?"

She nodded at the recollection and stood a little taller. "Yes, Jo and I helped you two escape Lucas's chains and free Queen Scarlett from his deceptions."

"I see you still have the pendant Mother gave you." Katerina pointed at Senora's necklace.

She looked down and held the pendent in her fingers. "Yes, I never take it off. Do you need it back?" She started to fiddle with the clasp.

Katerina waved her hands back and forth in front of her and shook her head. "No, it does serve as a good reminder."

The necklace fell dangling on her neck again as Senora looked up, puzzled. "A good reminder of what?"

Katerina stomped her foot and placed her hands on her hips. "How important family is."

She rubbed the back of her neck and nodded with uncertainty. "Is everything ok? How can I help?"

Katerina turned her back on her and hung her head. "There's only one way you can help me, Nora."

She crossed her arms in front of her and tapped her toe expectantly, "Anything."

Katerina turned sadly and stepped closer to Senora. "What would you do to see Trevor again?"

Senora jumped in shock at the mention of Trevor's name, her hand covering her mouth. "I miss him, but I know he's in a good place. I know I'll see him again at the right time. Kat, has something happened with Crystal or Scarlett?"

Katerina turned away and started pacing again. "Scarlett is fine. But she has her hands full."

"And Crystal?"

Katerina stopped in her tracks, fighting back the tears and trying to hide her sadness. "I don't want to hurt anyone. But sometimes, one does not have a choice. She lowered her head and looked at the red glowing gem in her hand and sighed.

She wiped away a few random tears and sighed. "I'm sorry, Nora."

"For what? Why are you sorry?" Katerina spun suddenly and swung her leg high in the air. Her foot connected with Senora's left temple and knocked her to the ground.

Senora lay unconscious in front of Katerina. There was a small trickle of blood on her eyebrow. Katerina bent down and pulled her hood over her head. She placed the gem in her pocket and leaned close to Senora's ear.

"I truly am sorry. He wants you out of the picture, and I'll not let him rip my family away from me again." She grabbed Senora's arms and dragged her into the barn.

Katerina looked around as she dragged Senora toward the back of the horse stalls. She spotted an old 4 X 4 fence post leaning against the wall. She placed Senora down on the hay and walked over to the fence post. She dragged it over to Senora and gently laid it on top of her. "There, that should hold you."

Katerina wiped a tear from her eye as she looked one last time at Senora. Panic filled her as she noticed the eagle pendant had fallen from Senora's neck. *Where is it?* She got down on all fours and started searching in the hay. Right then, she heard a car pull up the driveway. She stood and stepped back. Then, she turned, ran from the barn, and knocked over a lantern.

Sparks hit the hay, and smoke began to fill the barn.

As Robert approached Josiah's place, he heard the horses

stirring. That was when he saw smoke pouring out of the barn door. Robert blasted his horn as he pulled to a grinding halt.

Josiah and his parents came running out of the house as Robert jumped out of his truck. He tossed his cell phone to Josiah's mom. "Call 9-1-1. Jo, help me get the horses free."

Josiah followed Robert to the barn. By the time he reached the barn door, the smoke was so black he couldn't see in. As the horses emerged, his dad tried to help him round them toward the back field.

Robert made his way to the last stall, and the smoke burned his lungs. He managed to find and release the last stall door. As the last horse ran out, Robert tripped when his foot hit something. He tried to get under the smoke and felt around to see what he tripped over. *What's this fence post doing here?* he wondered. Soon he felt a leg below the post. Fear filled his heart. The flames crawled up the walls and rippled like waves across the ceiling above him. He caught a glimpse of Senora's face in the glow of the flames.

He quickly reached his arm under the fence post to lift it off of her. As his arm slid under the post, pain seared into his arm, and he flinched and pulled the post off. Robert placed his free hand close to Senora's nose and mouth. He breathed a sigh of relief as he felt her breathing. "Hang on, Nora; we're going to get out of here." Robert rasped as he started to cough. He dragged her toward the door.

As Josiah and his dad got the last horse into the back pasture, Josiah looked over his shoulder to see Robert emerge from the smoke, carrying Senora over his shoulder.

Josiah ran over to help Robert pull Senora to safety.

"What happened?"

"I don't know. When I pulled up, I saw the smoke. Why was Nora in the barn?" Robert yelled.

"I don't know. She was just on the bench swing on the porch," Josiah declared. Josiah's parents ran up.

"Is she ok?" Tanya asked.

"She's breathing but unconscious," Robert gasped through coughs.

"The fire department and EMS are on the way," her mom announced.

"You're bleeding." Josiah gasped, pointing at the bloody eagle shape burn on Robert's arm.

"Must have happened when I removed the fence post from Nora," Robert explained.

They sat there watching the fire engulf the barn. When the fire department arrived, they pulled their hoses off the trucks. One firefighter pulled debris away from the barn, while others turned on their hoses to drown the flames.

EMS arrived ten minutes later and quickly got Senora on a stretcher and placed an oxygen mask on both her and Robert. One of the medics bandaged up Robert's arm. Robert and Senora were loaded into the ambulance, and they sped away from the scene.

———

*K*aterina stood right out of sight and watched the brilliant lights of the ambulance. "I'm sorry," she said as she wiped a tear from her eye. She pulled the red gem from her pocket. "It's done." A red glow engulfed her and she vanished.

PART 2: DECEPTIONS

4

DEADENED VALLEY

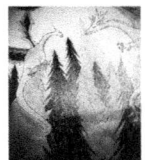

*T*he darkness weighed heavily with the blackness of night; a cool breeze rustled the leaves. A red glow illuminated the night sky and vanished almost as suddenly as had it appeared. Katerina sat there holding the red gem. Suddenly, she was startled by the sound of clapping behind her. She jumped up and quickly reached for her bow. But before she could reach her quiver of arrows, an eagle swooped down and snatched it away. "Now, now Kat, now that I have your attention. We had a deal," Lucas warned.

Katerina slowly stood and turned to face Lucas. "My sister. Where's Crystal?"

"So impatient. How do I know you did what I sent you to do?" Lucas asked.

"I'm here, aren't I? My sister, I want her back." Lucas stepped to the side, and Katerina saw Crystal still sleeping in the grass behind him. Katerina ran to her side and held her. "Crystal, wake up! Are you alright? Lucas, why won't she wake up?"

"Patience Kat. Just a little insurance on my part. I said you could have her back if Nora was eliminated from the picture. Only time will tell if you're true. You can take her, and I'll

47

decide when she'll wake or if she'll wake. Now, go back to your mother. She's about to get real busy," Lucas said with a smirk on his face. Katerina saw the trees shake as different creatures emerged from the shadows. Beasts with a glimmer of despair and anger driving them appeared.

"The Shadow Knights?" Katerina whispered.

"Oh, you've heard of them?" Lucas replied.

"I know they serve no one. They live for darkness."

"Yes, you're right about them living for the darkness. But they do serve someone. You'll see soon. Now, go with your sister before I change my mind." Lucas tossed Crystal's limp body onto a black horse Katerina had tied up before she used the gem earlier.

Katerina got on and rode quickly back toward the castle. *What are Shadow Knights doing in Treasure Kingdom? They never leave Shoel Mountain.* Katerina's thoughts raced. She looked back briefly to see even more movement behind Lucas.

"Why don't you let me kill her?" a dark shadow asked Lucas.

"She may be of more use. Patience. A kingdom divided against itself, will not stand." Lucas declared. "In time, you'll feed. Patience, Drayvon."

She rode into the castle and quickly called one of the guards to take Crystal to her room. "Lady Kat, is she alright? Where have you been?" the guard asked.

"Never mind that. She'll be fine. I need to see my mother." Katerina ordered.

"She's in the war room," the guard said as he carried Crystal up the stairs.

———

"*N*ow, we don't know when Lucas will attack, but we know he will. We need to prepare for all scenarios," Scarlett proclaimed.

"Yes, but how can we make a plan without answers?" Princess Delores asked.

"Light prevails over darkness. We cannot lose," Scarlett conveyed.

"You know Lucas is not to be underestimated," Sam warned. "He has been underestimated before."

"Yes, but the Silver Dagon's on our side this time," Scarlett announced.

"Careful. Lucas's unleashed." Scarlett heard the Silver Dragon warn from within her. She shook it off as if it were only an afterthought.

"Yes, Scarlett. I'll follow your command, whatever it'll be, despite the warning in my heart," Sam whispered. "I trust you and will follow you anywhere."

"We're strong. Lucas has been alone and in chains. We'll have victory," Scarlett declared.

Katerina entered the war room. "Mother, there's an army coming. I could see an army of Shadow Knights gathering at the forest near Sheol Mountain."

Scarlett looked over the map before her and pointed at Sheol Mountain. She slid her finger along the map to their castle, then pointed to a middle ground. "We'll meet them in the Deadened Valley. Lucas won't be allowed to cross that threshold. He mustn't be allowed any closer to the Fiery Crossroads." Scarlett indicated a triangle shape connecting Sheol Mountain, Treasure Kingdom, and the Fiery Crossroads. Deadened Valley and Treasure Kingdom stood between Sheol Mountain and the Fiery Crossroads.

"How can you be sure?" Sam asked.

"He deceived me once; he won't fool me again. The Silver Dragon's on our side, and Lucas' must not win her back. Now, rally the guards. Kat, you and Crystal will protect Treasure Kingdom. I won't leave these gates unguarded." Scarlett demanded.

"But, Mother. You always told us to use our surroundings and be strong, I can fight too."

"You're strong that's true. That's the reason I chose you to guard the castle." Scarlett pulled Katerina aside. "If we should fail today, if Deadened Valley falls, you'll be the only defense. Treasure Kingdom must have protection too. I need someone I trust here. That someone is you and your sister. Understand?" Scarlett turned toward the rest of the army leaders before Katerina could protest. "The rest of us will ride out and meet him, head-on. He likes to fight with darkness and fears; we'll force him into the light. Expose his deceptions and defeat his terrors."

"But mother."

"You have your orders. Relay everything to your sister; I'm depending on you both to stay strong and united." Scarlett proclaimed. Katerina nodded, turned, and left the room. "Now, Sam, you and I will trap Lucas's troops in. We, within our dragon forms, will set a flaming perimeter. Delores, you'll lead our troops to divide Lucas from his army. Force him to stand alone. We ride in an hour. Prepare the troops."

—◦◦◦—

ucas stood before a growing army of Shadow Knights. "So long you have been whispers in the night, only an afterthought, but now they'll see how great a threat you really are. Now's your time of strength. Now's your time to fight. We've strength in numbers. I've planted the seeds of doubt in Scarlett's ranks. It's time to water that seed and find our victory. Deceptions grow deeper than they could ever imagine." He panned the forest full of Shadow Knights gnashing their teeth and clawing the ground. Twenty, thirty, sixty, a hundred, thousand', and growing. The ground shook with their shrieking. "I'll give you the flesh you seek. The Silver Dragon has betrayed you long enough. I say, no more!"

The shouts, screams, and growls quivered the trees and as deafening as the sound was, silence fell as the terrifying site moved like a wave toward Deadened Valley. "Those strongholds will be transformed. No longer will they be a protection but a tomb," Lucas expressed as the army moved in unison, leaving the forest in silence once again.

———※※※———

S carlett mounted her horse and led her army toward the Deadened Valley. "To Victory!" she said as she rode out with her 20,000 troops following behind. The Red Dragon flew ahead to scout out what awaited them. Though it was already late morning and the sun high, she saw movement like a sea of ants swaying and moving in unison. She couldn't make out how many there were: despite the sunshine, they were shrouded in darkness.

She circled around to fly back to Queen Scarlett's side. "They move like a sea of darkness. The sun rises, but they're still shrouded in the blackness of night." Sam announced.

"Stick to the plan. We've strength and determination. The heat of day will expose them." Scarlett ordered, "Now scan the enemy and report back."

"Yes, my queen." The Red Dragon soared high into the air, hidden within the cloud. As she descended on the Deadened Valley, the sun reached its highest point. The sight below her instantly filled her with fear, for the scene looked unlike anything she had seen before. Both giant and scrawny black hairy creatures filled the Deadened Valley. There were so many the grounds were invisible to the eye. Their movements were swift, concise, and smooth. It appeared as though she was looking over a large ocean surface. She turned and flew back to Queen Scarlett's side. As she glided along, Scarlett looked at her expectantly. Scarlett's unrelenting determination motivated her to fly strong and true.

"Report," Scarlett ordered.

"It's like nothing I've ever seen. There's such a multitude: they move as one. They're inhuman and full of malicious intent," Sam warned.

"Find your courage. Stay true and focused," Scarlett said as she guided her horse and army up the final hill toward Deadened Valley, "We'll prevail."

The Red Dragon glided back into the sky and investigated the perimeter below. *Stick to the plan*, Sam reminded herself, as she circled down toward the wave of darkness. She took a deep breath and blasted a flood of fire, creating a wall of flames between the waves of blackness. Screams and yells reached her ears. Soon the Silver Dragon ignited the ground with flames on the other side of this sea of blackness. More screams filled the air. "Push them back," the Silver Dragon ordered Sam. Sam ignited the ground again, increasing the heat and dividing Lucas's army.

The Silver Dragon landed by Delores, who stood and secured both her and Scarlett's horses to a nearby tree, and the Silver Dragon transformed back into Scarlett. She grabbed her flail weapon from her saddlebag and stepped toward the approaching army. The mass of Shadow Knights invaded like a flood upon Delores and Scarlett's location. Delores aimed her bow as Scarlett readied her metal flail, its long chain swaying with a metal spiked ball on the end. Scarlett swung her weapon, embedding the metal spikes into several beasts' arms and sides, knocking them to the ground. Delores fired arrow after arrow, raining them down upon the approaching beasts. As this dark army dodged Delores's arrows, Scarlett saw the bloodthirst in their red eyes. Their fangs and claws were a mix of mud and blood that could be seen as they came closer.

Sam ignited the ground again right as Lucas came into

view. He stood on top a far hill, arms crossed, with a snug look of satisfaction and pleasure over the scene before him. "I only have use for one. Do what you wish with the others, but the Red Dragon's mine," Lucas ordered.

Turning toward Lucas, Sam ignited the ground before him, but Lucas stood firm. "Come little dragon. Just a little bit closer," Lucas said with a look of satisfaction on his face.

Scarlett moved forward, swinging her flail, sending several Shadow Knights flying in different directions. "We have victory. Continue to push them back," she yelled. Sparks flew as swords connected with claws.

"Their claws are as strong as metal," one soldier screamed. Lucas panned the battle below, seeking the next one to deceive. He connected eyes with that soldier, smirked, and visions of terror invaded this young soldier's mind. The soldier bent over screaming and madly swung his sword. He hacked away at anyone close to him, enemy or ally. Panic over-whelmed him to the point of eerie screams and convulsions. Soon he foamed at the mouth and fell lifeless to the ground.

Sam feared Lucas' mind-controlling attacks. She turned and darted down upon Lucas' position.

"That's it! Keep coming, little dragon." Lucas stood firm.

Scarlett spun her flail like a cyclone, sending Shadow Knights flying. She pushed forward as she looked up at the Red Dragon. "Sam, Lucas is mine," Scarlett proclaimed.

The Red Dragon turned to look toward Delores and Scarlett for a moment, the exact moment Lucas was looking for. "Now," Lucas ordered as a giant net was shot toward the Red Dragon, pinning her wings to her body. She fell with a thud.

"No! Give them nothing, stand true, and take away their power and control." Scarlett spat out her words.

Delores turned and, using the side of a large rock, propelled her body forward, flipping over a Shadow Knight as she embedded her last arrow deep into his skull. He screamed and fell silent. She landed, kicked another knight in the throat, and pulled a sword from a fallen soldier. Dipping and weaving, she rushed forward. Drayvon stepped between Delores and her fallen friend. Delores slashed downward as Drayvon stepped to one side. She stumbled forward with ripping pain as Drayvon's claws penetrated the back of her neck. Delores quickly pulled her sword upright in an attempt to slash his leg, knocking him off balance. Drayvon shrieked in agony, but in one fluent motion he spun, grabbed Delores's free arm and pulled her close. She swung her sword around and stabbed at his side. Drayvon bent over her, and sunk his teeth into her shoulder. Her arm went limp and the sword slipped out of her fingers. Drayvon tossed Delores like a shattered vase to the ground.

She forced herself to her knees, focused on Sam and crawled toward her. She reached in her boot and pulled out a small knife. "I'm coming, Sam. You're not alone. I'll cut you free," Dolores declared. Drayvon positioned himself over her and dug his claws into her back. Dolores's breathless scream came to an abrupt end. Tossing her over his head, he spun and threw her into Scarlett, sending them both crashing to the ground in a heap.

Delores and Scarlett staggered to their feet.

"Together?" Scarlett asked.

"Together," Delores replied.

The two rushed toward Drayvon in unison. Drayvon spun and punched his tail into Scarlett's stomach, knocking the wind out of her. Delores slashed her sword in an attempt to slice Drayvon from stem to stern. Drayvon bent forward as the sword passed a sliver of a hair from his ear. As Scarlett regained her breath, Drayvon acted quickly with a side kick to Scarlett's abdomen, doubling her over, her flail falling to the ground. Delores looked back and forth between Scarlett and Sam. As she decided on her next move, Drayvon punched Delores in the temple. Her world fluttered in darkness as she staggered to one side. She looked up at Drayvon and rubbed frantically to clear the blood pooling in her vision. Her eyes flashed with hatred as she tried to focus on her goal. *Deadened Valley must not fall.* Her movements were swift and concise as she made her way toward Sam. Scarlett pulled herself to her feet, picked up her flail and spun it at the back of Drayvon's head. While Drayvon staggered disoriented, Scarlett double-punched upward into Drayvon's back. She saw Delores heading to free Sam and turned her focus to Lucas. She pushed forward hard and fast, as her anger flared.

Lucas turned to make eye contact with her when her eyes turned glassy silver. "I tried to warn you," the Silver Dragon declared as Scarlett transformed into the Silver Dragon. The Silver Dragon took flight.

"What are you doing?" Scarlett asked from within the Silver Dragon's mind.

"Saving you," the Silver Dragon proclaimed. She circled the perimeter of the battle, raining fire down on the dark minions.

"No, I won't abandon my army; I won't leave Sam or Delores," Scarlett screamed from within. The Silver Dragon growled in frustration.

"But that'll be our undoing," the Silver Dragon warned.

"I don't run," Scarlett declared. "Land near Lucas, and we'll confront him head-on."

"Fine, but I don't agree with your tactics," the Silver Dragon argued as she turned toward Lucas and landed only a few feet away. The Silver Dragon transformed back into Scarlett. Scarlett inspected her surroundings; she saw Delores carefully dragging herself closer to the Red Dragon. *I need to buy her some time.* She reached for a sword, pulled it from a fallen Shadow Knight, and ran at Lucas. Lucas smirked at Scarlett and jumped into the sea of darkness, aimed his gun, and with a deafening shot, Delores fell. Scarlett's anger ignited the sword with flames as she jumped into the sea of blackness after Lucas.

"No, Delores. Say something," Sam said as she breathed out a blast of flames in an attempt to burn her bonds. Her tears burned as she looked upon Delores.

No, please be alright. Drayvon approached the Red Dragon. "Fight all you want, little dragon. But these bonds will hold true," Drayvon claimed.

"We'll see about that," Sam replied as she blasted a wave of fire toward Drayvon. Drayvon stood his ground, smirked, and turned toward Delores. "I should feast."

"No, please leave her be," Sam whispered as she felt her energy fading.

"Why not make things easier on yourself?" Drayvon asked. The Red Dragon transformed back into her human form in hopes that her bonds would fall off, but instead, they tightened more securely. She screamed in pain. Drayvon grabbed her and swung her over his shoulder.

Scarlett lunged at Lucas from behind. Lucas dodged, turned, and fired again, breaking the sword in two. In one swift movement, he grabbed Scarlett and pinned her arms behind her. He nodded at Drayvon, who secured Sam in chains and carried her away. As the sun fell on Deadened Valley, smoke rose on the defeated army. Delores's body lay in a pool of blood with no sign of Scarlett or Sam to be seen.

---

*K*aterina paced the courtyard. The last of daylight faded behind the far mountains, and she searched the horizon for any sign of the returning army. To her horror, she saw smoke rising in the silhouette of the final light. "Ready my horse." Katerina rushed for her armour and sword. Within seconds she rode her black horse at full speed toward Deadened Valley.

As she neared the top of the hill overlooking the valley, a wave of screams and tortured souls reached her ears. She madly panned the scene in horror at the deafening sight of guards fading in breath and strength. Searching each new face, she hoped to find someone she knew, but in her heart, she hoped she didn't find one. She stood on top of the hill, feeling desperate and alone.

She stepped carefully through the chaos of melted armour, broken bones, and smoldering flesh. To her dismay, her eyes fall upon Delores's lifeless body. "Delores!" Katerina screamed as she ran to her side, desperately searching for any sign of life.

"Lady Kat, you shouldn't be here," a wounded soldier said.

Katerina turned her pain-stricken face toward the soldier. "What happened?"

"Lucas. He was always three steps ahead. It was like he knew what we would do next before we even knew. I'm sorry, my lady. But it was as if we were defeated before we even arrived." The soldier gasped as he coughed up blood. Katerina carefully lay Delores's body down and turned to hold this dying soldier's hand. *Nobody should die alone*, Katerina thought as the soldier took his final breath. His eyes rolled back into his head, and his hand slipped from her grasp. Katerina lowered her head in defeat. *What have I done?*

A few random wounded soldiers drew close and surrounded Katerina and Delores. "I failed you, my lady," one soldier whispered.

Without looking up, Katerina sighed. "Salvage cloth. I'll prepare Princess Delores's body. She'll be returned to Treasure Kingdom."

"Right away, Lady Kat." Three soldiers searched among their fallen comrades for rope and cloth to bind Delores's body while Katerina slowly removed Delores' armour.

Katerina desperately rubbed the pooling flood of tears from her eyes as she focused on the task at hand. Her shoulder slumped as she thought about the first soldier's response. *If they only knew, I was the one who failed them...* Her thoughts were interrupted as the soldiers lay cloths beside her. She nodded a thank you and wrapped Delores's body. Once secured, she turned to the small group of soldiers. "I cannot lift the body. Can you place Delores on my horse?" Katerina asked.

Four soldier's nodded and carefully lifted Delores' body over Katerina's horse. Katerina gathered Delores' armour and said, "We will bury her armour here, with the fallen soldiers. This place will be a memorial for all we have lost." The four soldiers who had lifted Delores' body onto the horse hurried back to Katerina and started scooping mud and dirt away, forming a shallow grave beside Katerina. She slowly turned and slid the armour into the grave, and each one took turns throwing dirt over it. "As armour protects and unifies our army, so shall this unify the dead in their defeat," she said as she threw the last of the dirt over the armour. The last 8,000 soldiers and Katerina wasted no time as they built graves from Delores' armour and took the time to bury each fallen soldier.

It was the dead of night before Katerina, and the surviving soldier walked slowly through the castle gates. Four soldiers removed Delores' bound body from Katerina's horse and carried it into the castle. *What have I done? I don't deserve to serve. I'll find you, Mother and Sam. I'll get you back.* Katerina made herself a promise and followed the soldiers into the castle.

———

The ambulance pulled up to the hospital as nurses rushed out to pull Senora's stretcher into the emergency room. Robert slowly climbed out and was led to a different emergency room for another nurse to assess his wounds. "Don't worry about me. Take care of Nora!" Robert yelled.

"She's not my patient. Others are attending her. Now, lay back and let me look at your arm," the nurse demanded.

Robert begrudgingly lay down as the nurse cut away the bandages. "Strange."

"What's so strange? I burned myself on something when I removed the fence post to free Nora from the fire."

"What did you burn yourself on?" the nurse asked.

"I don't know. It was something hidden in the hay, I guess. Why?"

"Because it is in the perfect shape of an eagle."

"An eagle? Are you sure?"

"Take a look for yourself." Robert looked down at the bloody burn on his arm. *It looks just like Senora's eagle pendant.*

"Her necklace must have fallen off," Robert replied.

"Whose necklace?" the nurse asked. Robert's attention was drawn to the next room. He heard the nurses and doctors connecting machines to Senora's body. *Please let her be ok. We cannot lose her. Not now.*

"Nora has an eagle necklace that she always wore. But she doesn't have it on her now. So, it must have fallen off in the barn somehow. That must have been what burned me."

"Ok, it's fine. You'll just have an eagle scar on your arm that's all. Let me finish cleaning it so I can re-bandage it. Once you're all bandaged up, you'll be free to go."

"Go? I'm not leavin until I know how Nora is."

"Then, you're free to wait in the waiting room." She finished dabbing antibacterial ointment on Robert's wound, placed clean gauze and bandages over it, and handed him a glass of water and a cup with Benadryl to swallow. "There, you can go wait for your friend now." Robert stood and walked to the waiting room right as Josiah and Sylvia ran in through the hospital doors.

"Bobbie, are you alright? How's Nora? We brought your truck. Mom and Dad called your mom, and they're on their way," Josiah said as he handed Robert his keys.

"I'm fine. They didn't have to call my mom. I don't really want to see her right now. The doctors and nurses are still working on Nora. I haven't heard anything yet." Robert sighed as he sat in the waiting room with Josiah and Sylvia.

Josiah wrung his hands together, "Did you see the soles of her shoes when the ambulance arrived? They were completely melted. Why was she in the barn, anyways? The horse chores were already done. There was no need for her to be in there."

Sylvia placed her hand on Josiah's shoulder. "I don't know why, but we need to have faith Jo that God will bring her back to us."

"I know, Sylvia. I just don't do well when I don't have all the facts. How did the fire start, anyways?"

"The fire department will investigate that," Robert declared, trying to provide some comfort. Josiah's parents arrived with Robert's mom.

"Any news on how Nora is doing?" her dad asked.

"Nothing yet," Robert replied.

Robert's mom sat next to him and gently touched his arm. "You're hurt."

He pulled his arm away from her.

"You didn't need to come. As you can see, I'm fine. Just pray Nora's going to be ok."

"I…" Robert's mom mumbled.

"We're not discussing this now," Robert snapped sharply and stormed to the other side of the room.

Soon, the doctor entered the waiting room. "I would like to speak with the family of Senora Fredrickson." Senora's parents, Josiah, and Sylvia stood. "She's stable and resting. Her feet took the worst of it. But only second-degree burns. She should be up and running in no time."

Senora's dad shook the doctor's hand. "Thank you so much, Doc. Can we see her?"

"Yes, I'll have one of the nurses show you to her room," the doctor replied as he called a nurse over.

Robert turned and left the waiting room. He headed for his truck and drove away. *Thank God, she's going to be ok, but I need answers*, Robert prayed as he turned his truck down the gravel road toward the Fredrickson home. When he pulled up to the house, the barn still had smoke pouring out of it, and a few firefighters lingered to put out hot spots.

He slowly made his way to the spot where he had found Senora lying. The fence post lay where it was dropped. Kicking debris and ash around the area, he soon saw something metal. He ran over to one of the firefighters and asked for a cloth. The firefighter warned him he should not be there. Robert slumped his shoulders and ran into the house, grabbed a kitchen towel, and ran back where he found the piece of metal. Picking it up using the kitchen towel, he placed it in his pocket, and ran back into the house before the firefighters could protest. Using the kitchen sink, he unwrapped the metal and ran it under cold water. Soon, the eagle shape became more vivid. He tossed the kitchen towel in the sink and wrapped the necklace around his hand.

Robert ran out of the house, jumped back into his truck, and spun away, leaving a trail of dust behind him. He rushed down the gravel road heading back toward the hospital. *I need to get this back to Nora.* As he neared the stop sign, he stepped on the brakes, but the back wheel swerved. Robert tried desperately to regain control, swerved to the left, and back to the right. Soon his hood headed straight for the steep ditch. His truck nose-dived, flipped over, and the roof crushed down on Robert's head. Broken glass flew around him as the world spun out of control. The little truck finally came to a halt in a nearby farmer's field. Robert's bandaged arm hung out the driver's window. His face was full of cuts as it rested against the steering wheel, and his other hand hung freely between the seats. Blood dripped off his hand and down over the eagle pendant.

5

THE RESCUE

"I'm sorry to bring your family into our life traumas. I shouldn't have come," Robert's mom complained as she paced the hospital waiting room.

Senora's mom walked up to her and placed her hands on her shoulders. "You're speaking nonsense, Sarah. Robert was hurt too. You needed to come and see if he was alright."

Sarah hung her head, her shoulders shaking as she sobbed. "Yes, but now Bobbie has stormed to who knows where and I'm keeping you from spending the time you need with Nora."

Her mom shook her head and hugged Sarah. "It's fine. The doctor did say to not overwhelm her now that she's awake. So, keeping visitors in moderation is good. I'll see her in a few minutes."

"Thank you, Tanya." Sarah cried into Tanya's shoulder.

"Of course. What're friends for? If you want to talk about it, I'm here for you." Tanya rubbed Sarah's back to comfort her.

"I just don't know how to mend Bobbie's relationship with his dad. They both are so angry. At least Tony has been going through counseling in prison. He really has changed and wants to make amends with Bobbie. But even at the mention of his dad, Bobbie goes on the defensive and won't listen."

Tanya pulled Sarah out to look her straight in her eyes. "Maybe that's the problem."

Sarah shifted her feet and stared at the floor. "What do you mean?"

Releasing Sarah, Tanya placed her hands on her hips and tapped her foot. "You can't mend something that only God can. It's not your job to mend their relationship. Your job is to love them and pray for them."

Sarah nodded without looking up. She turned and shuffled toward an empty chair. "Thank you. Will you help me pray?"

Tanya relaxed her posture and slid into the chair next to Sarah, resting her arm around Sarah's shoulder. "Of course."

The two mothers bowed their heads to pray right as the ambulance pulled up. One EMS ran into the emergency room. "We have a young man, age nineteen. Head trauma, multiple fractures, victim of a motor vehicle collision."

Four nurses came running to help bring the young man into the emergency room. "Quick prep for surgery. Notify his family! We need to alleviate the pressure, or we're going to lose him," the EMS announced.

Sarah looked up with a start when she heard the age of the young man coming into the emergency room. She stood and looked over right in time to get a small glimpse of what looked like Robert on the stretcher. "No! Bobbie?" Sarah ran toward all the commotion. A nurse stepped in front of her.

"I'm sorry, but he needs to go into surgery immediately. You'll need to wait in the waiting room. What's your relation-ship to the victim?" the nurse questioned.

"No! No! What happened? He was just here. That's my son." Sarah yelled.

"I'm sorry; the doctor will update you when he can, but for now, I need to ask you to wait. If we don't prep him for surgery now, we won't be able to save him." Tanya ran to

Sarah and embraced her. The two ladies went back to the waiting room, looking back to get a last glimpse of Robert.

Josiah walked to the waiting room to see what had happened and saw Sarah crying uncontrollably into his mom's shoulder. "What's going on, Mom?"

"Oh, Jo, when it rains, it definitely pours. EMS just arrived with Bobbie. I guess he was in a car crash. He's in surgery now. We have to wait to hear from the doctor. I guess he has head trauma, and they weren't sure if he would make it through the surgery." Tanya whispered.

Josiah soaked a piece of gauze in a tap and dabbed the back of his neck. "I'm so sorry Sarah. If there's anything I can do, let me know."

"Pray," Sarah whispered, barely able to get the one word out between sobs.

"I am. We need to trust that no matter what happens, God still has a plan." Josiah walked toward Sarah and gently squeezed her shoulder.

"Thank you, Jo." Sarah's body shook with her silent tears.

"Mom, Nora wants to see you," Josiah said. Tanya nodded and stood. Josiah sat beside Sarah and held her hand.

Tanya entered Senora's room as she opened her eyes and looked toward the door. Seeing the torment behind her mom's eyes, she asked, "Mom, what happened?"

Tanya rushed to Senora's bedside and reached for her hand. "Do you remember anything?"

With her free hand, Senora rubbed her forehead. "Not much. I thought I saw someone I used to know."

Pulling a stair closer to the bed, Tanya sat down, taking Senora's hand again. "Who?"

The room spun as she tried to remember the events that had occurred. "I-I'm not sure."

Stroking Senora's arm, Tanya leaned closer. "Do you remember the fire?"

She sat up straighter in her bed, eyes growing wide. "There was a fire? Was anyone hurt?"

Tanya lowered her head and fiddled with the sheet on Senora's bed. "You hit your head."

Reaching to pull at the sheet to uncover her feet, Senora kicked and squirmed. "Why do my feet hurt?"

"They got burned. But the doctor said they will heal with time. Nora, Bobbie saved your life. He found you unconscious in the barn. Why did you go to the barn?"

"I…" Senora got a flash of Katerina's face. "I don't remember." Senora relaxed her feet and fiddled with the sheet, too, avoiding eye contact.

"Listen, you're just waiting to be transferred upstairs into a hospital room. But until one is available, you need to rest in the ER." Tanya stood and straightened her sheets, tucking them under the mattress.

Wiggling the sheet loose, Senora reached for her mom's hand. "What was all the commotion a bit ago?"

Tanya pulled out of Senora's grasp and stepped back. "You should rest now."

Senora painfully sat up in her bed. "Mom, what aren't you telling me?" Tanya's eyes filled with tears.

Wiping a tear from her eye, Tanya hung her head. "Nora, it's Bobbie."

She clenched her fists and madly pushed the sheet on the floor, swinging her feet over the side of the bed. "What? What about Bobbie? I thought you said he saved my life. Did he get hurt doing so?"

Tanya rushed to Senora's side and pushed her back into bed. "No."

Throwing her head against the pillow, tears tung her eyes. "Mom, what is it?"

As she picked up the sheet off the floor and placed it back on Senora, Tanya kissed her cheek. "Oh, Nora, after you were admitted into the hospital, Bobbie had a fight with his mom, and drove off. EMS just brought him in. He was in a car crash."

"What're you saying, Mom? He's going to be ok, isn't he?" Senora was filled with panic as she kicked at the sheet again to get out of the bed. It took all Tanya's strength to secure her.

"He's in surgery now. We won't know how he's doin until the doctor informs us. They weren't sure if he would survive the surgery." Senora sat there punching the bed, and Tanya embraced her. Holding her firm, Senora sobbed into her mom's shoulder.

"Mom, Bobbie's the strongest person I know. He has grown and learned so much in the last few years. His life can't end like this. I know he'll be alright; I just know he will." Senora reached for her eagle pendant subconsciously. *Wait! It's not there?* Fear bubbled below the surface; her jaw dropped. "Where's my pendant?"

"You must've lost it in the fire."

Discouraged and tired, Senora lay her head back down on her pillow.

"Mom, please let me know once you hear about Bobbie." Senora's mom slowly rose from the bed.

"I will, Nora. Rest now." Tanya left the room and walked back to the waiting room. She saw Sarah crying into her hands. Josiah and Sylvia sat praying next to her. Mark, Senora's dad, met her in the hallway and hugged her. The two joined the rest in prayer for Robert's surgery and recovery.

Three hours later, the doctor entered the waiting room. "I need to speak with the family of Robert Stevens."

Sarah stood. "I'm Bobbie's mother. How is my son, Doctor?"

"Well, he survived the surgery, but he's in a coma. When his car flipped, the roof came down on his head hard. I was able to reduce the swelling, but now the battle's up to him. Only time will tell," the doctor warned.

"Can I see him?" Sarah asked.

"He's stable, so yes, you can see him. Just one person at a time for now."

"Thank you, Doctor," Sarah replied as a nurse led her to Robert's room.

She entered and pulled a chair up to the side of Robert's bed. "Damn you and your temper. I just hope your stubbornness will keep you fighting. You've so much more left to live for." She kissed Bobbie's hand.

A nurse came in with a bag of clothes. "Sorry to bother you, but he had these things on him when EMS brought him in."

Sarah politely took the bag of clothes. Looking inside, she saw Senora's necklace. Pulling the necklace out, her rage began to rise. "Is this what you were doing? You risked your life for a stupid necklace?" Sarah threw the necklace on the hospital floor and walked out of the room. She walked back to the waiting room. "I can't see him like that. Can someone else please sit with him?" She stormed over to a waiting room chair and crumbled into it.

"I'll go," Josiah announced as he rose and walked to Robert's room. He walked toward the bed when his foot kicked something. He looked down to see Senora's pendant. "Wait, what is this?" He reached down and picked it up. "Nora's necklace? How did it get here? Bobbie, did you go back to the fire and get it? You know, your life is worth more than this piece of metal. You're not alone, and you're stronger than you think. Don't give up." Sylvia entered the room and placed her hand on Josiah's shoulder.

"Jo, is he goin' to be ok? If you need me to, I can sit with him for a while. You should let Nora know what's happening. Mom's trying to console Sarah."

Josiah nodded and left the room. He entered Senora's room down the hall. "Nora?"

Senora opened her eyes and slowly sat up. "Jo, any news on Bobbie? Is he out of surgery yet?"

"He's out of surgery. But in a coma right now. They're not sure if he'll wake up." Josiah moved the chair closer to her bed and sat down. Senora saw the eagle pendant in his hand.

"My pendant. Where did you find it?" Josiah handed the pendant to Senora.

"It was on the floor in Bobbie's room. He must have gone back to get it for you."

Senora placed the necklace around her neck again, and a lump formed in her throat.

Then, she looked up at Josiah. "Oh, Jo, I hope I'm not the cause of this."

"Why would you think that? Of course not," Josiah remarked.

"Jo, can you help me?"

"Sure with what?"

"I'm not allowed to walk on my feet because of the burns. Can you please get me a wheelchair and take me to see Bobbie?"

"I think I can do that. I'll be right back." Josiah rose and walked out into the waiting room. He saw a row of wheelchairs by the emergency door and wheeled one of them back to Senora's room. Helping Senora slide off the bed, he placed her into the wheelchair, trying hard to keep her off her feet as much as possible. Then, he wheeled her to Robert's room. Sylvia rose when she saw Josiah and Senora enter.

"I'll leave you alone," she said as she nodded and left the room.

Josiah wheeled Senora up to Robert's bed, and she touched the bandage on his arm. "Some are from the collision," Josiah declared.

"Some? Not all?" Senora questioned.

"The bigger bandage on his forearm is from the fire. He burned it lifting a fence post off you."

"Can I talk to him alone?" Senora asked. Josiah nodded and left the room. "What were you thinking, Bobbie? I know you have taken on the role of protecting me. Especially since Jo left for college. But running into a fire? What were you thinking? You have to wake up, Bobbie. I can't lose you too. You have taken on Trevor's role in my life. If I lose you, it will be like losing Trevor all over again. Damn your stupid pride. I can promise you, you're not your dad." Senora rested her cheek on Robert's forearm. A tear trickled down her cheek. As she lifted her head to wipe the tear away, another rolled down her other cheek, down her neck, and dripped off the eagle pendant. The tear absorbed into Robert's bandage. Senora thought she saw a slight glow, but she must have been mistaken.

———

*R*obert opened his eyes to find himself standing in an unfamiliar forest. "You're not alone." He heard Senora's voice as if it was just a whisper in the wind. He looked down at the eagle shaped scar on his arm. *Where am I?* Soon, the sound of footsteps interrupted his thoughts. He hid behind a tree to see what was happening. Five tall, hairy, wolf-like creatures walked past him, and he followed at a distance. Suddenly, the darkness was eliminated by the glow of what looked like campfires. The creatures entered a guarded camp.

"Victory's almost ours." Lucas stood on a tree stump. "Bring me the prisoners." Two young women in chains were dragged toward the man standing on the tree stump. One lady stood firm with golden blonde hair with a stern expression, while the other lady with fiery red hair stood with slumped shoulders.

Lucas approached Scarlett, and her eyes turned silver. "Lucas, what have you done?"

He bowed before Scarlett, grabbed her hand, and spun her around.

"What I originally planned to do. You distracted me

before. But my love, you freed me from love's bondage." He twirled her close into a hug, leaned toward her ear, kissed her neck, and smiled as he looked up at Sam. "Look at her." Sam slowly raised her green eyes toward Scarlett.

"Leave her out of this," Scarlett ordered. "It's me you want, isn't it?"

Lucas sat Scarlett down and walked toward Sam; he hit her on the cheek knocking her to the ground. Robert's anger flared up. Flashes of all the times when he had to sit and watch his dad beat his mom flashed through his mind, and he knew he had to save them. Lucas pulled Sam to her feet. "You see, these chains stop you from transforming. You'll help me one way or another, Sam," Lucas whispered in her ear.

"I'll never help you," Sam declared. "The horse is made ready for the day of battle, but the victory belongs to the Lord."[1]

"You're mistaken. You've already fallen. Victory's mine," Lucas proclaimed as he walked toward Scarlett. "You see, the Silver Dragon in all her wisdom and beauty bound me to her in love. But in her defeat, my love died. And so…" Lucas pulled Scarlett to her feet again. "I continue my rule." Lucas turned Scarlett to look at Sam.

"Lucas, my love, I was mistaken. Our love's bound for all eternity," the Silver Dragon replied. Lucas spun Scarlett to face him again.

"I do admit that I still hold the Silver Dragon with high regard. Your power's greater than this entire world. But…" His eyes glinted with mischief. "You, my love, have been corrupted with light. You no longer reside in the darkness kingdom. You no longer belong." Lucas spun Scarlett toward Sam once more and pointed his finger. "Now, a young naïve dragon? I can work with that. Mold it, and shape its path."

"You wouldn't." Scarlett gasped.

"Oh? I wouldn't? I thought you knew me better than that, my love. You see, you're trapped within this vulnerable body.

Scarlett has defeated you and you don't even know it. That was my mistake, but I'm here now to correct that little error," Lucas affirmed.

"Sam, no matter what happens remember you can do everything through Christ, who gives you strength," Scarlett declared.[2]

"Strength? The only strength here is mine. The age of the dragon is done." Lucas thrust a knife into Scarlett's side. Blood poured out, running like a river, as the ground hungrily licked it up. Scarlett fell. Sam ran toward her, but Lucas kicked her backward. "No longer will the Silver Dragon distract me." Lucas kneeled down and placed his right hand on Scarlett's gaping wound. He paused for only a moment before he stood and approached Sam as she tried desperately to crawl away on her stomach. "It's my time now. My rule. And you," Lucas said as he stood over Sam, reaching down and pulling her to her feet, "you, Sam, are going to be the undoing of everything." Lucas scoffed with a smirk on his face. "Take her away." Lucas tossed Sam like a rag doll into the hands of two shadowy creatures, who dragged her toward a tent in the center of their camp and pushed her inside. Robert watched in horror as Lucas kicked Scarlett's lifeless body out of camp and down a hill. He returned to camp and entered a tent on the far north end. Robert sat there feeling helpless.

This is crazy; I must have lost my mind or something. Maybe I'm dreaming? He climbed a nearby tree to get a better vantage point. Watching cautiously from a distance, he saw six of the hairy beasts patrolling the perimeter of the camp. Those were the strangest looking creatures he had ever seen. Like something from his nightmares. They were covered in thick black fur, and they had sharp fangs that would tear him apart if they got a hold of him. Their eyes looked like fire, and they had long crocodile snouts. Robert watched as they stopped at every second tree and clawed thick, deep scratches in the bark, almost like they were marking the border of their camp, warning others not to trespass. *These guys or creatures mean business. Maybe I'll wait here for now. Hopefully, I can find out where I am in the morning.* Robert rested his head against the tree and closed his eyes.

A blood curdling scream startled Robert awake, and he almost fell out of the tree. He looked on as Lucas pulled Sam out of the center tent and dragged her by her hair to the nearby fire. "Now, this is interesting. A dragon that's afraid of fire?" Sam spat in his face, and Lucas slapped her. "You may think you're tough, but I know what you truly fear. It's not me." Lucas stood Sam back up. "I'll break you, and you'll be begging me for mercy."

"I'll never give you that satisfaction," Sam replied.

"I don't need satisfaction to get what I want." Lucas dragged Sam over to a table and handed her a bowl of food.

"What's this? Poison?" Sam questioned.

"It's food. Eat; you'll need your strength," Lucas demanded.

Sam's hair glowed crimson. "You want to see my strength? Take these cuffs off and then we'll see. O Lord, my strength and my stronghold, my refuge in the day of trouble."[3]

Lucas leaned close and said, "I tear down strongholds, but you're right: this is only the beginning of days of trouble."

Sam sat up straight and yelled, "You're already defeated; your future has already been written!" Lucas pierced Sam's arm with a small needle and extracted some blood. Sam cried out with pain.

"We'll see. You say my future is already written? Well, now is my time. If you aren't going to eat then you can go back to your cage." Lucas pulled her away from the table and pushed her back into the center tent.

Robert turned his attention back to the beasts patrolling the perimeter. He noticed they always traveled together in packs of three. Three circled one way, while another three circled the opposite direction. *If I time things right, I can probably sneak in unnoticed. The problem will be getting out with this young lady. That's if she will even come with me.* He watched as one set of three beasts paused under the tree he was in. One by one, they took turns clawing the bark off the tree before moving on. He waited until they had moved down a number of trees before he climbed down. His thoughts returned to the night before. *I wonder about that other woman. The one who was kicked out of camp.* He swiftly slipped out of sight and neared the bottom of the hill where Scarlett's body lay. Carefully approaching her, he bent down and touched her face. *Still warm.* Scarlett's eyes fluttered and barely opened. "Who are you?" Scarlett asked, struggling to form each word.

"My name is Bobbie." Scarlett struggled to focus on Robert's face as she desperately gasped for breath.

"Bobbie? You must save them."

"Who? Do you mean that fiery redhead?"

"You must save them all. He is more powerful than ever. Soon, no one will be able to stop him."

"Who're you talking about? How can I help you?" Robert looked around to find something that might stop the bleeding.

"No, I'm done. My fight's over. Yours? Yours has just begun." Scarlett coughed and groaned. "Find the Saviour's words and wisdom. It's the only way now. Be strong." Scarlett's body went limp in Robert's arms and all colour faded from her face.

Robert gently laid her down and fought the urge to scream at the top of his lungs. *With her dying breath, she thought of others.* Robert shook his head in confusion. *I must find a way to free this young captive.* He raced back to the perimeter and studied the two patrol units carefully. When the nearest patrol passed his location, he quickly made his way toward the nearest tent. He tiptoed as quietly as he could, continuing this process until he finally found himself right outside the tent he saw Sam thrown into. He panned the gruesome crew for Lucas. He saw him in the distance as he headed into the north tent once again.

Now's my chance. Robert took a deep breath and entered the tent.

Sam stared at Robert with curiosity. "Who're you?"

Robert held up his hands to show her he meant her no harm. "Careful, I don't want to hurt you. I promise."

Sam looked away. "No promise is worth believing here. Did Lucas send you to try and soften me?" Sam turned and looked at Robert with hatred, a look Robert knew well.

"I don't know any Lucas, but I have seen how poorly you have been treated. I wish to help you escape."

Sam raised her handcuffed hands. "Can you unlock these?"

"I don't have the key."

"Key? Who needs a key? I haven't heard that word in years." Robert shook his head, wondering what she meant and planned to ask her once they were free from this place.

"I've been watching their patrol. Once those three move on; we'll have five minutes to run to the tree line."

"Do you not understand Shadow Knights?"

"What're Shadow Knights? Never mind. Can you run?" Sam nodded suspiciously but stood to follow. "Ok, let's go, but try to be quiet." Sam nodded again. They slowly made their way out of the tent and tiptoed around the back. *Do these creatures ever sleep?* He shook that thought away as he led Sam through the blind spots until they reached the perimeter. Once they got a few trees away from the camp, they both took off running. Soon, Sam pulled Robert to the side, and they both tumbled into a small hole. "What're you doing?"

"Shadow Knights can track the night. I'm surprised you could see their blind spots. That's a rare gift. Now, can you take these cuffs off?"

"I told you: I don't have the key."

"What do you think the key is? If you're true and wisdom guides you, the key to break the chains grows through the grace and forgiveness that will flow like rain through you."

"What does that mean?" Sam sighed and rolled her eyes.

"Fine, we can wait here until daylight, the Shadow Knights won't see our tracks as good in daylight. Rest now." Sam closed her eyes as Robert kept a look out. *Who's this strange girl, and where am I?* Robert's mind raced with unanswered questions. He must have dozed off because Sam startled him awake.

"Hey, it's time to move." Robert squinted at the sun's rays. Sam led Robert through the trees. "Come, we have a long walk ahead of us."

"Where're we?" Robert asked.

"We're in the Shadow Forest, the place where nightmares are born."

"What do you mean? How did I get here?"

"You don't know?" Sam spun around sharply and swung her chains at him.

"Wait, what're you doing?" Robert dodged; Sam flipped in the air and kicked Robert in the arm, sending sharp pain shooting up into his shoulder. He winced and fell. "I don't trust you yet." Sam punched Robert unconscious as she looked around her, finding something to release her bonds when she heard movement coming toward them. Quickly dragging Robert to a secure place, she saw a Forgiveness Eagle land, so she slowly tiptoed up to it.

"Kind Forgiveness Eagle, can you help me?" The great bird tapped her bonds with its wing as it flew away. Her bonds fell to the ground. She walked back over to Robert to inspect her strange rescuer. At closer inspection, she noticed the eagle shape on his arm. "Nora's pendant? How did you get this symbol?" Sam brushed Robert's hair away from his eyes. "I need to warn the others, but I can't leave you here alone." She stood and looked around. "Queen Scarlett." She gasped as she tiptoed back toward the camp and made her way to the bottom of the hill where she found Scarlett's body. "I'm sorry, my queen." Sam slowly and painfully pulled Scarlett's body back to where she had left Robert. *I'm not going to get very far like this.* She transformed into the Red Dragon, picked up Scarlett's body and Robert, and flew back to the castle.

Sam slowly lowered Robert and Scarlett in the courtyard and landed beside them. She transformed back into her human form. Katerina ran into the courtyard to meet them. "Sam, where have you been? Mother, no! It can't be!" Katerina screamed as she ran and embraced Scarlett's lifeless body. "What happened?"

"I'm sorry, Lady Kat. Lucas was too strong," Sam replied sadly. "They underestimated Lucas. I'm sorry, Kat. She didn't make it."

Katerina filled with guilt. *It's all my fault.* Turning her attention toward the unconscious man lying on the ground beside her, Katerina asked, "Who's this?"

"I don't know, but he helped me escape from Lucas's compound," Sam affirmed. Katerina called for some palace guards to carry Robert to a room, and ordered others to grab burial garments for her mother. Sam followed, still curious about the scar on his arm.

She watched from a distance as this strange visitor rested. Katerina approached and said, "Hey, Sam, what happened?"

Sam leaned on the doorpost and sighed. "One thing I learned in this battle is what Lucas is partially after."

"What do you mean?" Katerina shifted nervously.

"I'm vulnerable in my dragon state. Somehow, he manipulated me, and now Delores is dead."

"What do you mean? Manipulated?"

"You know he's king of deception. Delores died trying to free me. I jumped ahead and went after Lucas alone. I'm sorry, Kat. But I think Lucas is looking for something."

"Like what?"

"I don't know yet. But until I do, I think I need to refrain from being the Red Dragon for now. Scarlett and Delores trained me in combat just in case this were to ever happen."

"But the Red Dragon is a symbol of hope for our kingdom."

Sam sighed and placed her hand on Katerina's shoulder. "You forget, kid. The Saviour is our hope. 'Indeed, we felt that we had received the sentence of death. But that was to make us rely not on ourselves but on God who raises the dead. He delivered us from such a deadly peril, and He will deliver us. On Him we have set our hope that He will deliver us again.'[4] So, I will trust the Saviour's leading now. I'll refrain from using my dragon form until I feel it is safe to do so."

Katerina shifted her attention toward the man lying on the bed. "So, what is your opinion of him?"

"He's so mysterious. He carries a symbol of Scarlett's signet; you know, the one she gave to Nora. I don't know if I trust him. Deception seems to be thriving in many different places." Sam looked at Katerina.

Katerina squirmed in anticipation of her own deception. *Does Sam know what I did? Is Nora really gone? Will Sam see through me? Will Crystal ever wake up?* Katerina's mind spun. "In a time of deception and darkness, we need to unify. We need to prepare Mother's body for the funeral procession."

"We need to unite you're right. He'll try to divide us. We can't let him. But do you think when we're facing war, the time is right for a funeral?"

"Time for a funeral is never right. She's my mother and the queen. We need to mourn her."

"Sorry, Kat, my mind's wandering. But I'll find the answers I seek one way or another." Katerina left to regroup with the leading officials, while Sam remained at the door staring at this strange man.

When he stirred and sat up slowly, Sam cautiously approached the bed. *Who's this man? Where did his scar come from?*

"Where am I?" Robert asked.

Sam stopped half way into the room and folded her arms. "First, you need to answer some questions for me."

He rubbed his finger against his temple and glared at her. "You knocked me out; don't I deserve some answers first?"

She lowered her arms and approached the bed. Sitting on the side of the bed she looked intently into his eyes. "Ok, I owe you that much. What do you want to know?"

Adjusting his position on the bed, he fluffed his pillow and turned his attention fully on her. "Where am I?"

Spinning her hand to pan the room, she pointed out the window, and smiled. "You're at the Castle Calvarias. It stands to protect Treasure Kingdom. Now, you answer me this. Who are you?" In one smooth motion, she turned and pointed her finger at his chest.

Pushing her finger aside, he slowed his expression and looked up at her. "My name's Bobbie. What's Treasure Kingdom?"

Raising her eyebrow and tilting her head, Sam rose from the bed and turned toward the window. Pausing, she looked over her shoulder at him. "You sure aren't from around here, are you?"

"I guess not. Nothing seems familiar to me." Robert shrugged and looked around the room.

Sam pointed to Robert's arm. "That symbol? Where did you get it?"

Robert placed his finger on the eagle scar. "I got it saving a friend."

Rushing at the bed, she leaped at his arm, and Robert shuffled closer to the wall to make room for her. She asked, "Friend? Would this friend happen to be named Nora?"

With his jaw dropping, his eyes widened, and he raised his eyebrow, whispering, "What? Yes, how do you know Nora?"

She casually climbed off the bed again and stared out the window. Waving him off, she said, "We're old friends."

With a smirk he tilted his head and crossed his arms. "Funny, she has never mentioned you. What's your name?"

Swirling her hair between her fingers, she looked over her

shoulder and said, "My name's Sam. We met in a lighter time, a time of deception but she learned and brought the truth of the Saviour."

Chuckling, Robert scratched the back of his head and looked down. "That sounds like Nora. But why do you say lighter time?"

Getting very somber, she began pacing the floor. "Your arrival comes at a time of great sorrow and darkness. Now's a time for choices. I choose to stand for truth, I stand for justice, and I stand for the light! For darkness is forced to flee from the light, even if it happens to start from a small spark. The flame in all of us cannot be snuffed out. I choose to stand!" She punched her left fist into her right hand as she continued to pace.

PART 3: TESTED

6

THE CHOICE

Katerina made her way to the far side of the castle, out of sight of prying eyes. She walked to the end of a dark corridor and slowly opened the door. Walking up to the bed where her sister, Crystal lay, she said, "Crystal, I feel so conflicted right now. If you only would wake up. Things would start to make sense again. What have I done wrong? Why's God punishing me? It's my choice now, and I promise you, Crystal, that no matter what it takes, I'll bring you back to me. It's in my power to do so. I feel God has abandoned us; I'll prevail. I'll succeed where others have failed."

Lucas's words echoed around Katerina. *It's your choice. Did God really say that He would provide for all your needs and give you abundant life? Did He really say He would never leave you? Look at your life. You're alone.*

Katerina shook the thoughts away. "I choose to save you. Even if it'll destroy me, you'll survive. This is my promise to you, Crystal. Mother's gone; I can't lose you too. I only hope you wake to say goodbye to Mother with me." Katerina turned on her heel and left. With all the courage she could muster, she entered the war room where the other leading officials awaited her arrival. She nodded a simple greeting to each one.

"I'm sorry, Lady Kat. I heard about your mother and Princess Delores. Such a tragedy," Sir Gervon said as he handed Katerina a small token of sympathy, a simple green hooded cloak. "I have one for Lady Crystal too. Will she be joining us today?"

"Thank you no. She needs some time alone for now. I can take it to her."

Several soldiers and leaders of nearby territories gathered and handed Katerina tokens of sympathy and condolences. Katerina made her way to the front of the room and hardened her focus. "Now, enough with formalities, Lucas is more powerful than we could have ever imagined. Mother underestimated him. I won't. Now, we need a new plan, one he won't expect."

"What do you suggest?" a guard asked.

With fear, conviction, but determination in her eyes, Katerina announced, "I'm sending out for reinforcements."

"Good idea! As we gather, we can have a sendoff for your mother and Delores as well," Sir Gervon announced.

Katerina tried desperately to hold back her tears as she squared her shoulders and hardened her heart. *I can't afford to think about that now. There's too much at stake.* She panned the room as everyone nodded in agreement to Sir Gervon's suggestion. So, Katerina complied and nodded too.

———

*R*obert pondered Sam's words that weighed heavily upon him. "Sam, what do you mean I have to choose even if it means I'll lose what's most important to me? I fight for what's most important to me, not fight to lose it." Robert's muscles bulged as he thought of his mother, Nora, Josiah, and even Trevor. "I lost someone close to me before. It nearly tore me apart. I won't choose to go through that again."

Sam stepped back almost in fear. "You are angry just like Lucas. How can I trust someone so agitated?"

Robert felt as if he had been punched in the stomach with Sam's words. *How can I trust someone so aggressive?* He remembered thinking these same words when he thought of his dad. *I won't become my dad.* He fiddled with the blanket on the bed and slowly made eye contact with Sam. "I'm sorry; I just get so upset at the thought of someone hurting those I care about."

A knock at the door started both of them. A guard entered the room and said, "Sorry to disturb you, but Lady Kat's requesting your presence in the war room, Miss Sam."

Sam nodded and turned away from the bed. Robert touched her arm. "Will I see you again?"

"Of course, I still have more questions, and you don't have my trust yet." Sam nodded her goodbye and left the room. *You don't have my trust yet* still echoed in his mind. His thoughts turned to Senora; he had to earn her trust back too. He remembered the time he tried so desperately to get her attention, but that was the wrong way. Despite all that, she chose to save him and introduced him to Jesus. If it wasn't for Josiah and Senora, he wouldn't be alive today. He remembered that night like it was yesterday how he was so broken. He felt worthless and not deserving of any love or forgiveness.

So many times, Robert had tried to do the job only God could do. His mind wandered to a new memory. "How many times do I have to attend church before I can consider myself a Christian?" Robert asked.

Senora covered her mouth, stifling a laugh as she searched her thoughts for the best words to use to explain. "Ummm, well… going to church doesn't make you a Christian."

Puzzled, he scratched the back of his head and leaned closer to her. "What do you mean?"

Twirling her eagle pendent between her fingers, she looked up to the sky. "Being a Christian is being a Christ-follower. It's a relationship, not just routine and stuff to do. Your relationship with God isn't based on anything you can do. It's a free gift."

Taken aback, he stood and paced in front of her. "If we can't do anything, then how can we become a Christian?" He desperately shook his finger at her.

Senora stood and lowered his hand and placed her other hand on his shoulder. "It's based on what Christ has already done for us. With God, nobody's forgotten. Nobody's unlovable. No matter where or how far someone runs, they can't escape God's love for them."

His shoulders slumped, and he shook his head. "But how do we become a Christian?"

Rubbing his back, she explained, "You need to accept, repent, and receive."

Shooting his head up, he shrugged away from her and stomped to the curb and sat back down, resting his elbows on his shoulders and staring at his feet. "What do you mean by accept, repent, and receive?" Robert scratched his head in confusion.

Walking up and sitting next to him, she stared straight ahead. "Accept that you're a sinner you've made mistakes in your life. Repent means to surrender your sin into God's hands because the result of our sin is death. Christ took your sin upon Himself when He died. When He came back to life, He conquered death and gave us the free gift of friendship with Him. You need to search your heart and ask yourself if you believe God loves you."

"That's hard to believe. I've made so many mistakes in my life, I still feel like a worthless rag waiting to be used and abused." He looked over at her with tears streaming down his face.

Placing her arm around his shoulders, she gave him a

gentle squeeze. "I understand that feeling, but as you grow and spend more time with God, you better understand who God is creating you to be."

"What do you mean by spending more time with God? How do you spend time with God?" He picked up a random stone and tossed it in the grass beside them.

Pointing to her chin, then waving her hand in a circular motion, she said, "You get to know God. I mean, think of it this way. Let's look back at how you interact with Trevor and Mark."

Shaking in confusion, he raised his eyebrow and looked out of the corner of his eyes at her. "Mark? Mark and I aren't friends."

Raising her hands in surrender, she said, "Just hear me out. What's the difference between you and Trevor compared to you and Mark?"

He picked up another stone and tossed it on the grass. "First off, Mark and I aren't, nor will we ever be, friends."

Turning her head and twirling her hair, she asked, "Why?"

"Mark's a jerk! We have nothing in common. For starters." He threw his hands in the air stood, and started pacing again.

"I used to feel that way about you, and now we're friends."

Robert stopped in his tracks and stared at her with his mouth open. "What does that have to do with anything?"

Pretending to wave the white flag of defeat, she motioned for him to sit down again. "Ok then. What made you and Trevor friends?"

He sighed and shifted back over and sat beside her again, pulling at some blades of grass. "That's easy. We liked the same things and spent time with each other."

She smiled and snapped her fingers. "That's it!"

"What's it?" He shrugged in confusion.

"You made time to spend together. That's what you need to do with God." She picked up a stone and tossed it ahead of them.

"How do I do that?"

She reached into her backpack, pulled out her Bible and placed it into Robert's hands. "Reading your Bible, going to church, praying. Study the Bible and apply what the Bible says."

Holding the Bible close to his chest, he turned his head to look at her again. "Ok, so as I become closer to God and understand Him then I'll be a Christian?"

He twirled her hair again and shrugged. "That's part of it. Talk to Him and allow Him into your life. Make Him your center and accept His forgiveness and love for you. It's all about you entering into that friendship with Him."

"Thank you, Nora. Can you pray with me?"

Being pulled from his thoughts, he heard some guards talking outside his room. "Strange day. Hey?"

"You can say that again. First Delores and Scarlett. Now, this strange man, Bobby. Makes you wonder what the creator is doing."

"Tell me about it. I know He doesn't make garbage but what masterpiece is He planning now? I just wish He would give us more details at times."

"You got that right. Come on, let's go relieve the front guard."

As their voices faded away, the thought, *He doesn't make garbage but what masterpiece is He planning?* hung in the air as Robert was reminded of a youth retreat Senora and Josiah took him to a year ago. The speaker sat in front of the microphone talking, *"Jesus is God son. and He created me. He does not make garbage: He created masterpieces.:* A love overpowered him that night; life would never be the same. He felt as if someone grabbed him by both arms, picked him up and, with a firm hand on his back, led him to the stage. His whole body shook; he couldn't contain his tears. A young girl approached him and simply said, "Can I pray with you?"

With a lump in his throat, he fell to his knees. "God, if

You can hear me, help me to believe. Change my heart, renew my hope, enter my heart, and forgive me." He raised feeling thankful the speaker listened to God's call despite his pain. He recalled the speaker mentioning being involved in a hit and run only two weeks before coming to the conference to speak, explaining his need for speaking on stage in a wheelchair.

His life didn't change overnight. But he began an amazing adventure. He had many unanswered questions. Even after God entered his heart, he still made bad choices. Even though his dad was still an angry drunk, he now had a Heavenly Father who loved and accepted him. It wasn't his job to save everyone; he had to surrender that choice into God's hands because God was the only one who could change a person's heart.

With time for everything, he needed to trust in God's timing. Yes, he had made mistakes, but God would never give up on him. "So, no matter how hard things get, there's always light somewhere. Even if it may be small, it's always there. Once you find that light, hold onto it because darkness will always flee from the light, and in turn, that small light will grow." Senora's words hung in the room, and his thoughts returned his focus back to his present surroundings.

———

*S*enora leaned close to Robert's hospital bed and said, "So no matter how hard things get, there is always light somewhere. Even if it may be small, it's always there. Once you find that light, hold onto it because darkness will always flee from the light and in turn that small light will grow." She spoke barely above a whisper. Reaching for Robert's hand, she continued, "You're one of the strongest people I know, Bobbie. Never give up. Remember your battle's not alone." Sarah entered the room, startling Senora.

"Nora, how's he doing?" Sarah asked as she approached the bed.

"He's strong, but he still has not opened his eyes."

"I just got word that the police want to talk to me. Are you ok with sitting with Bobbie a little longer?"

"Yes, that's fine. I'll be here. You go do what you need to." Sarah hugged Senora as a thank you and left the room again.

Two police officers met Sarah in the hallway. "Sorry to bother you at this time, but they just towed your son's truck to the impound lot. Would you like to go through the car and get any personal belongings? We have ruled the collision as bad road conditions, due to the gravel road. So, you're welcome to go through things," an officer stated.

"I don't have a vehicle here. I came with some friends," Sarah replied.

"I can drive you over and after you're done, I'm willing to bring you back."

"That would be nice. Thank you." Sarah smiled gratefully. The two officers led Sarah to their patrol car and drove her to the impound lot.

An officer led her to what remained of Robert's truck. The sight of crumpled metal shocked Sarah. "It's a miracle your son's even alive," the officer declared. Sarah nodded as the second police officer pried open what remained of the passenger side door. Sarah leaned in and looked around at broken CDs and shattered glass.

She carefully felt around in the seat cushions and along the floor. Her hand touched a crumpled envelope, and she pulled it out of the car. *It's the letter from his dad unopened.* Sarah grabbed the letter, turned, and looked at the two officers. "This is all I need. Everything else is either broken or garbage. Can you please take me back to the hospital now?" The officer nodded and took her back to their patrol car and drove her away. Sarah thanked the two officers for their help and returned to Robert's hospital room.

Senora looked up as Sarah entered. "Is everything alright?"

"I don't know," Sarah whispered as she approached Senora. Sarah placed the unopened envelope on Robert's bedside table.

"What's that?" Senora asked.

"Partly the cause of mine and Bobbie's fight. It's a letter from Tony, Bobbie's dad. I just wish he could see that Tony has changed."

Senora stiffened a little at the thought of Robert's dad. "Only time will tell. Let's just hope Bobbie wakes up."

Sarah nodded and pulled a chair close to Robert's bed. Senora excused herself and wheeled herself back to her room to rest. Sarah reached for the envelope and opened it, reading out loud for Robert to hear:

Dear Bobbie,

It pains me to think of all the darkness I have brought into your life. I do love you; I just don't know how to show that. If only you could understand the pain I grew up with. I'm not trying to make excuses, but the thought of never speaking to you again is tearing me to the core. I'm sorry, and being able to win your trust and forgiveness is my new goal. I pray that you won't allow your hatred toward me to destroy you. Talk to me. Please forgive me. I have found forgiveness through Jesus, but I have so far to go. I want to start with my relationship with you. I know I don't deserve it. I have taken so much from you; I hope in time you will be able to forgive me.

Love,
Dad

7

CAVE OF EXPLORATION

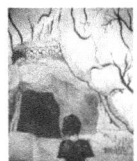

*R*obert sat up when Sam entered his room. "I don't have much time before I have to rejoin the war room meeting. I just wanted to see how you were getting along." Sam said.

"I'm getting better. How're you doing?" Robert replied.

"The Lord will provide; as it is said to this day, 'On the mountain of the Lord it shall be provided.'[1] Even though I still don't trust you, I have to admit, the Lord did provide you when I needed help. I want to thank you for being my provided escape."

"You're welcome. I don't like to see a woman getting hurt by anyone." Robert clenched his fists.

A guard entered the room and stood at attention. "Miss Sam, you're wanted back in the war room now." Sam nodded and left the room.

She re-entered the war room, and Katerina looked up at her, "So, how's your rescuer doing?" Katerina teased, attempting to lighten the mood.

"He's recovering nicely. Now, do we have a plan?" Sam asked.

"We'll need all hands in on this one. In my experience,

93

Lucas always seems three steps ahead. He must have been planning this from the beginning. He took my mother from me; we need to take his power away from him." Katerina turned her attention to Sam. "Now, your rescuer, what do you know about him? Where did he come from? Is he a spy?"

"What? A spy? If he was a spy, why would he go through such great lengths to rescue me? When I was already Lucas's captive?"

"You know Lucas' deception runs deep. You need to keep an eye on him, Sam. We don't need any more distractions." Sam agreed, trying to hide her excitement at getting to know more about this stranger. She felt strangely drawn to him.

"Now, we need to rest. We'll regroup in the morning. I want you all to think about a plan of attack. When we meet in the morning, we'll combine our thoughts and hopefully destroy Lucas once and for all. I sent out the call. I know The Called will come; we just need to give them time. Dismissed." Each guard nodded and left the room, leaving Katerina and Sam alone. "Sam, I wanted to talk to you in private."

"Yes, Lady Kat? What is it?"

"Your rescuer. When do you think he'll be well enough to move?"

"He's recovering quickly. He should be good to go by tomorrow. Why?"

"I don't trust him. I think he should go into the cellblock until we know more."

"Wait! What? He risked a lot to get me back here. I'll watch him. He won't cause any problems."

"And if he does?"

"Then I'll take the blame." *There's something different about him. I don't trust him, either, but he knows Nora, so he can't be that bad.*

"Fine, you need to watch him closely. Dismissed." Sam nodded and left the war room. Katerina exited through the hidden entry and followed the chamber halls toward Crystal's room. Careful not to make a sound, she entered and sat on the side of the bed. Soon, a flash of red appeared behind her, and she turned with a start. There stood Lucas.

"Lucas, what are you doing here? You killed my mother, and my sister isn't waking up."

"Now, now, Kat. I'm the only person who can wake Crystal. I need Sam."

"Sam? I won't betray anyone else."

"Betray? No, you misunderstand me. I just need you to separate her from everyone else. I'll do the rest. You want Crystal to wake up, don't you?"

Katerina's heart fluttered with regret. *I'll never forgive myself if I had a way to wake you Crystal and I didn't take it.* "What do you want me to do?"

———≈≈≈———

am entered Robert's room. "Sam, what is it?"

"I told you: I don't trust you. Why should I trust you? Give me a reason."

"I can't give you a reason. Personally, I'm pretty worthless. My own father saw me as trash," Robert said.

Sam walked right up to him and looked him square in the face. "God doesn't make trash, and I believe he has a plan for everyone. We just need to discover what that plan is."

"If God has a plan for me, then why do I fail at everything I do?"

"You saved me. That is not a failure." Sam proclaimed. "You get some rest. Tomorrow, your day starts early." Sam turned and walked to the door. She looked back at Robert over her shoulder and smiled.

"Early? What do you mean?"

"You start your training."

"Training? For what?"

"We'll need to be ready for whatever Lucas throws at us.

I'll help you prepare." Sam left the room before Robert had time to object.

He rested his head; deep down, his heart leaped at the thought of spending time with this fiery redhead. *She intrigues me*, he thought as he closed his eyes.

———∽∾∽———

*R*obert was surprised awake when a shirt was thrown onto his face. He removed it to see Sam standing before him in full armour. "Ok, get dressed. I'll meet you in the courtyard," Sam commanded as she turned and left the room. Robert stood, stepped into his pants, and pulled the new shirt over his head. He slowly made his way down to the courtyard where Sam waited for him. As he walked up to her, she tossed a sword at his feet. "First, hand to hand combat."

"What? Combat? I won't hit a girl."

"Pick up the sword."

"No, there has to be another way."

Sam swung her leg and knocked Robert over. "What was that for?"

"Everyone needs to know how to fight. If you don't, you're already dead."

"I know how to fight; I just won't fight you."

Sam kicked Robert's side. "Fight me. You won't hurt me. You have seen what Lucas can do. Defend yourself." Sam swung her fist toward Robert's face, but Robert caught her fist and pushed her away.

"I said I won't fight you."

"Good, you do have some skill. Fine, if you won't fight me, pick up your sword and defend yourself." Sam kicked the sword toward him. He saw a knife fly through the air, and he dodged as it stuck in the ground beside him. From beside Sam, a guard readied another throwing knife to toss his way. The second knife flew his way as he rolled to his side, picked up the sword and knocked the knife off course, sending it to the ground. Sam walked up to Robert and pulled him to his feet. She leaned close. "Defend yourself," she said right above a whisper as she moved to one side. Another three knives flew toward him. He swung his sword to the left, knocking one knife down, then swung to the right, knocking the second knife down, but missed the third knife as it skinned his right arm.

"You'll learn. Not bad for your first try. Again."

"Wait! What?" Robert questioned as another three knives flew at him. He turned and knocked two knives to the ground simultaneously and swung his sword in front of himself as the third knife hit his sword. The third knife fell as Sam swung a sword at him. He blocked, and the two were engaged in a heated combat. Sam kicked the sword out of Robert's hand.

"You learn quickly. Come with me. There's somewhere you need to be." Sam walked out of the courtyard toward the stables. She emerged on a horse and rode up to Robert. "Do you ride?"

"No, I have never been on a horse in my life." Sam reached her hand down and pulled him up behind her.

"Ride with me."

"Where're we going?"

"To the Revealing Cave of Exposure." *I have too many unanswered questions that need to be exposed. I need to understand this stranger if I'm going to trust him in battle. Kat saw him as a threat, I need to prove he isn't a spy.* Their horse galloped away from the castle.

—⁓⁓⁓—

S am slowed as they rode along a narrow ridge on the cliff side of a mountain. "This is mount Divulge." They turned around a narrow corner, and there before them, stood a large cave entrance. Sam dismounted as Robert fell off the horse. She chuckled as she helped Robert to his feet. "You need to go in there. Alone," Sam declared.

"What will I find in there?" Robert asked.

"It's different for everyone. But what's hidden in the darkness will be revealed in the light."

"What if I don't go?"

"You must. If you want to be prepared for Lucas, you need to know yourself."

"I don't want to know myself."

"You must. Go."

"Do I have another option?" Robert struggled to swallow the lump forming in his throat.

"No, this is the only way."

I will not give in to fear. Robert squared his shoulders and made his way into the cave. The farther he walked, the darker his surroundings became. He shivered. Soon, he found himself standing alone in the darkness. A small sound reached his ears. *What's that?* Robert thought. *Is that crying? What? Is someone hurt?* "Hello? Is anyone there?"

"Please, go away. I'm Nobody," a small voice warned. Robert ran toward the voice. "Stop! I said I'm Nobody. Leave me be." Robert soon came up to a small boy who sat in the crevice of a rock, appearing to hide.

Robert held out his hand. "Come, let me help you. What're you hiding from?"

"My uncle. He'll hurt you, too, if he finds you."

"We can stand together. Nobody should hurt someone else." Robert reached for the young boy's hand. "What's your name?"

"Nobody. At least that's what my uncle called me."

"I'm Bobbie. What does your mom call you?"

"Mom's gone. It's only Uncle and I, but she called me Tony."

"Tony? Ok, I'll call you Tony." Robert smiled as he kneeled to look level in the boy's eyes. The boy grimaced but chose not to pull away.

"Why would you want to help me?"

"I believe everyone has the right to live and be known."

"That's nice."

"Now, do you know what we're supposed to do here?"

"I hide. I want to fade away; if he can't see me, he can't hurt me no more. I won't be like my uncle."

Robert scratched his head. *This boy sounds like me. I refuse to be like my dad.*

"Nobody! Where are you?" A cruel voice floated in the air.

"My uncle. Quick, we need to run." Tony took Robert's hand and led him farther into the darkness. Soon, Robert ran by himself, the small boy nowhere to be seen, and a small light formed ahead of him. He knelt down to take in the sight. Soon a middle-aged man appeared pulling Tony by the arm.

"Nobody, you piece of garbage. Why are you so stupid?" Robert watched in horror as the man shoved Tony's little head under water. Tony's little feet shook trying to get balance and pull himself free. "Nobody, you need to learn respect." The man released Tony as the little boy fell backward, coughing and sputtering for breath.

"I'll never respect you." The man grabbed Tony by the ear and dragged him to his feet.

Robert snuck up behind the man and punched him.

"Come on, Tony! Run. You're free." He led the young boy away from the scene.

"I'll never be free. Bobbie, you don't understand. I'm unlovable."

"I feel that way at times, but life isn't hopeless."

"You don't know anything. There's no hope for me. I must hide." Tony looked up with red eyes.

Robert backed away. "What do you mean?" Tony pushed Robert away and ran into the darkness again. Robert sat there alone feeling confused. "I need to help this boy. No person deserves to be treated this way. God doesn't create garbage." Robert stood and walked with a newfound confidence toward the direction Tony ran. Soon, he heard yelling ahead.

"You worthless piece of skin. You'll learn your place." Robert heard Tony's uncle again. He looked ahead, and he saw Tony on the floor. His uncle stood above him, kicked him, and shoved him against the wall. "You're Nobody, and that's all you'll ever be."

"Stop." Robert shoved Tony's uncle away and pulled Tony into the darkness again.

"Why do you keep saving me? I told you I'm not worth saving."

"I don't believe that. God says, 'You did not choose me, but I chose you and appointed you so that you might go and bear fruit-fruit that will last-and so that whatever you ask in my name the Father will give you.'"[2]

"I told you I'm Nobody. I'm not worth saving. I'm garbage just as my uncle says."

"No, the Holy Father knew you before you ever took your first breath. He chose to give you life. There's forgiveness and love for you."

"You say that, but do you truly believe that?" Tony disappeared into the darkness again. Robert followed him. Light shone before him as he found himself standing in what looked like his old basement. A lump formed in his throat. He turned at the sound of voices coming from upstairs. He slowly climbed the stairs, then stopped when he saw his dad slumped at the table. He appeared to be crying. Robert sat at the top of the stairs and watched in the shadows. "I'm Nobody," his dad whispered.

Soon a younger version of Sarah walked up behind him and said, "That's not true. Tony, you're going to be a father."

Tony clenched his fists.

"Why would you do that to me, Sarah? All I've ever known is worthlessness and hopelessness."

"This baby could be your second chance. Tony, I love you."

"I won't be like my uncle."

Robert shook in horror. *Is it true? Is Nobody, a younger version of my dad?* Soon Robert found himself back in his basement crouched in a corner. He saw himself and Trevor talking. "No, I could never forgive him for this." Robert shuts his eyes as he heard the gun blast. He forced himself to look as he saw Trevor's lifeless body on the floor. Robert turned and ran away from the scene, trying desperately to escape the painful memory.

"This is all on you, boy," Robert's dad's voice echoed behind him. He stumbled and soon found himself in a prison cell. His dad sat alone on his bed. "I'm Nobody. I don't deserve my son, I don't deserve forgiveness, and I don't deserve love. I broke my promise. I promised I would not be like my uncle. Now, look at me." Robert fell to his knees to see this broken shadow of his dad.

The scene shifted, and he found himself kneeling in the dark cave alone. *I'm Nobody.* He heard the small boy's voice echo around him. He looked up and saw the young boy standing before him, eyes red from crying. "Now that you know the truth, do you agree with my uncle?" the boy asked.

"What do you mean?" Robert asked.

"I'm Nobody. A spawn of bitterness, only created to be tortured and forgotten."

"I believe everyone has a purpose."

The boy before him transformed into his dad. "Even me? I spoke the lies I grew up with. It's in my nature. People are worthless and are only there to be used and abused."

"No, I don't believe that."

"Then, you must be that waste of skin that came from Nobody."

"No." Robert forced himself to look at his dad. He clenched his fists and ground his teeth.

His dad lunged at him and shoved him against the rock wall.

"What're you going to do, boy?"

"You aren't Nobody." Everything went black, he fell to the ground, and the silence weighed heavily on him.

"What do I do? I don't understand," his dad asked.

"Life's full of choices. No matter the choice you make, you will lose everything that's important to you." He heard an unfamiliar voice.

"You stand at a crossroads. You need to choose," Nobody's voice declared, but it was too dark to see the little boy.

"What are my choices? What choice is there? I hate him for what he did to Trevor. I can't forgive him."

"You could forgive because Christ has forgiven you," the voice claimed.[3]

"How can I forgive such pain?"

"I never forgave the pain my uncle caused," Tony stated.

"It destroyed me. Nobody is my name, and Nobody is all I'll ever be."

"No."

"Whoever is forgiven little loves little, but whoever's forgiven much loves much." the voice declared.[4]

"I don't know if I can forgive."

"Let me help you." Sam's voice whispered. "The Saviour's with you always. Open yourself to hurt and allow Him to teach you forgiveness."

Soon, Robert stood alone in the dark cave. The cave was illuminated with the glow of fire. Robert walked along the rock wall toward the glow. He was shocked at the sight of a large Red Dragon standing before him in the cave. "The fire will purify, but you need to accept purification." A blast of fire shot from the dragon's mouth and rippled up the cave walls. Sweat dripped off Robert's forehead. "Unforgiveness will lead you to anger, deception, destruction, and you'll become everything you have fought to destroy. Deception will lead you down a path to the father of lies. You can't serve two masters. Choose!"

The heat of the fire started to suffocate Robert. "I yield. I choose."

"What? What choice will you make?" Sam asked.

Robert fell to the rock floor, gasping for air. "I choose to forgive." Robert spat out the words as he fell to the ground.

Sam transformed back into her human form and ran to Robert's side. The flames went out, and the two sat in the darkness. "Have you ever felt like your entire world was crashing in on you? You stand at a crossroads with many choices before you, but no matter what choice you make, you'll lose what you thought was most important to you? When all hope is lost and darkness is thriving, you stand at the brink of destruction. When you feel defeated, what choice will you make?" Sam whispered in Robert's ear.

"What choice is there?" Robert gasped.

"War is upon us. You may have passed this test, but when the time comes, will you know what choice to make? Forgiveness is key. I can see now the Saviour's with you. You hold His words within your heart just as Nora did."

"How was this a test? I barely survived."

"Just think about this: when your entire world is crashing in on you, you face a crossroad with many choices, but no matter what choice you make, you'll lose what's most important to you. What choice will you make?"

"Honestly, I don't know. How can you ask me to choose something that'll cause me to lose what's most important to me?"

"You're a treasured possession. I can see the same thing in you I once saw in Nora. 'For you are a people holy to the Lord your God, and the Lord has chosen you to be a people for his treasured possession, out of all the people who are on the face of the earth.'"[5] Sam touched Robert's cheek and brushed a loose strand of hair from his forehead.

PART 4: FORGIVENESS

8

BROKEN BONDS

*W*alking through the dark tunnel illuminated with intense heat, Senora looked around as flames rippled like waves along the rock wall. She saw movement ahead. Cautiously approaching the scene, she saw Robert surrounded by a tornado of flames. She ran toward him. "Bobbie," she said at the top of her lungs, but her voice was drowned out by what sounded like Sam's voice.

"You must choose," Sam's voice reached Senora's ears. She stopped in her tracks seeing Robert fall to his knees.

"Bobbie," Senora called sitting up in her hospital bed. *Was that a dream?* The fire was weeks ago, and Robert still had not awakened. She turned to look at her clock. It read 3:00 a.m. She swung her legs over the side of her bed, reached for her crutches, and stood to her feet. As she winced in pain, she limped her way down the hallway to Robert's room and sat in a chair next to his bed.

"Hey there, Bobbie. It's me again. I had another dream about you. Only this time, you were surrounded by fire. I heard an old friend's voice. I'll tell you about her, I promise. You just need to wake up." Senora took hold of Roberts hand and brushed his forehead with her other hand. "You're burning up." It worried Senora to see his face turn fire red and beads of sweat forming on his forehead.

Senora pressed the call button, followed by "code blue" alarms. Robert started shaking and appeared to be having a seizure.

"Nurse, please help."

The nurses rushed into Robert's room and quickly ushered Senora out.

"Help him," Senora demanded.

"I'll update you, dear. Try to rest," a nurse said as she closed the door. Senora stood there feeling helpless. She turned and made her way to the hospital chapel.

Sitting down in one of the pews, she prayed, "God, please heal Bobbie. He has so much he hasn't done yet."

"See now that I, even I, am He, and there is no God beside me, I kill and I make alive; I wound and I heal; and there is none that can deliver out of my hand."[1] Senora looked up from her prayer and was startled to see the Tall Bearded Man towering before her.

Taken a back, Senora nearly toppled out of the pew. "What're you doing here? I haven't seen you in two years. Now you return? And how're you here and not in Treasure Kingdom?" Senora stammered over her words, as she clutched at her chest, gasping for air from the shock.

"I come to bestow wisdom upon you," he declared as he gently sat in the pew in front of her so he could look her in the eyes.

She looked around as fear began to rise up within her. "What sort of wisdom?"

"The illusion of safety is a hard thing to give up." He gently placed his large hand on her shoulder.

Before fear could take control, she grasped the back of the pew in front of her and dug her nails in. Taking beep breaths to calm her nerves, she asked, "Safety? Is Bobbie in danger?"

"Sometimes God needs to pin someone down in a place

where they have nowhere else to run and are forced to face Him, when they choose to depend on their comfort zones instead of God. It is natural for people to fear losing the things they possess and have control over. These are the things that will cost us in order to behave as God's children. We are to show sacrificial love and care to the most vulnerable, ones who could never repay us." He spoke as softly and gently as he could.

Senora shuttered and shrugged the hand free from her shoulder. She stood and walked around the room, pondering, "I admit it is hard to see Bobbie in such a vulnerable state."

"The only way to obey God's law is to believe that God exists, that He is good, and that He rewards those who seek Him. There's no other way. God has your back." He stood and moved in front of her, stopping her and forcing her to look up at him.

Tears streamed down her cheeks, and she considered the consequence that might be before Robert. "I do believe. But what does it mean that sometimes God needs to pin down someone? I am scared to lose Bobbie."

"The only way to overcome the fear of losing the things or people who give us a sense of security is to overcome that with a greater fear. If you've heard God speak, if you've heard the lion roar, then the fear of turning down God overrides your fear of everything else."

Senora stood taller as confidence and peace filled her up. She could feel the fear melting away. "I believe nothing is impossible with God, and Bobbie is in His hands. But will Bobbie die?"

"For He wounds, but He binds up; He shatters, but His hands heal."[2] The Tall Bearded Man turned and walked back to a nearby pew and sat down.

She placed her hands on her hips and stomped her foot defiantly. "Why do you speak in riddles? I don't understand."

"A time to kill, and a time to heal; a time to break down, and a time to build up."[3]

She slumped her shoulders and walked over, sliding into the pew next to him. "Please answer me plainly. What time is it?"

"And when Jesus heard it, He said to them, those who are well have no need of a physician, but those who are sick. I came not here to call the righteous, but sinners."[4] He tapped his hand on her knee to assure her everything would be ok.

"Will you heal him? Please grant me a piece of wisdom." She turned to face him more directly and grabbed the back of the pew once again.

"He has his own journey. Don't give up on him. He's strong, but he'll need you in time." Suddenly, Senora was alone. She stood and hobbled back toward Robert's room. A nurse met her in the hallway.

"There you are. You need your rest, dear," the nurse stated.

As Senora wrapped her arm around the nurse's neck, she leaned on her for support. "Bobbie? How's Bobbie?"

"He's stable. Let me help you back to your room. Rest now, and you can see him again in the morning," she said while directing Senora back to her room.

Senora nodded and leaned on the nurse for support as they walked back to her room. Senora sat on her bed as the nurse helped lift her tender feet. Senora rested her head back on her pillow and closed her eyes. "Thank you."

"You're welcome." The nurse covered Senora with a warm blanket. "Rest now." Senora watched as the nurse left the room. She caught a glimpse of the Tall Bearded Man smiling, nodding, and fading away as she closed her eyes.

———

S am and Robert returned to the castle and rode up to the stables. As Sam dismounted, two guards approached them and pulled Robert off the horse. Robert struggled to get free and regain his balance.

Tossing the reins to a stable boy, Sam stormed up to the two guards. "Wait. What's the meaning of this?" she reached for one of the guard's arms and tried to pull Robert free.

"Lady Kat's orders. He's going to the cell block," the guard said as they dragged Robert away as he kicked at the ground and struggled to get free.

"Believe me; I'll have a talk with that young lady," Sam declared as she crossed her arms, and her hair glowed crimson. She turned on her heel and headed to the throne room, entering the room with a bang.

Her eyes shot up toward the door as Katerina jumped at the sound. "Lady Sam, please come in."

Sam speed-walked right up to Katerina with determination in her eyes. "Why did you order Bobbie to the cell block? Is he our prisoner now?"

She rolled her eyes and looked back down at the map before her. "I don't know him, and you said it yourself: you didn't trust him. I'm preparing to fight Lucas; I don't need a spy with us who can betray us at any moment."

Sam placed her hands on the table as fire flared in her eyes. "I understand, but he passed the test."

Without raising her head, Kat stared at Sam's hands as they began to glow. "Test? What test?"

Smoke started to rise from the table just below Sam's hands. "I took him to the Revealing Cave of Exposure."

Katerina lunged at the table, slamming it slightly into Sam's stomach. "What? If he was working for Lucas, you might've endangered us all. How dare you reveal part of our training grounds!"

As she regained her balance, the glow subsided. She took a deep breath and stood her ground. "He passed."

Kat tossed the map aside and jumped on the table, and within seconds, she was standing in front of Sam. "That's not the point."

Turning her back on Katerina, she tossed her hair and stared out the window. "I didn't expect you to understand. You're just a child."

Katerina grabbed Sam's arm and turned her to face her. "You're lucky Princess Delores held you with such regard, or I would send you to the cell block."

Brushing Katerina's grasp on her arm, she stared down at her. "I'm sorry, but I told you I would keep an eye on him, and I have. He hasn't done anything out of the ordinary that would cause him to go to the cell block. Please, release him."

Busying herself with gathering the maps and supplies she had knocked off the table, Katerina looked up briefly. "What's he to you? Won't he distract you?"

Sam knelt and helped Katerina pick up the mess on the floor. "I can focus. You know this."

Sighing in defeat, she stood, tossed the mess on the table, and yelled, "Fine! Guards."

Three guards entered, "You called, Lady Kat?"

Pointing at Sam, she nodded toward the guards, "Yes, bring the one they call Bobbie here."

The guards bowed and back out of the room. "Yes, my lady. Right away."

Sam tossed the rest of the mess on the table and started organizing it again. She reached out and squeezed Katerina's shoulder. "Thank you."

Looking up with concern in her eyes, Kat stared at her. "You think you can trust him?"

"I do trust him; he has earned that. There's also something that draws me to him," Sam pondered as the guards returned with Robert in tow.

"Sam, what's going on?" Robert looked back and forth between the two, examining their expressions to see if he should be preparing for another fight or if this would be a friendly gathering. The guards shoved him forward and he fell before them on his hands and knees.

Squaring her shoulders and attempting the most demanding voice she could, she said, "Silence! I'm Lady Kat. Sam has spoken to me on your behalf. To test your true loyalty, I am sending you two on a quest."

Sam walked over to Robert and helped him up. Startled by Katerina's words she looked over her shoulder in surprise. "Quest? What kind of quest?"

Turning her back to them she spoke softly, "You're to go to the Waterfall of Tears, find the Crystallite Truth Gem, and bring it to me,"

"We can do that. Right, Sam?" Robert replied. Sam just glared at him, turned her attention back to Katerina, and bowed her head.

"As per your request," Sam replied. She grabbed Robert's arm and pulled him out of the throne room.

"Hey now! Why the hostility?" Robert asked Sam once they entered the courtyard.

Stopping abruptly, she turned and found herself standing nose to nose with Robert. "Why did you say that?"

Staggering back, a little off balance, he scratched the back of his head in confusion. "Say what?"

Pacing back and forth and throwing her hands in the air, she said, "That we could do that?"

Robert walked up to her and placed his hands on her shoulders. He leaned in and smiled. "You don't think we can?"

Turning away again, she kicked at the ground and stared up at the throne room window. "You don't understand. You don't know the terrain. The Waterfall of Tears? The Crystallite Truth Gem? Shadows at every turn?"

Robert stood in front of her and took hold of her hands. "Hey, I believe in you. We escaped Lucas once. Right? Besides, what's a Crystallite Truth Gem?" Sam looked into Robert's dark eyes and saw such confidence behind them.

Relenting in her protest, she released one hand and lead Robert toward the stables. "It's a Jewel of Truth. When someone holds it, they're forced to only speak the truth."

"Oh, so it's like a truth serum but in the form of a crystal."

Stopping and considering his analogy, she just smiled and continued into the stables. "Um, sure. If you say so."

He squeezed her hand, and as their hands swung back and forth together, he smiled. "We can do this together."

"I know we can do it. It's just…" Sam looked back at the castle. "Kat."

Looking over his shoulder at the throne room window, he shrugged. "Lady Kat? What about her?"

Sam rubbed her chin between her fingers as she considered all the angles. "I'm not sure. It could just be her grieving the loss of her mother, but I felt she was hiding something."

Confused, he looked back at Sam. "Hiding something? What made you think that?"

She shrugged and pulled her hand away. "Just a feeling I get. Why on the brink of war would she send us away? Especially, to find something that has only been whispered about."

Speed-walking to keep up with Sam, he got in step with her. "What do you mean, whispered about?"

"Never mind! She has requested. It's not my place to question." Sam mounted her horse; she reached out her hand to pull Robert up behind her. They rode out of the courtyard and turned toward the Sheol Mountains.

Robert jumped at the clap of thunder when he looked toward their destination. "That looks like quite the storm brewing," Robert said as he pointed toward the mountain.

"That's Sheol Mountains, the border of Shadow Dominion," Sam declared.

"Shadow Dominion? I thought we were going to the Waterfall of Tears?"

"We are, but the Waterfall of Tears is on the other side of Shadow Dominion."

"What? You mean we have to go through Shadow Dominion? Why didn't you say that before?"

"Why do you think I glared at you?" Sam directed her horse closer to the building storm.

———————

*S*enora was startled awake by a clap of thunder outside her hospital window. "Quite the storm brewing," a nurse said as she entered Senora's room. She turned to close the blinds on the window.

"Could you please leave them open?" Senora asked as the nurse paused to give her a strange look. "I like to watch the colours of the lightning." The nurse smiled in amusement and left the room again. Just then, Senora saw a big spark of forked lightning shoot across the sky followed quickly by a giant clap of thunder, which sent the walls of her room shaking.

Senora shivered with delight. "God, you're so creative and powerful. Thank you for sharing this beauty with me." Soon, Senora's thoughts turned to Robert. She stood, reached for her crutches and limped to his room. Making her way to his bedside, she sat down in the nearby chair, and held Robert's hand. "Hi, Bobbie. Just wanted to tell you of the beautiful storm we're having. Such majestic colours. You should wake up and enjoy the sight with me. Jo and Sylvia had to return to work and school. They send their love. Your mom should be by later today to see you. She would be overjoyed to see your dark brown eyes again." Senora jumped at another clap of thunder. "My feet are healing nicely; I think I'll be off the crutches in a few weeks. They remove the bandages in just a few days. Your mom dropped off another letter for you. I'm not sure if you want to hear it or not. She read you the first one, but she wanted you to wake up and read this one yourself."

Another clap of thunder rattled the hospital walls.

———∞———

*R*obert jumped as another clap of thunder shook the ground beneath them. Their horse stumbled and paced. Sam dismounted and grabbed the reins to calm the horse. As the horse reared slightly, Robert fell to the ground.

"Easy now. Are you ok, Bobbie?" Sam asked.

"I'll be fine." Robert stood and brushed the dirt from his pants, feeling a little embarrassed.

"We're close. I'll send the horse back. He's too jumpy and will draw attention to us." Sam turned the horse around and released it to return to the castle. "He knows his way back." Another clap of thunder turned their attention toward the mountain. "Be on your guard, for Drayvon attacks your dreams. He could turn your dreams against you, and they'd become nightmares."

Waving off her warnings, he put on his bravest face. "My whole life, I've lived in a nightmare, and I'm still alive. I'll not be shaken, not even by this Drayvon person."

"Many others have underestimated him, even me. Don't be so sure." Sam said as she gathered some supplies in a satchel she had taken from her saddle before the horse left. She tossed it over her shoulder and looked Robert in the eyes.

Placing his hands on his hips and hanging his head, Robert quickly scratched his nose and placed his hand on his hips again. "I've already lost so much-lived in terror and torture. What more can he do to me? Except take my life?"

Storming up to Robert, she punched him in the shoulder. "Don't say that, Bobbie. Drayvon has a way of smelling your fear. More than you might like. Just be careful. We're at the border of Shadow Dominion. Why would Kat send us this way?" She breathed heavily through her nose as she stared into the thick forest before them.

Following her gaze, he said, "Do you have doubts?"

Shaking her head sadly and with less confidence than he had seen in her before. Sam said, "she just seems off."

He reached for the satchel on Sam's shoulder and took a step closer the forest's edge. "She just lost her mother. She's young."

Shrugging, she tilted her head slightly and smiled. "That must be it."

Looking up toward the storm raging overhead, he looked at Sam with concern. "Is the Crystallite of Truth worth the risk?"

Squaring her shoulders, she punched Robert again in the shoulder and stepped into the forest. "I don't know. But she's acting queen right now. I have to follow her orders."

Turning his attention back to where Sam just vanished into the trees he shrugged and followed. "Is there a way around Shadow Dominion?"

"It would take too long. Lucas's growing in strength. We need to defeat him." Sam looked over her shoulder at him and smiled again.

"The storm's gettin worse." Sheets of rain pound down on their shoulders. Shielding his eyes from the rain he blinked at Sam, "Should we wait for it to let up?"

"It'll never let up. It's always dark and stormy in Shadow Dominion. We just need to keep moving forward. Be alert! You never know who's watching." Sam took Robert's hand and led him up the mountain; a bolt of lightning struck the side of the mountain and sent rocks tumbling straight for them.

SHEOL MOUNTAIN

*W*ith the fast-moving rocks sliding toward them and the ear-piercing sounds, Sam took no time. "Quick! Follow me," she said as she leaped into the air and started gliding over the rocks. Robert was mesmerized watching Sam gracefully surf over the sliding rocks. *I must be careful not to reveal our presence here. The Shadow Knights will fall on us in seconds, and we'll be overrun. I must use every precaution I can,* Sam thought.

Sam turned to look over her shoulder, and to her horror, Robert was still where she had left him and was now buried up to his waist in rocks. She took immediate action as she shifted her weight, leaped over each sliding rock with ease, and made her way back to Robert. "Hang on! I'll get you out," she said as she quickly pushed and tugged the rocks away from his body. She managed him free, and with a firm grasp of his arm, she hauled him over the sliding rocks. Robert was amazed at how smoothly and quickly she moved as she tugged him along. He slipped and stumbled over every sliding rock until Sam drew him close. She hugged him firmly to a tree as the rumbling slowly diminished.

"Are you all right?" Sam asked when silence surrounded them again.

Robert looked down into her deep, emerald green eyes. He was captivated by her intensity and compassion. Sam stood there, bracing Robert to the tree, feeling safe and at peace. She unconsciously brushed a piece of hair away from his eyes, leaned close to him, and felt magnetized to his very soul. Robert's face leaned closer to her own as his arm moved up behind her head.

Sam quickly pushed away from him. "The rocks have settled now; we should keep moving."

Almost in a dizzy trance, Robert rubbed his hand behind his head, feeling embarrassed. "Um, yeah, you're right. Lead on."

Was that a little rosiness in her cheeks? Robert was not sure. Sam turned and walked confidently into the tree line. Robert speed-walked to catch up to her. "How did you do that?"

"Do what?"

"That thing with the rocks?"

"Oh, that's training." Sam shrugged nonchalantly and continued walking. "We're entering Shadow Dominion. Be on your guard. Drayvon's crew monitors these borders well, and they don't like unwanted company."

Robert kicked at some small rocks at his feet. "I understand," he said as they continued walking. Soon, a strange mist fell heavily upon them.

Sam shivered a little and said, "It's getting late. We should camp tonight and continue at daylight."

"Sounds good. I'll collect some wood for a fire." Robert quietly shuffled away.

Sam busied herself with making a shelter. Robert disappeared as he searched the ground for kindling. "Come to me," a whisper floated to his ears. *Who's that?* he wondered as he searched about. *Nothing.* The mist seemed to press in on him;

he shivered with the damp feeling but shrugged this uneasy thought aside as he continued collecting wood. "Come to me." Robert jumped at the request.

"Who's there?"

"Come and see." Robert looked around at his surroundings but couldn't see anything past the mist. "Did God really say you would never be alone?" Robert shook his head at such a strange question. "I could make sure you were truly never alone. I could give you what you seek."

"What's it you think I seek?"

"Acceptance, forgiveness, the control to protect those you care about."

"How could you do that?"

"Come and see. What would you do to protect the ones you love?"

"I would die for them."

"What would you say if I told you I could teach you how to be stronger?"

"I would ask, what's the catch?"

"I could give you a demonstration."

"What sort of demonstration?"

"Come, just come closer, and you'll see. I'll show you more than you ever thought possible. Come, I could teach you to save them all. I could make it so nothing happens to them ever again."

"How?"

"You've known such sorrow and pain. You've a strong heart." Robert took a step forward as the wood he collected fell from his arms. The mist lightened. He saw a faint image of a cave appear before him. "I can bring you wholeness and peace. Come and see."

Sam finished the last of tying a shelter together when her thoughts wandered to Robert. *Where is he? He should be back with that firewood by now. I should go look for him.* She turned in the direction she had last seen him. "Come to me, Bobbie," she heard. Immediately, she shivered and bolted in the direction from which the voice had come. "Come to me, Bobbie," a faint voice on the wind called out again. She took off running in the direction of the voice.

Please let Bobbie be ok. I warned him to be on his guard. Drayvon's smart. Sam could mostly make out a silhouette of Robert as she saw darkness looming about him. She jolted forward and grabbed the back of his shirt to pull him away from it.

"What? Sam? What's going on?"

"We're not alone. Come, Drayvon is coming, and he knows we're here. We need to guard our thoughts; he knows your fears. Don't let him in!" Sam yelled with such conviction in her words. Robert filled his thoughts of Sam and tried to push thoughts of his mom away. Sam pulled him back toward the shelter she built and they hid inside.

"I heard a voice. It promised to teach me how to save and protect those I love, and I promised I would not let anyone hurt my mom again."

"He knows that. He'll use that promise against you. Besides, we all learn through pain. I too, have lost much, but I can't allow my grief to give him a foothold. The Lord is a stronghold for the oppressed, a stronghold in times of trouble."[1]

"Who is he?"

"He is ruler of the Shadow Knights, and it appears he has joined forces with Lucas. He feeds on deception, worry, and fear. Right now, you stink of worry and uncertainty. You need to focus on something positive. Or your anger will open you to his control."

"Control? I'll never be controlled." Robert gritted his teeth.

"That's what I mean. You need to let go of that anger." The air fell heavy around them, and Robert fell to his side, gasping for air. "Fight it, Bobbie." He could barely hear Sam's words as he heard his mom screaming and the thumping of his heart against his ribs. Sam shook Robert's shoulder. "Fight! You need to stay strong." Robert heard Sam's words, but only at a distance, almost like a dream. "Enough!" Sam yelled as a blast of flames exploded in a circular border around them, rippling outward. Robert opened his eyes to see Sam holding him close in the shelter. The mist had disappeared. All was silent.

"Sam, what happened?"

"Drayvon attacked you. I had to act fast. I knew this was a mistake." Sam let go of Robert and scooted away from him.

"Sam? What do you mean, you had to act fast?"

"Never mind that. We aren't safe here. We need to keep moving." Sam climbed out from under the shelter. Robert crawled out behind her.

"Where did the mist go?"

"I have to recover. I hit it pretty hard."

"It? I thought you said Drayvon attacked. Isn't Drayvon a him, not an it?"

"Deception is one form of illusions Drayvon uses to control others. We need to be extra careful stay together; we're in his territory now, where he's the strongest. I don't know when he'll attack again, but I know he will. We're unwanted guests here."

"Is the Waterfalls of Tears much farther?"

"No, but my fear is what we may find when we get there. Drayvon knows we're here; we need to be diligent. The more times he attacks us, the more he knows how to defeat us."

"You said you injured him. How?"

"I'm not without counter measures." Sam quickened her pace. Robert almost had to run to keep up with her.

"I heard my mom screaming."

"It wasn't real."

"How do you know?"

"He uses his attacks through fear and manipulation. So, therefore, not real."

"Well, that's good to know." Soon, Sam jumped into a nearby bush pulling Robert in with her. "What?"

"Shh, he's coming." Sam pointed at the same shadowy figure Robert had seen the night he rescued Sam.

"Is that Drayvon?"

"Yes, he's guarding something. But I can't see what." They watched as Drayvon paced back and forth only a few feet from them, as if he was a caged animal. Sam leaned closer to get a better look without revealing their hiding place.

"The Waterfall of Tears will overflow. Guard and let no one get through," Sam heard a voice say.

"She's strong. But I'm stronger," Drayvon announced.

"Yes, you're strong, but my plan has been put in place. Don't allow your pride to jeopardize that plan." Sam leaned closer, trying to place the voice. "I have a spy on the inside: I'll win this war," the voice disclosed.

"As you wish." Drayvon turned uneasily in a circle and wandered off the path.

"Who was he talking to?" Robert asked.

"I know the voice, but I can't place it right now," Sam pondered.

"Has he gone? Can we continue moving?"

"Drayvon's guarding this way to the Waterfall."

"Is there another way?"

"Yes, but it's not easy."

"You think this has been easy? I'm not sure if I want to see what you think is hard, but do we have any other choice?" Sam slowly crawled away and headed back toward their previous shelter without saying a word. Robert shuffled to catch up to her. "So, what's this other way?"

"You won't like it."

"Hey, we're in this together. So, tell me."

"We need to go back to the mountain and make our way around the narrow path and come in on the back end of the falls."

"That doesn't sound so bad."

"The narrow path is treacherous, full of spies, lots of eyes, and hard not to be seen. Only the true of heart can find their footing."

"True of heart? What does that mean?"

"The Saviour will guide us, but we need to be guarded." They passed by the shelter and made their way up the side of the mountain once more.

I thought this was hard during the day, but at night, please, Father, be our guide, Robert prayed. The night sky was illuminated with flashes of emerald and red, giving only enough light so he could see Sam moving ahead of him. Slowly, they made their way over the loose rocks. Sam leaned close to the edge of the flat side of the mountain and disappeared.

"Sam? Where are you?" Robert shuffled closer to where he last saw her. Sam peered her head around to look at him.

"The ledge is narrow. One false step, and you could fall." Sam moved her head out of sight again. Robert moved closer to where he last saw Sam. He peered around and saw Sam pinned flat against the side of the mountain; her toes balanced uneasily. "Stay focused on your next step, and each new step will bring you closer." Robert tried to swallow the lump forming in his throat as he pressed himself flat beside Sam. Sam turned her head and continued forward. The two shuffled along in silence for a few minutes. "We're almost on the other side" Sam turned to reassure Robert, but her foot slipped, and Robert reached out his hand to catch her.

Robert's body cried out in pain as he struggled to maintain his balance and hold onto Sam. "I won't let you fall."

"Can you swing me? I see the other side. But you need to swing me and let go at the highest point."

"What? Let go? But you'll fall." Robert's muscles strained to keep hold of Sam.

"Do you trust me?"

"Do I have a choice?"

"Swing me, now!" Robert swung his arm with all his might, and Sam slipped from his hold.

"No, Sam!"

"I'm here, Bobbie. I made it. You only have a little farther." Sam's voice trailed off. Robert shuffled forward and soon stumbled onto the surface of the other side of the mountain. Terror filled him as he saw Sam battling off a dozen of those hairy beasts. He was enthralled with her swift movements, watching her take a flying leap as she kicked one beast in the abdomen. In one fluid motion, she swung her arm around elbowing another in the side.

Robert looked around as he heard movement coming up the side of the mountain. *We're going to be overrun. What should I do?* He searched his surroundings for something to stop the flood of beasts about to descend upon them. Sam turned to face Robert, and he saw even more beasts jump on her; the weight of them dragging her down.

A dark hood was pulled over his head as he felt himself being bound and dragged away. "Master Drayvon will be pleased," he heard a shrill voice reply.

"Robert!" Sam screamed.

——❧❧❧——

S am found herself chained to a chair in a dark room. She sensed someone staring at her. "I know you're there. Bobbie, is that you?"

"Bobbie, eh? So that's the stranger's name." Drayvon gleefully announced. "Where did this Bobbie come from?"

Sam filled with regret at unknowingly giving Drayvon information. "Drayvon, what do you want?"

"You know me: power and authority." Drayvon leaned close to Sam's ear. "Control." Sam was filled with panic.

"Control? Control of what?" Sam feared his answer.

"You have lost everything and everyone, yet you still question? What hope is left? You're alone."

Sam squared her shoulders, focused all her courage, and looked into Drayvon's red eyes. "No, in all these things we're more than conquerors through Him who loves us."[2] Sam felt her courage growing.

"You won't be so courageous when he arrives. He still has plans for you." Drayvon smiled mischievously as Sam struggled to maintain her confidence.

As her courage wavered, she prayed quietly, *God please protect me and keep me guarded.*

"What have you done with Bobbie?"

"What do you care? You're alone; nobody's coming for you this time. Besides, you don't need anybody." Drayvon left the room as Sam lunged forward, only to be pulled back by her bonds.

———

"Where am I? Someone better give me some answers or else," Robert demanded as loud as he could. He kicked one beast in the shin as the beast tried to restrain him, managing to free his one arm while he elbowed another beast. "I'll fight anyone who threatens me." He growled and punched toward the first beast he kicked.

"Enough," Drayvon yelled. Robert froze at the sound of anger in his voice. His fight melted away as he was forced to sit and felt his hands and feet being bound. The hood was yanked off his head. He looked angrily at Drayvon. "Bobbie, right?"

"Who're you?"

"I like your spunk. I could use you."

"I'm no one's puppet." Robert tried to fight against his bonds.

"Leave us," Drayvon ordered the others out of the room,

leaving only Robert and himself. "Easy now. I'm on your side. I can help."

"Help me? How?" Robert questioned as his posture relaxed a little.

"You're a stranger here. Am I right?"

"Yes, but what does that have to do with anything? Besides, if you were on my side, why am I tied to this chair?"

"You're fighting; you're bound for protection until I know if I can trust you." A smirk formed on Drayvon's face.

"Sorry, I usually fight first and ask questions later."

"A man after my own heart. I can help."

"Help me how? What help do you think I need?"

"I can help you get home. Protect your family from hurting again."

Robert relaxed more as he considered this creature's offer. "What would you want in return?"

"Nothing major. Something you probably won't even miss."

"What?"

"Let me ask you: what's your family worth to you? If you leave and forget about this place, no harm will come to you or your loved ones."

"Why do you want me to leave so badly?"

"Suit yourself; I'll let you think about my offer. But it expires once my lord arrives." Drayvon slunk out of the room.

———

S am closed her eyes and focused her thoughts on Robert. Her hair glowed crimson red as her mind's eye floated down corridors, past several Shadow Knights, and past Drayvon. "Bobbie, where are you?" Her thoughts brought her to an old wooden door; beyond that door, she saw Robert tied to a chair. "Bobbie." Robert jumped and looked around the room.

"Sam? Is that you? I don't see you."

"It's me. Our thoughts are connected somehow."

"How's this possible?"

"It might be the same reason I'm drawn to you. Something's connecting us. I'm not sure what yet. Are you alright?"

"Other than being bound, I'm fine. How about you? Are you ok?"

"Good to know I'm not alone." Sam breathed a sigh of relief.

"I met someone. He says he can help."

"Here? Nobody here helps another. Not without a sacrifice. Was there an offer made?"

"Sacrifice? What do you mean by sacrifice?"

"Nobody offers something without getting something in return."

Robert shifted in his chair. "What if I could get us out?"

"I wouldn't risk it. Be careful who you trust. Did he give you a name?"

"No."

"How're you doing this?"

"Just be careful." Sam wavered and lost her connection with Robert as Drayvon entered the room again and smacked her in the face. "Your tricks don't work here but don't worry. Soon, you'll lose that inner strength."

"What're you going to do to me?" Sam asked.

"I told you: you're part of Lord Lucas's plan."

"What plan is that?"

"You'll know soon enough. Now, sit tight no more tricks. You hear me?" Drayvon smiled and left as quickly as he entered. Sam closed her eyes once more and tried to focus on Robert again. Her thoughts drifted down the hallway, past the same knights, and up to the same wooden door.

"Bobbie?"

Robert looked around the room again, "Sam, where'd you go?"

"I need to warn you."

"Warn me? About what?"

"Lucas."

"Lucas? Who is this Lucas you keep mentioning?"

"He was in Eden, the garden of God; every precious stone his covering.[3] He was the anointed guardian cherub, and he was on the holy mountain of God; he walked in the midst of the stones of fire."[4]

"I don't understand."

"Lucas was blameless in his ways from the day he was created, till unrighteousness was found in him."[5]

"What do you mean, unrighteousness?" Robert squirmed as his thought drifted back to his dad in the cave.

"In the abundance of his trade, he was filled with violence, and he sinned; He began to want more, and greed set in. So, God cast him as a profane thing from His Holy Mountain."

"He lived in God's presence and still sinned? Is there any hope for us?"

"His heart was proud because of his beauty; he corrupted his wisdom for the sake of his splendour. So, God cast him to the ground and exposed him before kings, to feast their eyes on him. By the multitude of his iniquities, in the unrighteousness of his trade, he profanes his sanctuaries; so, God brought fire out from his midst; it consumed him, and God turned him to ashes on the earth in the sight of all."[6]

"If he was consumed by fire, how is he still here?"

"He has fallen from heaven and is cut down to the ground.[7] He said in his heart, he will ascend to heaven; above the stars of God he will set his throne on high; he will sit on the mount of assembly in the far reaches of the north; he will ascend above the heights of the clouds; he will make himself like the Most High."[8]

"I ask again, how can he ascend if he has been consumed by fire?"

"Bobbie, he is the king of deception. Just be on your guard."

Suddenly, she found herself face to face with Lucas. Almost as if she was punched, she flinched back into herself and fell backward in her chair, crashing to the floor. Soon, a Shadow Knight rushed in and pulled her upright again and left without saying a word.

———⋘⋙———

*R*obert sat alone in his room of solitude. "Sam? Are you there?" he called out. His words were met with an eerie silence. Soon Drayvon re-entered the room.

"Have you given my offer some thought?" Drayvon asked.

"I don't know."

"What do you mean you don't know? I thought you wanted to keep your family safe?"

"I do. It's just..."

"Just what?"

"I'm not sure if you are able to get me home and keep my family from harm. Or if you will just put them in more danger. This doesn't sound like a fair offer or even one you can pull off."

"I know you're not strong enough by yourself. No one will be safe. I give you this choice. You need to choose: are you part of this war or not? If you choose to stay here and not go home, you will be forced to choose a side. Who'll you follow? Your time to decide is running out." Drayvon left the room again.

"I just don't know who to trust. What am I even doing here?" Robert asked as his thoughts wandered back to Sam. *I hope she's ok.* He was suddenly startled out of his thoughts with an ear-piercing scream. "Wait. Sam. What're they doin' to you?" Panic filled Robert's heart and mind. He frantically tried to loosen his bonds as he crashed his chair on its side. At this very moment the only thing that mattered to Robert was protecting Sam. He violently kicked his feet snapping the chair legs in two. With his feet free, he leaped up and slammed his shoulder into the wall, breaking the chair back and arms. Soon, his hands were free as three Shadow Knights dashed through the door to investigate the noise. Robert wasted no time and reached for one of the broken chair legs and swung it at the first knight, knocking him to the floor. He spun and slammed the chair leg into the second knight's knee, causing him to collapse on the floor screaming in pain. The third knight rushed Robert and kicked him in the side. Robert teetered and spat blood. The knight spun to punch Robert, but Robert caught the knight's fist in his hand. Robert stood and shoved the knight backward. The third knight stumbled and hit his head on the wall, falling to the floor. Robert ran out of the room and down the corridor. *I need to find Sam.*

Suddenly, five knights rushed toward him from around the corner, and Robert stumbled backward. He swung the chair leg toward the nearest knight but missed. The knight grabbed his arm and forced the chair leg from his grip. Two knights secured him in a kneeling position. The first knight took the chair leg and swung it across Robert's forehead. Robert fell to the floor with a thud. "Take him back to his room. Lord Lucas and Master Drayvon have more questions." The first knight ordered the other two knights, who had originally secured him, to drag Robert back to his room. "He'll weaken as time goes on."

—⋙✦⋘—

Senora's feet had healed from her burns. She paced the hospital hallway outside Robert's room. It had been a month of up and down care but Robert still lay in a coma. *Will he ever wake up?* Her mind wandered back to his seizures and the night she saw the Tall Bearded Man. *What did he mean that Bobbie would need me?* Senora's mind was a jumbled mess of questions. She paced as she waited to hear from a nurse that she could return to Robert's room. *God, what's happening to Bobbie? Please help him wake up,* she prayed. A nurse walked by Senora's room. "Excuse me, can I see Bobbie now?" Senora asked.

"Soon, dear. They're just cleaning him up. But to reassure you, he has been stable for a while. He just had a minor fever this morning. The doctor just wanted to examine him for any change. It shouldn't be long. Will his mom be by today?" the nurse asked.

"No, she has to work a double today and she wanted to visit her husband. His parole hearing is in a few days."

The nurse nodded but was startled by the code blue bell suddenly chiming from Robert's room. She rushed to Robert's room once again without a word. Senora prayed more earnestly as she rushed to the chapel, a familiar place of solitude for her lately. "God, You're in control, and You know what's going on with Bobbie more than anyone. Please bring him back healthy and strong."

Suddenly, the Tall Bearded Man appeared before her again. "Remember to do your part. Is it not so, oh Nora, that God gives examples to help you know how to follow what is right? Punishment is unavoidable for three transgressions, and for four, He will not revoke the punishment. When God punishes your own sin, there is no escape. No matter how fast you think you are, you will not escape God. You think you're strong, not strong enough to resist Him. You think you're brave, not when God comes in judgment. Whatever strength you have came from Him, and it's powerless to resist Him. Sometimes, God's people persist in sin because they mistakenly feel safe in doing so. Because God is slow to act does not mean He will not act. God is a God of love, but there are consequences to Bobbie's sin."

"Consequences? Does this have anything to do with his coma?" Senora wrapped her arms around herself in a hug.

"Through repentance, there will be purification."

Fear started to bubble beneath the surface. "What do you mean by punishment?"

"Because we have security systems around us, we feel we have a safety net. You are really smart and have a great network of friends, excellent health. All of those things offer protection against something but not protection against God. The people who bear God's name are not exempt from judgment. They are held to a higher standard."

"I trust God's leading. Is there a way I can help Bobbie through this purification to ease the pain of punishment? The fire of God will purify me, and even though it'll be painful, I trust I will come out stronger."

"A father and his daughter are walking through a field, and out in the distance, they can see smoke billowing before them. By the time they realize the fire is out of control, they know the wind is against them, and they will not outrun the fire. The father knows there is only one way to escape. He quickly burns his own fire right there in the middle of the grass to burn a large patch off. When the large fire comes near, they stand on the section they had already burnt. The girl is terrified by the large flames but the father reassures her that the flames can't reach. They were standing where the fire had already been. Trusting God as your Saviour, you are where the wrath of God has already been. God's wrath toward your sin has not been cancelled. The punishment has not been revoked, but it has already been burnt. Jesus took your place, satisfied God's wrath, and satisfied His judgement. The only safe place to stand when the fire of God's wrath comes is where God's wrath had already burnt. As His child, do you live like you understand that?"

"I know I make mistakes, but I trust in Jesus's victory in my life."

"Nora, Bobbie needs you more than he knows. The battle isn't an easy one."

"What do you want me to do?" Senora asked.

The Tall Bearded Man looked at Senora with both concern and compassion in his eyes. "It's time." The chapel filled with blinding light, and suddenly, Senora and the Tall Bearded Man vanished.

10

DECEPTION IGNITED

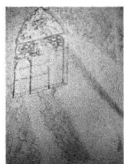

*S*enora blinked to adjust to the bright light. When her vision focused again, she realized she stood in front of the secret cave leading into Delores' castle. The Tall Bearded Man stood beside her. "'Be on your guard. For behold, I send you out as sheep in the midst of wolves, so be wise as serpents and innocent as doves.'[1] The castle's not as you remember," the Man warned with great conviction in his voice.

"I'll have to confront Kat. I know she didn't want to hurt me. I saw the conflict within her," Senora said.

"Watch and pray that you may not enter into temptation. The spirit indeed is willing, but the flesh is weak.[2] When the battle is raging, remember to stand where it is already burnt." Senora looked down the dark cave, her heart filling with uncertainty. "Bobbie needs you now more than ever."

"Wait, what do you mean Bobbie needs me? If he needs me, why did you bring me here? Shouldn't I be with him at the hospital?"

"Bobbie's here and there."

"How could he be in both places?"

"The mind's a powerful part of one's body. You could use

your mind to dwell in both worlds. Bobbie was torn between worlds, and this made him vulnerable and open to deception. You must remind Bobbie what the truth is. If you abide in Jesus' word, you're truly His disciples, and you'll know the truth, and the truth will set you free.[3] Of truth, God will not do wickedly, and the Almighty will not pervert justice.[4] He who walks blamelessly and does what is right and speaks truth in his heart; He who does these things shall never be moved."[5]

"Will you go with me? Will I see Delores or Sam or Scarlett?"

"The way before you is dark. Allow the truth to illuminate your soul. What you're about to face will test you to your breaking point. Hold onto truth, speak truth. Both Bobbie and Sam need you. I'm now sending you." The Man vanished from sight. Senora stood before the dark cave, remembering the last time she entered the castle two years ago. She searched the entrance for a light, and noticed her necklace was glowing. Removing the necklace from her neck, she held it firmly in her grasp as she carefully made her way toward the broken wooden door that led up that old familiar staircase.

As Senora reached the top of the stairway, she quickly made her way to the nearby room and closed the door. She listened at the door, but all was quiet. "I need to talk with Scarlett. Maybe she could bring some answers." Senora made her way into the secret passageway leading to the throne room. She pressed her ear against the old entrance to listen for any conversations. "All's quiet." Upon entering, she spotted a figure standing by the ornate throne. *Who else would be standing by the throne? This must be Scarlett?* Senora cautious approached. "Scarlett?" The figure jumped at the sound of Senora's voice and suddenly turned to face her.

Senora was surprised to be standing face to face with Katerina. "Kat? Where's Scarlett?"

"Nora? What're you doing here? You've brought death and doom to us all. You shouldn't be here."

"Kat, I know you didn't want to hurt me. Please, fill me in and let me help you."

"With you here now, I might as well face the facts."

"What facts?"

"Come with me." Katerina walked out of the throne room. Senora shuffled to keep up. The two walked past the guards who stared curiously at Senora down several dark and dusty corridors to the end of a long hallway. Katerina led Senora to an old door, and as the two entered, Senora saw Crystal sleeping on the bed.

Senora walked up to Crystal and reached for her ice-cold hand. "What happened?"

"Lucas he escaped. He did something to her. I can't wake her up. He promised me if I silenced you, he would return her to me. But now that you're here, I fear I've lost her forever, like I lost mother."

"What happened to Scarlett?"

"He killed her and Delores too. I'm alone. Oh, Nora, I'm not deserving your help or your forgiveness. I deceived you, Sam, and Bobbie."

"Bobbie? How do you know him?"

"He's with Sam. I sent them on a quest. One Lucas told me to send them on, one that took them into the heart of Shadow Dominion."

Senora placed both of her hands around Crystal's cold hand with the eagle pendant wrapped tightly in her left hand. As Katerina stared, the eagle pendant started to glow. "Wait. Is that?"

Senora nodded. "The pendant Scarlett gave me? Yes."

The girls watched the glow of the pendant move through Crystal's fingertips, up her arm, over her shoulder, and into her cheeks. Suddenly, Crystal's eyes fluttered as she looked up at Senora. "Nora? Is that you?" Crystal asked.

Katerina embraced Crystal in a strong hug. "Crystal, it's a

miracle! Thank you, Nora! You brought my sister back to me!"

"I felt blanketed in darkness, and just now, I saw a bright light, walked toward it, and opened my eyes to see Nora. How did Nora bring me back?" Crystal asked.

"She brought it! In turn brought you back from the darkness." Katerina cheered.

Senora released Crystals hand and unraveled the necklace chain from her hand, placing it back around her neck. Crystal's eyes widened as she pointed. "Mother's pendant! You still have it?"

"Of course, it has always been a reminder of what I learned in Treasure Kingdom and of my friends Sam, Delores, Scarlett, and you two," Senora replied.

Solemnly, Crystal turned her eyes toward Katerina. "What have I missed?" Crystal asked as Katerina flooded her shoulder with tears.

"Kat will fill you in later, but for now, where's Shadow Dominion?" Senora asked.

"Shadow Dominion?" Crystal said with panic. "Nobody goes there, but if they do, they're lost forever."

"I need to help Bobbie and Sam," Senora stated.

Confused, Crystal locked eyes with Katerina. Her sister pulled away. "Who's Bobbie? Why would Sam even consider going there?"

Flinching, Katerina looked down. "I thought I'd lost you. I couldn't lose you too. Lucas was too strong," Katerina whined.

"Mother always told us we have strength in numbers. Ask her she will tell you." Crystal said.

"I-I don't know what to say," Katerina stammered.

"Where's Mother?" Crystal asked.

"Lucas escaped and put you under a spell. Chaos ran rampant; Mother, Delores, Sam, and Drayvon." Katerina stammered.

"Wait, since when does Drayvon's name go with Delores, Mother, and Sam?" Crystal interrupted.

"Scarlett and Delores are dead." Senora's words fell heavy upon Crystal's ears.

"How long have I been out?" Crystal asked.

"Two months," Katerina replied.

"Two months? Where's Sam?" Crystal asked.

"Lucas promised if I did what he asked, he would release you," Katerina revealed.

"Kat, what did you do? Have you forgotten Lucas's deception? He only tells lies." Crystal slammed her fist on the bed.

"I think Drayvon has them. Soon they'll be in Lucas' hands," Katerina said.

"Kat, the horse is made ready for the day of battle, but victory belongs to the Lord," Senora said.[6]

"If we stand together, we're never alone. Delores taught us that. Lucas thrives on dividing us. Scarlett wouldn't allow Lucas to destroy everything that's important. I'll fight him." Crystal's anger boiled up. She crossed her arms and glared at her sister.

"I'll find a way to free Sam and Bobbie. Kat and Crystal, are you willing to gather your army to fight to free Treasure Kingdom from Lucas' tyranny?" Senora asked.

"You mean, you're still willing to trust me, even after my betrayal?" Katerina replied.

"We all waver in our decisions, but when you face truth, darkness is forced to flee," Senora declared.

I can't believe Nora is willing to forgive so easily. I won't be duped; Kat will have to earn my trust back. How could she even consider thinking that behaviour would be ok? Rolling her eyes, Crystal took a deep breath. *This will have to wait until another time, Nora needs my help.* "Kat, please. Lucas can't win," Crystal begged.

"We will stand with you, Nora."

"Thank you. Before you start gathering your armies, can

you guide me to where I can start looking for Sam and Bobbie?" Senora asked.

Katerina shuffled her feet. "It'll take a while to gather an army willing to fight Lucas. Plus, I've planned a funeral procession and farewell for Mother and Princess Delores. Right now, we have our local leaders, but I've been calling more to our aid. We need to give them time to arrive."

Crystal rolled her eyes and scrunched up her nose. *Here we go with the excuses. Hasn't my sister learned anything?* "When's the farewell? You weren't going to have that without me, were you?" Crystal asked.

"I…well..." Katerina paced the room. "I didn't know if you were going to wake up. Sir Gervon's here, and he's helping keep the peace. You know how he is."

"Fine. I can show you, Nora." Crystal offered as she slowly stood from the bed. "I say again, when is the farewell?"

"I think the day after tomorrow."

"We'll return with Sam and Bobbie. I promise you that. No thanks to you, Kat." Crystal spat her words and stormed out of the room.

Squeezing Katerina's shoulder, Senora turned to leave. "She will come around. Give her some time. She has a lot to process."

"That is just it. I don't deserve your trust or her forgiveness," Katerina stated.

"Everyone deserves forgiveness. Trust has to be earned," Senora replied while following Crystal.

Crystal led Senora to the barn, saddled two horses, and handed the reins of one horse to Senora. "You can ride, can't you?"

"I'm a natural, and I have my own horses back at home," she said as Crystal mounted her horse with ease. Senora put one hand on the horn of the saddle and the other on the back brim and quickly mounted. She nodded to Crystal to lead on. They rode out the castle gate.

Senora galloped to keep in stride with Crystal's horse. It amazed her how natural and graceful this young twelve-year-old was on the back of her horse. It had taken Senora years of training and riding to get this confident on a horse. *I wonder how long she has been riding?* The thought hung in her mind, but she didn't feel right to ask. She needed to focus on how she was going to save Sam and Robert.

PART 5: HEALING

11

STORMS OF DECEIT

*R*obert sat in a dark room, flexing against his bonds. "Easy now. Are you the one they call Bobbie?" Lucas spoke through the silence.

"You know my name, but what's yours?" Robert asked.

"My name's not important right now." Light illuminated the room; Robert's eyes burned at the intensity. His eyes slowly adjusted while he looked around the room. It surprised him to see how large and cluttered the room was.

"One can easily get lost in here," he said.

"One can lose themselves only to become anyone they want to be," Lucas replied.

"What do you mean by that? Where are you? Show yourself."

Lucas stepped out from behind a large pile of dusty file folders and random scraps of papers on top of a table. He bowed toward Robert and grinned. "Welcome." As light radiated from all around Lucas, Robert fell back in shock and covered his eyes for protection.

"You make it sound like I'm a guest."

"Not just a guest but my honoured guest."

"Do you chain all your guests to a chair?" Robert rattled the chains with his hands, out of frustration to get free.

"Let me take care of that." Lucas simply snapped his fingers, and two Shadow Knights appeared at the door.

"Yes, Lord?" the first knight declared.

"What's the meaning of chaining my guest to a chair? Release him immediately," Lucas ordered.

"But you said…" The Knight started but quickly silenced his protest at the glare and sheer darkness he saw flaring in Lucas's eyes. He jumped at Robert and released his bonds, gathered the chains, and shuffled out of the room.

"There, you see, my guest." Lucas reached out his hand.

Robert raised his hand to grab Lucas's but hesitated. "Where's Sam?"

Lucas leaned close to his ear and whispered, "Walk with me. Let me show you around." Robert stood and followed, almost feeling as though he were in a trance. Lucas led him out of the cluttered room, down a dark rock tunnel.

"Where're we goin'?"

"To where it all began."

———

S am sat bound to her chair in the small, dark room. "You're not strong enough," Drayvon whispered through the darkness.

"Strong enough to defeat you. 'The Lord is my strength and my song, and he has become my salvation; this is my God, and I will exalt him. The Lord is a man of war; the Lord is his name.'[1] Stop hiding in the shadows and face me. You'll soon learn how strong I truly am."

"If you were strong enough, why didn't you save them?" Suddenly, Sam found herself sitting in her dragon form in the Dragon City, where she grew up.

"Starstorm." Sam jumped at the sound of her mother

calling her long-forgotten name. "Come, Starstorm, they're coming," Rhaegal called.

"Who's coming, Mama?" Her mother drew her close in her wing to protect her from a fireball blast. Sam felt the heat surrounding them. "Mama, I'm scared."

"It's alright, little one; I need you to do something."

"Anything," Sam declared. Her mother wavered as another fireball blast knocked her off balance. "Mama?"

Rhaegal drew Sam close and whispered, "Stay strong. Transform."

"But, Mama, you said transforming was forbidden."

"I need you to transform. You're the only one who can other than the Silver Dragon. It's a gift the Saviour gave to only you and the Silver Dragon. That's what makes you so special. You need to survive." The little Red Dragon transformed into a small red-haired girl with emerald green eyes. With Rhaegal's red tail she surrounded Starstorm and lifted her safely into a high tree. "I love you, my little Starstorm. Never forget who you are. The Tree of Hope will protect you." Sam watched in horror as the Silver Dragon dove on top of her mother.

"Where's the little whelp?" The Silver Dragon yelled.

"I won't allow you to corrupt her!" Rheagal yelled.

The Silver Dragon lunged at Rheagal's throat and sank her teeth in. Rheagal's cries reached Sam's little ears. "No, she'll be your undoing." Rheagal fell as the Silver Dragon ignited the body and surrounding area with fire, leaped to flight and flew toward a cluster of dragons in the distance. Little Starstorm sat helpless in the burning tree.

Sam covered her ears and closed her eyes. "Make it stop," she pleaded.

"Why didn't you save her?" Drayvon asked.

"I was just a child. I couldn't save her."

"You weren't strong enough. You couldn't do enough to save her."

Sam hung her head as she saw the hopeful memory of Princess Delores finding her. "Come down, child. I won't harm you. What happened here?" Delores questioned. Sam climbed down from the Tree of Hope, looked at her surroundings of the city in ruins, and took Princess Delores' hand. "Come you're safe now. What's your name?"

Sam looked down at what was left of her mother's body, swallowed hard, and said, "You can call me Sam."

"Not only are you not good enough, but you're a liar too. Not even those who thought they knew you actually know your real name," Drayvon claimed.

"I had to protect my true identity. I didn't know where the Silver Dragon was or what she would do to me if she found me," Sam replied.

She tried desperately to hold onto the memory of the Tree of Hope, "The LORD will fight for you, and you have only to be silent.[2] Just listen to the Saviour; He will guide you in His truth, little one. Jesus Christ is the same yesterday and today and forever."[3] Delores whispered in Sam's ear.

The memory of Delores' lifeless body lying in a pool of her blood invaded her memories. "She died not knowing who you really are. Why didn't you save her?"

"How could I? You had me bound."

"You're alone. You're a liar. You're not good enough, and you're not worth loving."

"Not true. I'm born of the blood of Jesus; I am adopted, chosen, I'm a child of God."

"We'll see. I'll break you." Sam stared confidently with a tear-streaked face, but with determination in her eyes.

—◦◦◦—

*R*obert cleared his throat as they exited the cave into a thick forest. "What do you mean where it all began? Where what all began?" Robert asked.

"Let me tell you a story," Lucas replied.

"What kind of story?"

"A story of love. It was just beyond the Forest of Truth when I saw her, full of power, authority, and beauty. I knew right there I needed her for my empire."

"Your empire? I don't understand."

"Oh, you will." As they stepped out of the Forest of Truth, Lucas pointed off in the distance. "Look: what do you see?"

Robert stared toward where Lucas pointed. "It looks like the ruins of an old city."

"You're right. We're nearly there."

"Where, exactly?" The two walked along silently for a few hours and emerged at the entrance to the ruins. "What happened here?"

"You know, control, power, greed. Welcome to the Dragon Kingdom. Home of the Silver Enchantress."

"Who's the Silver Enchantress?"

Lucas lunged at Robert, grabbed the front of his shirt, and shoved him against a wall. "Only I can call her that. She belonged to me!" he yelled, then almost instantly softened, released Robert and continued walking. Robert straightened his shirt and ran to catch up.

"What happened to her?"

"She was corrupted. We had it all. Only one could stop us from moving forward in the plan."

"What plan?"

"Well, only one is what I thought. I never considered the power Scarlett held until her undoing." Lucas ignored Robert's question.

"Let me ask you: what would you do to keep those you love safe?"

Robert shifted his weight and avoided Lucas's question. Lucas turned and got right in Robert's face. "If their lives were threatened, would you kill to save them?"

"What? I would do anything to save them."

"Anything? To Anyone?"

"I don't understand." Robert's uneasiness began to rise within him.

"Never mind. We should go back."

"Go back? Now? We've already been walking for hours." Lucas simply tapped Robert's forehead. Robert blinked his eyes, and to his surprise, he found himself back in the cluttered room again facing Lucas. "How did you do that?"

"I can teach you if you'd like. In fact, I can teach you a lot of things."

"Can I see Sam?" Instantly, Lucas's smirk faded.

He snapped his fingers, and three Shadow Knights rushed in and secured Robert's arms. Robert instantly started kicking and fighting them off. "I thought I was your guest."

"A guest on my terms." Lucas turned toward the door. "You're a fighter. I like that. What would you say if I told you I could teach you to fight so you could never lose and all who you cared about would always be protected?"

"I would say, what's the catch?"

"No catch. I can help you save everyone who's important to you. You have lost so much."

Immediately, Robert found himself kneeling at the bottom of his stairs with blood-stained hands, looking down at Trevor's bloody body.

"You couldn't save Trevor. Just think about the control and power I am offering you." Soon, Lucas left Robert alone in the dark room once more. Hanging his head and feeling defeated, Robert pondered what Lucas had told him.

———

Senora flinched as she looked ahead of Crystal at the sight of the large mountain that came into view. Everything around her appeared to be engulfed in stormy darkness. Soon, her horse veered up and sent her flying to the ground with a loud thud, filling her shoulder with stabbing pain. Crystal quickly dismounted, secured both horses, and ran to Senora's side. "Nora, are you alright?" Crystal asked.

"My shoulder hurts, but I'll be fine. How much farther?" Senora replied as she carefully sat up.

Crystal turned to look toward the mountain. With her arm extended, she pointed. "That's the entrance to Shadow Dominion; the Sheol Mountain is its border. I'll wait here and keep the horses calm and secured so we've a way back home. But you need to be on your guard. Darkness rules there. Time has no boundaries. You can't trust what you see. The Shadows and especially Drayvon live on deception, lies, and fears. The moment you lose truth, you've lost," Crystal warned. "The storm's great right now; Drayvon's using the storm to guard his borders. This'll be a good time to try to sneak in. You might be able to stay undetected if you go now. As long as he continues the storm, his focus is elsewhere."

"Please pray with me. That the Saviour will guide me and surround me with His protection and truth." Crystal bowed her head. The two prayed together as Senora prepared for the next leg of her journey.

"Dear Heavenly Father, You know the journey that's before me. You know the dangers and trials I'll face. Please guard my heart and my mind. Give me wisdom and strength. I lift up Sam and Bobbie to you. Fill their hearts with truth. Guard their minds from the attacks of the evil one. Remind them they're not alone. In Jesus' name, amen," Senora prayed. Senora hugged Crystal and slowly stood. Crystal gave her a confident nod as Senora stepped into the storm cloud raging around the mountain.

The moment Senora entered the cloud, she was instantly shrouded in darkness. The weight that pressed in on her made it hard to breathe. She pushed forward. *When I pass through the waters, You'll be with me.* She felt warmth surrounding her as light illuminated from her eagle pendant. She was amazed that as the storm raged about her, she was untouched by it. A barrier of protection surrounded her. *Thank You*, she prayed.

—◈◈◈—

"Tell me about your dad," Lucas prompted. His question startled Robert.

"Why do you want to know about him? He's nothing special," Robert snapped.

"I just want to get to know you. Why you do what you do. I shared with you from my past. Now, it's your turn."

"There isn't much to tell. He's quite private and a hypocrite."

"Why do you say hypocrite?"

"Don't get me wrong. He can be a good guy. I mean, when he wants to. He can be quite likable. He taught me to fish and shoot. But when the booze comes out, he's a completely different person."

"Go on. Ohh… do tell." Lucas rubbed his hands together gleefully.

"I learned a long time ago to make myself scarce when I saw the vodka and scotch bottles come out."

"How was he different?"

"Let's just say things got broke."

"What sort of things?" Lucas questioned, his eyes greedily drinking in all the details.

"Oh, you know. Walls, sticks, chairs, tables, arms, noses. If he wasn't beating on me, he was beating my mom."

"Did you ever try to stand up to him?"

"Once."

"What happened?"

"You know, he was beating on my mom for not getting the dishes done right after supper. He was plunging her face into a full sink of soapy water. I pulled at his feet caused him to fall backward as Mom limply fell to the floor, gasping for air. I was only eight at the time. He turned violently toward me, gripped me by the hair, dragged me out of the house, my feet scuffing against the gravel stones in the driveway. Then, he picked up a thin stick and pulled me into the woodshed."

Lucas licked his lips, almost as if he was deliciously drinking in every word. "Tell me more."

"He bound my wrists extended outward to two hooks on the wall. I stood helplessly facing the wall. And the stick slammed upon my back. Again and again. I lost count of how many times the stick hit, but when his rage subsided, he threw the stick at my feet. I looked down, not willing to give him the satisfaction of a tear. He would not break me. No matter how bloody he made that stick. Dad just turned and left me barely hanging there with my wrists bound to the wall. You know what he said to me?" Robert looked up at Lucas for the first time.

"What?"

"That'll teach you to get in my way. I hung there for hours before Mom came out and unbound me. She acted as if this was normal and told me to go to bed. What parents do that to their child?" Robert's muscles constrained, he took low shallow breaths, and the heat rose up into his face. Clenching his fists, he bit his lip to fight back the tears.

"You deserve better. I can teach you so you don't ever hurt like that again. You can get even."

"There is only one Lawgiver and Judge, the one who is able to save and destroy. But you who are you to judge your neighbour?"[4]

Lucas stood and paced the cluttered room, swung his arm, and knocked the pile of papers on the floor. He left the room without saying a word.

12

LOST TO UNFORGIVENESS

*S*enora saw movement ahead. She dodged behind a tree and peered out to see what headed her way. She saw a strange-looking, tall, hairy beast-like humpbacked creature emerge from the storm. "Patrol the perimeter, patrol the perimeter I'm patrolling. One wrong choice leads to the possibility of getting stuck in a patrol with everyone else." The beast sarcastically yelled out, "It's not like anyone will try to penetrate his storm! They wouldn't dare. Doin' the wrong thing is like getting' shot by an arrow. It's usually a long-lastin' pain that doesn't go away. The Master holds all the power The Master has the control. But yes, I'm out here patrollin'. Patrol is a boring man's game that never ends. You can't quit. Soon, she'll fall, I'll find the hidden entrance to the rest of the dragons and nothin' will stop The Master." The beast walked past the tree Senora was hiding behind and cackled like a hyena. She watched and slowly followed quietly behind this strange creature.

"Chester, pay attention." Senora darted away as another hairier beast approached. "You spend too much time distracted in your thoughts; there are gaps in your patrol."

"The Master asked me to patrol. So, I patrol. Don't take life too seriously. You'll never get out alive," Chester whined.[1]

"Oh, never mind you. Go back to the hidden entrance, but pay attention," the hairier beast ordered. Chester shrugged and lumbered off away from the Shadow Dominion border. Senora quietly snuck away and continued to follow Chester.

"They never know what they want. Patrol, guard, pay attention, demand, demand. Some people just need a high-five. In the face. With a chair. Things will be different when Master has won." Soon a rusty door came into view. Senora knelt and watched as Chester looked around. He reached down and grabbed a handful of mud and smeared it over the doorposts. Soon, the door opened, and Chester entered. The door slammed shut behind him.

What are these creatures? Are they the Shadow Knights? The ones Katerina mentioned? What should I do now? Please help me know what I should do, Senora prayed.

"You have all the answers you seek. Just open your eyes and face your fears. When you face your fears, you find your courage. For when you're weak, His strength shines through you." The Tall Bearded Man appeared behind Senora. She jumped at his sudden appearance. Scurrying to his feet, she brushed off her pants and tried to clear her dripping hair from her face. "Remember, you're never alone. I'm your guide, but He rules your heart. The Saviour's always with you."

She nodded as she gathered her thoughts. *I need a plan.* Senora's courage filled her as she stood, nodded, and approached the rusty door.

As she rubbed her hands along the frame of the door, she asked, "What'll I face in there?"

"Now war arose in heaven, Michael and his angels fighting against the dragon Lucifer.[2] He rose up against the Saviour, tried to claim His eternal authority, but the Saviour is unchanging and all powerful. You will not be alone. Despite the dangers awaiting you in the dark, you will be protected." He patted her shoulder and gave her a reassuring wink.

"Dragon? What dragon?" Senora's thoughts returned to the Silver Dragon and her friend Sam. She hugged her arms and rubbed them vigorously.

Ignoring her question, he continued with his story, as if he was recalling a distant memory. "The dragon and his angels fought back."[3]

Turning, she pressed the palm of her hand into his chest and look up at him. "Wait. You said his angels. Who's he? I only know of the Silver Dragon and the Red Dragon."

Looking down at her, his face grew sad as he continued. "But he was defeated, and there was no longer any place for them in heaven. And the great dragon was thrown down, that ancient serpent, who's called the devil and Satan, the deceiver of the whole world he was thrown down to the earth, and his angels were thrown down with him.[4] Lucifer and His angels were cast out and renamed."

"Wait, deceiver of the whole world? Do you mean Lucas?" she asked as her hand shot up to her mouth in shock.

He picked her up in a warm hug and released her, holding her shoulder firmly. He smiled and nodded toward the door. "Therefore, rejoice, O heavens and you who dwell in them! But woe to you, O earth and sea, for the devil has come down to you in great wrath, because he knows that his time is short."[5]

Touching the door frame again, her mind was spinning with this new knowledge. "What do you mean, his time is short?"

"And if those days had not been cut short, no human being would be saved. But for the sake of the elect those days will be cut short.[6] Guard your mind darkness thrives here.

Lean on the Saviour's strength and fill your mind with His truth."

"Will you go with me? I don't know the way." Senora looked over her shoulder, but the Man was gone. She looked back at the door, reached down, grabbed a handful of mud, and took a deep breath. "Well, here goes nothing. I hope this works." She smeared mud over the doorposts, and soon, the door opened. She carefully stepped through as the door closed behind her.

———

"What was your mom like?" Lucas asked as he leaped into the room. Robert jumped back and bumped into a nearby filing cabinet.

"Why do you keep asking me about my family?" Robert growled.

Lucas calmed his expression and leaned close. "I think you need to walk with me again. Once again, Robert rose and followed Lucas out of the room. They turned right and walked down several dimly lit caves. "Where're we going now?"

"You'll see. Just open your mind and focus your eyes." They soon emerged into the Forest of Truth, past the ruined city of Dragon Kingdom, and suddenly Robert found himself standing next to a strange-looking tree.

"Is this the Tree of Hope you were talking about before? Why is it called that?"

Lucas smiled mischievously as he leaned against the old, large tree. "The dragon's believed that the Tree of Hope would be a beacon of light for the Saviour's arrival. But with the fall of my Silver Enchantress, their defeat was at hand." He ran his palm along its bark as if in gleeful triumph.

Jumping in shock, Robert braced himself for a fight. "Defeat? I thought you said you loved her?"

Lucas looked at the ground, shook his head, and chuckled. "Oh, but I do. She was my half that made me whole. But when Scarlett deceived the Silver Dragon to the light, I realized that love was only bondage."

Robert shoved Lucas away from the tree and punched him in the mouth. "No, I don't believe that."

Lucas staggered and spat out some blood. "You don't?" Regaining his composure, he stood and walked around the tree again. Grabbing ahold of the tree trunk, he swung around it and glared at Robert from behind the tree. "Tell me about your mother."

"She was just as manipulative as my dad. It took all her strength to keep our life a secret. She would put on her fake smile and pretend we were the perfect family. I wasn't allowed to speak in public. She didn't want me to slip and tell anyone. You see, family problems are just that; they're to stay behind closed doors. But as I got older, I realized something."

Lucas licked his lips and leaned closer to Robert as he turned his eyes to the ground. "What did you realize?"

"That my worthless life was a lie. My friend Trevor believed in my worth. His friendship gave me hope and purpose. He showed me there's a way out. His little sister, Nora, taught me about the Saviour."

Lucas squirmed at the mention of the Saviour. He quickly turned and tapped Robert's forehead, and he fell back against his chair in the cluttered room once more. "I have to go, but we'll talk tomorrow. I'll give you some much-needed insight." Lucas left the room.

Robert stood and walked to the clustered mess Lucas left on the floor. He knelt and slowly picked them up and placed them back on the table. Strangely, most papers appeared to be blank. He searched around the maze of filing cabinets and chairs scattered throughout the room. After trying to open one filing cabinet, he realized they were all locked. He walked to the door, but it was locked too. *Guest on his terms,* Robert reminded himself.

He made his way back to the middle chair and slumped onto it. *When Dad went away to prison two years ago, I made myself a promise. I will not allow that man back into my life. He won't be allowed to hurt anyone again,* Robert reminded himself as he drifted off to sleep.

———

*S*enora found herself standing in a damp, dark, and rocky tunnel. The air was dense, cold, and foul. She covered her nose and tried breathing through her sleeve. "Not much place to hide here. God, please protect me." She slowly shuffled down the tunnel, the only light coming from the glow of her pendant. Soon, she heard Chester's laughter up ahead. She leaned against the rocky wall, but the wall shifted, and she stumbled behind a hidden boulder. *How'll I ever get around him? And how'll I ever find Bobbie or Sam? This tunnel seems to go on forever.*

"Oh, I wish they would make up their minds. Patrol, go inside, report," Chester grumbled as he stumbled over his feet. "It takes real skill to choke on air, fall up the stairs, and trip over nothing. I have those skills. Patrol is so boring my mom won't even do it," Chester sighed, "And yet, I could be useful. The nice part about being a pessimist is that you're constantly proven right or pleasantly surprised.[7] One will see I prove my loyalties. Yes, I could." Senora watched silently as Chester lumbered past her, heading back toward the rusty entrance. She shivered at the sound of Chester's high-pitched laughter. Relief returned as Chester's laughter faded. She swallowed her fears, moving forward.

———

*R*obert sat in the chair. He felt utterly defeated, unloved, and alone. His mind raced, and he felt dizzy. *You're alone. You're a liar. You're not good enough, and you're not worth loving.* Lucas's words danced in his mind, tormenting him.

Lucas entered the dark room. "Let's take a walk," Lucas declared like he had every day for the last two weeks. Robert's mind spun in a fog. Between these walks and being bound, his mind struggled to make sense of his surroundings.

"What is it you want from me?" Robert asked.

"What makes you think I want anything? I'm teaching you."

"Teaching me what exactly?" Robert questioned. "And why won't you let me see Sam? Where is she?"

"After everything I've done for you?" Lucas punched Robert in the cheek. "Why're you so ungrateful? Maybe you need some discipline." Lucas swung his fist at Robert's face again but this time, Robert caught Lucas's fist in his hand and pushed him away. "Good reaction time. There's hope for you yet. Maybe tomorrow, you'll be more willing to listen and talk. Your dad caused so much pain; your mom pretended like nothing was happening. What would you say if I could take your parents out of your life?"

"No, I've forgiven my dad." Robert's mind wandered back to the tornado of fire, and the child called Nobody. *Forgiveness is the key to healing*; the thought ran through his mind.

"They don't deserve forgiveness. You said you wouldn't let him hurt you or your mother again. Right?"

"I know, but I don't need to lose myself to unforgiveness."

"You just think about the power, protection, and control I offer." Soon, Robert was alone in the cluttered room once more. He hung his head in despair.

"I can't do this anymore. I'm unlovable, I'm alone, and I'll never be good enough. I've already seen so much, or at least what Lucas allows me to see, and yet, I still can't find Sam."

"No, His divine power has given *you* everything *you* need for a godly life through knowledge of him who called *you* by his own glory and goodness. Through these he has given *you* his very great and precious promises, so that through them you may participate in the divine nature, having escaped the corruption in the world caused by evil desires."[8] The Tall Bearded Man appeared before Robert. Being caught off guard with the Man's sudden appearance, he toppled backward, and crashing to the floor, he bumped his head on one of the cabinets.

Sheepishly rubbing the back of his head, he jumped to his feet to hide his surprise. "Who're you?"

The man calmly walked around the cabinets, keeping an eye directed on Robert the whole time. "I'm the divine servant of the High King of kings, the great I AM."

Skeptically leaning against a cabinet, he asked, "Who am I that the Saviour would send me such a loyal servant?"

Waving a gentle hand toward him, the Man kept walking around the room. "You've found favour with God."[9]

"Why do you say favour? I'm worthless, worse than nothing, unlovable, and I'll never be good enough." Robert fell to his knees, feeling broken.

The Man stopped at a far cabinet, and Robert looked up without moving his head as the Man forced the cabinet open and pulled out a file. "You're a child of God, you're justified completely, you're free from condemnation, you've the mind of Christ, you've been made righteous, and you've been blessed with every spiritual blessing."[10]

Scurrying to his feet, he scratched his head. "How did you?"

The Man opened the file and started leafing through it. He continued walking around the room as he spoke and reviewed this file.

"As a father has compassion on his children, so the LORD has compassion on those who fear him; for he knows how we're formed, he remembers that we're dust. We've this treasure in jars of clay to show that this all-surpassing power is from God and not from us. For you're a people holy to the LORD your God, and the LORD has chosen you to be a people for his treasured possession."[11]

Shaking his head, he slunk back in his chair, resting his elbows on his lap and placing his head in his hands. "Why would He choose me? I'm not even worth loving."

With each step, the Man's words became bolder, and full of compassion. "*You*'re loved with an everlasting love; therefore, *He* has continued *His* faithfulness to you.[12] Even before he made the world, God loved *you* and chose *you* in Christ to be holy and without fault in his eyes. God decided in advance to adopt *you* into his own family by bringing *you* to himself through Jesus Christ. This is what he wanted to do, and it gave him great pleasure."[13]

When the Man stopped in from of him, Robert looked up with sadness. "Why would God care about me? He has been silent for years."

Robert watched as the man flipped through the file more vigorously, appearing to be searching for something. "Even the very hairs on your head are all numbered. So, don't be afraid; you're worth more than many sparrows."[14]

"This is an impossible situation; it can't be fixed. Lucas has already won."

"Jesus looked at them and said, 'With man this is impossible, but not with God; all things are possible with God."[15]

Clenching his fists, he turned and punched a nearby cabinet. "I'm too weak, I just can't fight anymore."

The Man smiled as he pulled a piece of paper from the file, looked up with such conviction, and said. "My grace is sufficient for you, for my power is made perfect in weakness."[16]

"God has forgotten me."

"Can a mother forget the baby at her breast and have no compassion on the child she has borne? Though she may forget, *God* will not forget you! See, *God* has engraved you on the palms of *His* hands. Stay strong in His strength 'He is with you always, to the very end of the age'. God has said, never will I leave you; never will I forsake you.'"[17] The man placed the paper into Robert's hands. "I'm sending you one who's wise in the faith. She'll remind you of a time you've forgotten. Stay strong you're not alone."

The Man placed his large hand on Robert's back and nodded toward the paper. He turned and walked back to the far file and placed the folder back in the cabinet. "You need to come face to face with God's judgment on your sins today because the longer you avoid what God says to you, you are unable to help others. No one else can hear of God's love for them through you if you are living in denial of your need of saving. When you are brought low at the cross of Christ and confess your sins and acknowledge the punishment falling in Christ, other people will notice and be drawn to the truth. No one can earn their salvation. God can save anyone. Sin will not go unpunished, but God's judgment will be merciful in the way He spares His people because He has good intentions toward those who belong to Him. What will God bring forth after you have gone through the judgment to be refined, purified, and restored?"

"I fear the consequences. I am afraid that there will be nothing left of me."

"Read the paper. You cannot deny this truth. Courage is found in unlikely places, like fear. The fear of saying no to God will override the fear of everything else. If you fear the right thing. If you fear the Lord and cultivate an awareness of Him and His goodness by fearing His word, then the fear of everything else must get smaller by comparison. If it doesn't, then you haven't understood what God has been saying to you. If you will listen, you will be brought near to hear the roar of the lion and will show you must fall down and get low in reverence to God. Let God's voice be your source of conviction and truth that shapes the way you worship, the way you live, and the way you treat your neighbours. Christ's righteousness is made available to you. He has not held it back. Stay strong in His strength, and the truth will set you free."

Robert looked around the dark room. He felt confused, but held on to a small glimmer of hope. Looking down at the paper he saw a photo of himself. Stamped across the photo it read *Chosen. Robert is my adopted son, whom I love.* Robert sat in silence as the darkness no longer felt as heavy.

———

*S*enora shuffled along silently for what seemed like hours in the darkness, when suddenly, a dull glow appeared before her. She cautiously approached the light. Crouching at the end of the dark hallway, she found herself facing a large, pillared room full of glowing candlelight. Statues lined the outer walls. Each statue was a beast-like creature with the face of a man. As she focused on the statue closest to her, she wavered as a shiver of fear hit her. The face was that of Lucas. "No, not Lucas again," Senora gasped barely above a whisper. Her eyes scanned the large room in search of other tunnels or entrances she could slip into. She caught a glimpse of two hairy beast-like creatures emerging from the other end of the room.

"They'll soon be overcome. Master Drayvon will prevail. Lord Lucas is almighty." One creature laughed with glee.

"They'll soon see they're alone: nobody's coming for them," the other declared. Senora dove behind the nearby statue as the two creatures walked past and entered the dark tunnel she had just come out of. Sighing out of relief of not being seen, she quickly jumped and dodged behind each statue, bringing her closer to the other entrance. Cautiously sliding into the darkness, she reached her new destination undetected.

The hallway was still cold and damp, but the air was not as foul. Senora pressed against the side, rock wall in hopes that if any more creatures came her way, she would be able to slip past them unnoticed. She hid the glowing eagle pendant in her pants pocket and continued on her way.

—⟨⟨⟩⟩—

*A*s Lucas strolled into the room once again, Robert quickly folded the paper and shoved in into his jeans pocket. "Have you considered my offer?"

Robert stood and paced the room. "I'm not willing to gain the whole world if it means I lose my soul,"

Lucas squeezed the brim of his nose between his fingers and rubbed his forehead. "Who said anything about your soul? I offer you a way out of here; I offer a way home. I offer you freedom and peace away from your parents. Maybe you just need more time to think it over. I'm patient. Why continue on a path of failure, when I offer you the tools to be strong?" He moved some of the papers around on the table as he spoke.

Robert stopped and scratched the back of his head. The room felt as though it was spinning. Reaching for a nearby cabinet, he braced himself. "Your words ring true to my ears, but they don't feel right inside."

Lucas leaned right into his face and firmly stated, "You failed to protect your mother. You failed to protect Nora. You failed to save Trevor. Now, I offer you a way to be strong, and you say you don't feel right?" He pushed Robert backward. "What does feeling right have to do with anything? I offer you strength and the ability to save everyone; I only ask one small thing. You probably won't even miss it. I'm the only one you can trust right now. Think about it." Lucas slammed the door behind him.

Robert slumped in his chair. "I can't take this any longer. I just can't help myself. I'm such a failure, I'm inadequate. I'm just a nobody. I don't matter to anyone. I can't do anything right." Robert sighed in defeat. *I'm just Nobody.* The words of little Tony sang in his ears. Concern and worry filled his heart. Suddenly, the Tall Bearded Man reappeared before Robert. Robert staggered in fear.

"See what great love the Father has lavished on *you*, that *you* should be called *a child* of God! And that's what *you* are!"[18] The Man reached a grabbed his hand to stabilize him. "To all who receive Him, to those who believed in His name, He gave the right to become children of God."[19]

Robert pulled the folded paper out of his pocket again. "A child of God, yes, but why does God still love me when I keep making the same mistake all the time?"

The Man pulled him close into a big hug, lifting him of the ground. When he placed him firmly on his feet again, he nodded and said, "In love He predestined *you* for adoption to sonship through Jesus Christ.[20] Everyone born of God overcomes the world. This is the victory that has overcome the world, even our faith."[21]

Filling with anger, he tore the paper into small pieces and threw it on the floor. "I'm a failure and not worthy of sonship." Turning his back, he stomped over to the table.

The man walked around the cabinets as he spoke. "He gives *you* the victory through our Lord Jesus Christ."[22]

"How could I trust God? Just look at my life nothing seems to get better." Robert tossed the papers off the table.

"My God will meet all your needs according to the riches of His glory in Christ Jesus.[23] He will not let you be tempted beyond what you can bear. But when you're tempted, He'll also provide a way out so you can endure it."[24] The man walked up behind Robert.

Placing his hands on the table, he hung his head and dug his fingernails in. "You don't understand what I'm going through."

Placing a hand on his shoulder and giving a squeeze, he said, "*You* do not have a high priest who's unable to sympathize with *your* weakness, but *you* have one who has been tempted in every way, just as *you* are yet He did not sin."[25]

Robert pounded his fists into the table a few times. "I'm so angry with my mom. I can't forgive her for allowing him back into our lives. I know I'm called to forgive her, and I've forgiven my dad, but that doesn't mean I welcome him back into my life to hurt me again. I don't think I can forgive her."

"*You* can forgive because Christ has forgiven *you*."[26] The Man placed the now intact paper on the table in front of Robert. Reaching for his hand, he placed it firmly on the paper.

Taking a deep breath and crumpling the paper with his fingers, he stared at the Man. "I don't deserve to be forgiven."

"It's by grace you've been saved, through faith and this isn't from yourselves, it's the gift of God-not by works, so that no one can boast."[27]

"I'll never change. I'll always be a mess."

The man tapped the table with his finger. "He who began a good work in you will carry it on to completion until the day of Christ Jesus."[28]

He picked up the paper and shoved it in his pocket once more. Gritting his teeth, he spat out his words. "God can't use me, and I'll never figure this out. God has forgotten me."

"You didn't choose me, but I chose you and appointed you so that you might go and bear fruit—fruit that will last.[29] Trust in the LORD with all your heart and lean not on your own understanding; in all your ways submit to him, and he'll make your paths straight.[30] Cast all your anxiety on Him, because he cares for you."[31]

Grabbing the edge of the table, he flipped it on its head

with a loud crash. "I know that in my mind, but it's hard to believe in my heart."

"For *He* formed *your* inward parts; *He* knitted *you* together in *your* mother's womb.[32] *Your* frame wasn't hidden from *Him*, when *you* were made in secret, intricately woven in the depths of the earth. *His* eyes saw *your* unformed substance; in *His* book were written, every one of them, the days that were formed for *you*, when as yet there was none of them. How precious are *God's* thoughts, how vast is the sum of them! If *you* would count them, they are more than the sand."[33]

His head shot up, and his eyes grew wider, "God thinks of me?"

"For I know the plans I have for you, declares the LORD, plans for welfare and not for evil, to give you a future and a hope. Then you will call upon me and come and pray to me, and I will hear you.[34] Stay strong in the strength the LORD provides. I'm sending someone who'll remind you of the truth. You're not alone. It is time."

"Time? Time for what?"

"Time to stand in the fire, face your fears. Courage is found in unlikely places. Your courage will be refined in the fire as you face your fears." The Man vanished, and Robert pulled the paper from his pocket and read the word again, *Chosen*.

Robert looked around, questioning what had happened. *Did I just have a vision? Or was that man really here?* His mind raced for answers.

———✷✷✷———

Senora stayed as quiet and as still as she could and listened to a conversation unfolding before her. "She's almost ready for you. I've almost broken her," Drayvon declared.

"Good, my plan's working perfectly," Lucas said gleefully as he rubbed his hands together.

"What sort of game are you playing with him exactly?" he asked while he pulled a random flea from him fur.

Stroking his chin, a flicker of mischief flashed in his eyes. "I'm building and replacing his bond with her. I'll show him true power. He'll come to desire it, and the truth will become hazy to him." He snapped his fingers and pressed his hand into Drayvon's thick chest.

Backing away and scraping his claws on the cave wall, he licked his lips and howled. "How're you going to do that?"

Leaning against a wall, he folded his arms and grinned. "He's almost ready for another walkabout."

With a growl, Drayvon stood twice as tall in front of Lucas. "What's the point of these walkabouts? Are you not just revealing more of my kingdom to him?"

He chuckled, placed his hand firmly on Drayvon's chest and pushed him aside. "Not your kingdom. I'm just shedding some history into the boy. Maybe tomorrow we will visit the Forgetful woods. A few days there, and Sam won't even be an afterthought."

Nodding and scratching at his side, he howled in agreement. "You're the master of deception."

Bowing his approval, he looked up and winked. "Why, thank you. Soon, their connection will be severed, and their division will be the foundation of their demise. I'm training him."

Wiping some drool from his chin and clawing at the wall, he looked up at Lucas, puzzled. "Training him for what?"

He placed his hands on his hips, threw back his head, and laughed loudly. "For the ultimate deception. Soon, their hope and faith will be gone. No more protection for them. I'll destroy the last of the dragons and take the power that's rightfully mine." Lucas rubbed his hands together greedily.

Dragon's power? Ultimate deception? What does he mean? I have to find Sam. Senora's thoughts raced. Looking around the corner, she could see one of the largest and scariest creatures she had ever seen. She shuddered at the thought of what demise they'd been referring to. She squirmed in fright but remembered God's greater than all things. Her confidence wavered when she caught a glimpse of who Drayvon was talking to. "Lucas," she whispered with a gasp.

13

FORGOTTEN SECRETS REVEALED

"I'll inform you at once the moment she breaks. But what about the other?" Drayvon asked.

"He's breaking; I need to raise his fear to the surface. He's a fighter; I need to use a different attack with this one. But I've seen him waver. In time, he'll lose himself," Lucas stated.

Drayvon smirked a devilish smile as he turned and walked down a dimly lit tunnel.

It's like a maze down here. How'll I ever find my way back out once I find them? She shook off her questions. *I need to focus now. If I follow this creature, maybe he'll lead me to Sam.* Senora moved closer to Lucas. She froze in place as Lucas turned toward her. *Please LORD, protect me now,* she prayed. Lucas shifted closer to her location as Senora was strangely filled with peace.

"Lord Lucas, sorry to interrupt, but there's movement on the northern border. Do I get Master Drayvon?" Lucas turned abruptly around to face a skittish Chester.

"Gather a small group. Have them investigate. I've a meeting with someone now." Lucas replied as he stormed away.

"Yes, Lord, right away," Chester said as he shuffled past

Senora toward the other large lit room she had just left, leaving a trail of faint hyena laughter behind him. Senora quickly made her way down the tunnel Drayvon had entered. After a short run, she caught sight of Drayvon. She watched as he opened a door. Then, she caught sight of *Sam* as the door closed. Senora ran up to the door and listened.

———◦◦◦———

*D*rayvon entered the room. Sam locked defiant eyes with him as he entered. She squinted at movement from behind him. *Was that Nora I saw? No, it can't be.* Sam stared, puzzled with what she thought she might have seen, and Drayvon closed the door. Drayvon moved quickly toward Sam and struck her cheek knocking her and the chair to the ground.

He swiftly pulled her up against the wall and stared deep into her eyes. "What hope do you hold onto? I could break you in one swipe," Drayvon warned.

"Then why don't you?" Sam challenged. "You need me. I just don't know for what yet."

"Need you? I need no one. You just happen to be part of the plan." Drayvon released her and Sam crashed to the floor. The chair broke and dug into her arm. Sam cried out in pain as Drayvon pulled her up and bound her to a different chair. "Oh, this is going to hurt." Drayvon pulled the piece of chair out of her arm as blood oozed out. Sam screamed in pain, then bit her lip so she wouldn't give Drayvon the satisfaction.

"Where're you finding this strength? Remember, no one's coming for you. No one even remembers you. You're the last of your kind; it must be lonely for you. No one understands the loss you've endured."

Sam looked at Drayvon with such hatred that her hair glowed crimson, and her green eyes ignited like lasers.

Drayvon lunged at her and dug his claws into her wounded arm. "There it is," Drayvon stated with glee as he squeezed her arm, and Sam felt as though part of her was draining away. She felt so weak. The fire went out of her, and she hung her head. "Lord Lucas will be pleased," Drayvon whispered as he drifted back to the door and was gone.

———⦻———

*I*t horrified Senora to hear the painful and terrifying screams from her dear friend Sam. *What's he doing to you?* Senora wondered. She wanted to dart right into the room and make the pain stop, but if she revealed herself now, all would be lost. She held her breath and silently prayed. Soon, the door flew open, Drayvon stormed out, slammed the door shut, and walked gleefully back down the tunnel.

Now's my chance, Senora thought as she ran toward the door, opened it, and walked up to Sam. Senora knelt down in front of her friend and touched her hand. *It's so cold.* Senora feared for her friend's life. She reached for Sam's chin and lifted it to look into Sam's face. Sam's eyes were closed, and her breath was weak. "Sam? It's me, Nora. I'm here to help you. Sam, open your eyes." Sam's eyes fluttered and rolled back. "Sam, I'm here! Look at me. Please come back. You're not alone."

Sam rolled her eyes forward and opened them only a little, trying to focus on the figure before her. "Nora? Are you really here?" Senora hugged her friend and quickly unbound her.

"Can you walk?" Senora asked.

"I don't know." Sam's eyes opened more to better focus on Senora's face. "Is this a dream?"

"No, Sam. I'm really here. There's still hope. If we could get out of this place, then we could regroup. Crystal's waiting just beyond the Shadow Dominion border. I need you to stand." Senora reached out her hand, but she noticed Sam's arm. "What did he do to you?"

"Nora, tear a piece of cloth from my shirt. You need to stop the bleeding." Sam gasped for breath. Senora nodded, stood, and ripped a piece of cloth. She wrapped it around Sam's wound and tied it tight. Sam winced in pain but refused to cry out. Senora stood and reached out her hand to help Sam to her feet. Sam leaned on Senora for support as they made their way to the door. The two opened the door and shuffled toward the hiding place.

"I guess it's my turn to save you," Senora said as she playfully laughed. Sam closed her eyes and smiled. "Sam, do you know where they're keeping Bobbie?"

"So, you do know Bobbie? It's strange."

"What's strange?"

"With Bobbie, I feel a connection like I've never felt before. Earlier, I was able to see the path to where they held him. But whatever Drayvon did to me, I can't seem to find him again."

"Think about what you saw before. Do you think you can guide me?"

"I don't know. I also saw Lucas there."

"I saw him talking with that creature earlier. I could lead you to where they were talking. Maybe you'll remember from there?" Sam nodded weakly. "But we need to be careful that we don't run into any of those creatures."

"They're called Shadow Knights. Drayvon's their ruler; he's the one you saw with me." The two quietly made their way back to the opening of the dimly lit tunnel. Senora saw the boulder she had hid behind earlier and helped Sam slip in behind. "I need to rest. I feel so weak."

"Stay with me, Sam. Does anything look familiar from your vision?"

Sam looked around the boulder at several different tunnels.

"They all look the same." She closed her eyes and tried to remember her vision of Robert. Soon, she opened her eyes back up and pointed down the corridor leading downhill and to the right. They rested behind the boulder as Chester entered the crossroad of tunnels and scratched his head.

"Gather a group. Gather a group? Grr." Chester grumbled under his breath. "People say nothing's impossible, but I do nothing every day." Chester turned and entered a different tunnel leading back toward the large room again.

"He's a strange one," Senora whispered. Helping Sam to her feet, they entered the tunnel Sam indicated. It was quite a steep decline, so they both leaned on the rock wall to maintain their balance. At the end of this tunnel, there was a wooden door. Senora leaned Sam against the wall in the darkest part of the tunnel. "Lucas might still be in there," Senora said with concern.

Sam tried to think of Lucas, but fear held her in bondage. *What did Drayvon do to me?*

"Sam, let's rest for a bit. You're weak," Senora said as she looked nervously at the door.

Chester stumbled toward the wooden door. "Lord Lucas!" Chester shrieked. Lucas jumped out the door as Chester slammed right into him.

"You better have a good excuse for this intrusion," Lucas warned.

"That prisoner. You know the one. Sam, is it?" Chester started to say but shrunk back at the rage growing within Lucas's eyes.

"First movement on the border. What's this about Sam?" Lucas demanded.

"She's not in her bondage anymore," Chester mumbled.

"What? Find her." Lucas pushed Chester against the wall, and he fell with a thud. "You waste of brain cells. Move." Lucas and Chester rushed back up the steep tunnel and out of sight.

"Wait here, Sam." Senora rushed toward the wooden door and burst through.

"I've considered your offer," Robert whispered as he looked toward the door. "Wait, Nora? What're you doin' here?"

Senora ran toward Robert, hugged him and untied his bonds. "Let's get out of here first, and then I'll fill you in."

"What's the matter, Bobbie? Let's go," Senora replied.

"I don't know. I mean, I'm his guest."

"Guest? But you were just tied to a chair. Who ties their guests to a chair?"

"I'm free to roam as long as I don't ask about, well, you know."

"Ask about what or who? You're not making any sense. Come, Sam's just outside. She's hurt; we need to get her out of here. Snap out of it, Bobbie. We need you." Robert convulsed as if fighting off an unseen battle. Senora grabbed both of his shoulders and shook him. Robert slowly focused on Senora's face as his eyes became less dazed.

"Nora? Did you say Sam? Where is she?"

"Just out in the hall, but we need to get her out of here. She's hurt." Robert quickly jumped into action and followed Senora out of the room. He stood almost frozen when he saw Sam leaning weakly against the wall.

"Is she goin' to be alright?" Robert's heart went out to her. He ran to her side and embraced her to keep her safe.

"We need to get her out of here. She's very weak. Can you help her?" Senora asked.

Robert nodded and picked Sam up in his arms.

"I can carry her. But how'll we find our way out?" Soon, they heard chuckling from behind Robert.

"I can help. Besides, I led you in, didn't I? Never follow anyone else's path. Unless you're in the woods, and you're lost, and you see a path. Then, by all means, follow that path."[1] Chester laughed sarcastically. "They treat me as stupid my advantage. Come, I will show you the way." Robert looked at Senora with uncertainty.

"Do we have a choice here? He was the one I followed in," Senora said. The two quickly ran to catch up to Chester, nearly bumping into him. Chester grabbed both Senora and Robert and pulled them out of sight and behind a statue pillar. Senora looked around to see hordes of beast-like creatures running in all directions.

"Come, must go around. Come, I help you." Chester slunk swiftly behind each statue with ease, waving for the others to follow. Sam rested her head weakly on Robert's shoulder. Robert nodded at Senora as they moved swiftly to keep up with Chester. Chester led them quietly down the tunnel toward the rusty door. Their breath caught within themselves as they burst through the rusty door out into the storm now raging even stronger than before. "Master's angry. Fear's what keeps me going. That's why I have you around."

"Why did you help us?" Senora asked.

"Master's angry, but Lord's worse. I die either way. Might as well die doing what's right. If you don't know where you're going, you might wind up someplace else.[2] Now, go!" Chester said. Robert and Senora rushed into the cold storm, the ice crystals scraping at their faces. Robert stumbled, and both he and Sam crashed to the ground. Senora rushed toward them and pulled them behind the shelter of a fallen tree.

"This storm will be the death of us if we don't find shelter," Robert stated. Senora suddenly remembered her eagle pendant and pulled it out of her pocket. It was still glowing, and she placed it around her neck.

She stood and reached for Robert's hand. "Will you trust me?"

Robert took hold of Senora's hand and felt instant warmth rush down his arm through his spine and down into his toes. He nodded and picked Sam up again. The two stood and walked through the raging storm, unharmed by its effects.

Within a couple of hours, they emerged from the storm to find Crystal waiting patiently with the horses. The glow of the pendant died out as the three approached Crystal. "You found them. Are you alright? What's wrong with Sam?" Crystal asked.

Robert lifted Sam's weak body onto a horse. "I don't know what they did to her, but she's very weak."

Senora placed her hand on Robert's shoulder. "Likewise the Spirit helped us in our weakness.[3] *What* is sown in weakness; it is raised in power.[4] She's stronger than you think. We need to regroup. Sam's too weak to ride on her own. Crystal's the best rider. She should ride with Sam. You can ride with me," Senora replied.

"Sure, since dismounting seems to be a challenge for me." Robert laughed. He mounted the horse clumsily but made it before helping Senora climb on. The horses galloped back to the castle.

Senora's thoughts wandered as she remembered Chester, Robert, Sam, Katerina, and Crystal. So much had happened in such a short time. She thought about Josiah, Sylvia, her mom, her dad, and Robert's mom. She considered the letter Robert's mom read to Robert at his hospital bedside. The anger Robert must be holding onto toward his dad. *Should I tell Robert about the letter? About him in the hospital bed? About him being torn between two worlds? So much to tell him, but how? Would he believe me? What should I share with him, and what should I allow him to discover on his own?*

Senora was pulled out of her thoughts as Crystal turned to the right and quickly dismounted her horse. Senora turned after her, but in doing so, Robert leaned too far over and pulled the both of them off the horse, crashing onto the ground. Crystal only shook her head and rolled her eyes at them. Robert sheepishly stood as Senora got control again of the horse. "Why did we stop?" Senora asked.

Crystal pointed toward the castle. They saw movement,

but Senora couldn't make out what it was. "We need to wait. That's The Called," Crystal revealed.

"What's The Called?" Robert asked.

"The Called is when all seems lost, and kingdoms are called to stand together against a common enemy. My sister is calling those to her. It'll be the greatest battle. Good vs. evil. 'Proclaim this among the nations: Prepare for war! Rouse the warriors! Let all the fighting men draw near and attack.'[5] 'Together they'll be like warriors in battle trampling their enemy into the streets. They'll fight because the LORD's with them, and they'll put the enemy horsemen to shame.'[6] 'They gathered the kings together to the place that in Hebrew is called Armageddon,'" Crystal gasped.[7]

"What do you mean by Armageddon?" Robert asked.

"It's the ultimate battle, which has been foretold over the decades of long ago, one that will surpass worlds. If Lucas wins, no one will be safe. The Crosswords of Fire will ignite and threaten not just our world," Crystal said as they watched several armed soldiers march toward the castle. Senora saw movement in the grasslands to the left of the castle too.

Senora tapped Crystal on the shoulder and pointed toward the movement. "What's that?"

"Oh, more of The Called. They're swift and cunning. Worthy warriors, they come from the Grasslands of Sheava. They're always prepared for an attack because they move faster than your eyes can see, in their fighting style. The only one you'll see is their leader during the war meeting with Kat," Crystal declared.

Robert stared in awe as the masses flocked to the castle and prepared for battle. *What am I even doing here? I'm not strong enough to even stand up to Lucas by himself, let alone an army.* Senora sensed his doubts. She turned and faced him. "Finally, be strong in the Lord and in the strength of his might. Put on the whole armour of God that you may be able to stand against the schemes of the devil."[8] Senora said with great confidence in her voice. Robert felt his courage return.

Soon the roar of the armies died down. "Let's go! We can continue now," Crystal proclaimed as she mounted her horse again. Robert lifted Sam up behind Crystal. He climbed onto Senora's horse with a little more ease this time. They rode off toward the castle once more.

PART 6: UNIFICATION

14

THE CALLED

*R*obert dozed as they drew closer to the castle. He was jolted awake when Senora slowed the horse to almost a dead stop. His eyes widened at the sight of so many different people groups and creatures of different shapes and sizes. Senora carefully led her horse next to Crystal's. "Are these more Called Ones?" Robert asked.

Crystal nodded. "They all come to honour princess Delores and Queen Scarlett. The funeral procession's tomorrow." She pointed to each different group. "Those tall ones in the mossy green armour, they're the Riverglade Mapleflecks, and they use tree vines in a whipping style that could snap one in two with just a single hit. Those small creatures covered in spikes are called the Stalkers. They're master swordsmen in the east from a place called the Combatant Valley. The glowing laser creatures are called the Truthtellers from Flashgrove. They hold all wisdom of the Saviour," Crystal revealed as Senora stared in fascination.

"I've never seen such magnificent people and creatures alike. Are they all allies?" Senora asked. She caught a glimpse of a different group of people. They were small and clothed in mud and seemed to stay on the outskirts of the entourage. She pointed at them. "What about that group?"

"Oh, those are the sneakiest and strongest. They're called the Stonewall Radissons from Radisville. They cover themselves in mud to camouflage to their surroundings better. Don't be fooled by their appearance. They've never lost a battle," Crystal said.

Senora's focus turned to Sam, who seemed barely conscious. "Is Sam going to be ok?"

"She's strong, but I don't know what Drayvon did to her. I hope my sister, Kat, will be able to provide some answers. But this is going to take a while. This group isn't moving quickly and there's no way around them. Just hold on Sam," Crystal said. The four rode along silently with the slow-moving crowd.

After about an hour of silence, Robert cleared his throat.

"How would Kat know what Drayvon did to Sam when you don't?"

"Well, we were captive to Lucas for a number of years. She was more intuitive to his tricks and schemes than I was. Maybe during that time, she might've heard something about a plan. I know he had, in the past, tried to eradicate the Dragon Kingdom with the aid of the Silver Dragon. Maybe when Scarlett turned the Silver Dragon against him, he took up that old desire for ultimate power." Crystal gasped.

"What do you mean dragon? Should I be concerned?" Robert asked. "I mean I want Sam safe. I don't want to see her as dragon food or anything."

Senora couldn't help but chuckle. Robert glared at her. "Sorry, I couldn't help but laugh. I can confirm there is no chance of Sam being eaten by a dragon. That's for sure." Senora laughed as both she and Crystal shared a knowing look.

"What're you not telling me?" Robert asked.

"It's not my secret to tell." Senora claimed. She looked

ahead with anticipation as the castle came into view. "Look, there's Castle Calvarias. We're almost there."

As the front of the group reached the draw bridge, the crowd slowed even more. Crystal steered her horse off to the side of the group and dismounted. Senora followed. She dismounted first, then Robert followed a little more carefully and managed to stay on his feet this time. Crystal secured both horses to a nearby tree. "If we walk around the back ledge, we could get in through the back tunnel. Do you remember, Nora?"

Senora nodded and led them away from the crowd. Robert rushed to Crystal's horse and helped Sam off the horse. She wavered. "I don't have the strength to stand. Maybe you should just leave me. I'll only slow you down," Sam announced.

"Nonsense, I never leave anyone behind." Robert picked Sam into his arms and turned to follow Senora and Crystal. His courage faded when he saw what Crystal meant about the back ledge. "Not sure if I can balance that narrow ledge and carry Sam at the same time."

Senora stopped and turned toward Sam. "Can you manage?" Senora asked.

"Unfortunately, no." Sam sighed.

"Is there another way?" Robert asked.

"Only if you go back and enter the gate with the crowd, but it'll take you longer. Time is of the essence," Crystal declared.

Senora saw the concern growing within Robert and Sam. "Crystal, you go ahead. Bobbie and I'll go with the crowd to take Sam in. Maybe you could warn Kat. Maybe she could make a way for us to get through faster," Senora suggested. She saw the relief forming in both Sam and Robert's faces.

"Alright." Crystal maneuvered along the narrow path toward the hidden cave entrance.

Senora walked over to Sam and touched her cold and clammy forehead. "What did he do to you?" she asked.

"I honestly don't know." Sam rested her weak head against Robert's chest.

"Let's head back to the front," Senora offered as Robert agreed and followed. The crowd had grown so thick it was oozing along at a snail's pace. The group of three slowly made their way through the crowd.

<hr />

$\mathcal{K}$aterina was staring out the throne room window when a guard entered. "Lady Kat, your sister, Lady Crystal has returned," the guard declared.

"Send her in," Katerina ordered. Crystal entered the throne room and hugged Katerina. Katerina looked behind her sister with concern. "You're alone. Where're the others?"

"They're trying to enter through the crowd. Sam was too injured to enter the secret way," Crystal said.

Katerina filled with more regret and fear. "Guards!" The guards entered and bowed.

"You called Lady Kat?" a guard asked.

"Yes, take a small patrol out through the entering masses. Nora, Sam, and Bobbie are there. Bring them to me," Katerina ordered.

"Right away, my lady," the guard said and jumped to action.

When the guard left the throne room, Katerina looked at the floor with sadness in her eyes. Crystal got right up in her face. "Don't you do that. She was my mother too. Princess Delores mentored both of us. You won't carry all the grief alone. I won't allow you to steal that from me."

Katerina glared at her sister. "You don't have to carry everything. I do. Lucas must pay for what he did. I'll grieve when I can. But for now, I need to be strong."

"Let us both be strong. But tomorrow, let us both say our goodbyes. Together, ok?"

"I know you're right, but as soon as the process is over, we must prepare and gather for war." Crystal hugged her sister.

———❦———

*T*he masses of different people and creatures alike fascinated Senora, but what fascinated her more was the focus and attention Robert had on Sam. *He seems so protective of her. I've never seen him so attentive. Does this mean he is learning to feel again?* Senora filled with excitement at the thought. "How's Sam doing?" she asked.

"Not sure. She appears to be tired and weak. I wish I could've saved her from that torture," Robert said, as his muscles flexed and tightened.

"I understand. They always had a plan. You're no good to Sam if you allow your anger to blind your focus," Senora said. "Be angry and do not sin; do not let the sun go down on your anger, and give no opportunity to the devil."[1]

"Anger gives me strength to protect others," Robert declared.

"Yes, but when you use your anger in the wrong way, it's like gaining the whole world but forfeiting your very soul," Senora stated.

Robert pondered her words, and they felt heavy upon his heart. He remembered what he said in the cave with his father. *He was just a boy, endured such torture himself, and promised he would not be like his uncle. But that was what happened. Am I doomed to make the same mistakes?* Four castle guards approached them, interrupting Robert's thoughts.

"Lady Kat has sent us to you for private escort into Castle Calvarias. Come quickly," the guard ordered. Robert readjusted his hold on Sam and nodded. "Would you like me to carry her the rest of the way to lighten your load?"

"I'm fine. Lead the way," Robert replied with both conviction and determination in his voice. The three followed as the crowd parted to make a way for them. When they finally reached the courtyard, Kat and Crystal met them. Kat stopped in her tracks at the sight of Sam.

Her hand covered her mouth with shock at how weak and pale she looked. *I've never seen her like this; she has always been the strong one. What have I done?* A wave of guilt and despair slammed against her, filling her with panic and fear. *We are all doomed, and Lucas has already won.* She gasped for air as her breath left her. Crystal reached for her arm to stabilize her.

"It's ok, Kat. 'Fear not, O land; be glad and rejoice, for the LORD has done great things.[2] 'And, do not fear those who kill the body but cannot kill the soul. Rather fear him who can destroy both soul and body in hell," Crystal declared.[3]

Katerina found her confidence again as she remembered what Delores told her when she was younger: "So we can confidently say, 'The Lord is my helper; I will not fear; what can man do to me.'"[4] Katerina focused on the three new arrivals. "Take Sam to a bedroom to rest." A guard approached Robert to take Sam from him. Robert pulled her closer to himself protectively.

"Lead the way I'll take her," Robert said. The guard looked over his shoulder toward Lady Katerina and Lady Crystal. Katerina only nodded, and the guard turned on his heel and led Robert up the long winding staircase that took them to the main chamber bedrooms. Katerina turned to focus on Senora.

"Nora, is there any information you can share with us that could better prepare us for the battle that's ahead?"

Senora approached Katerina and bowed. "Can we talk in private?" Katerina nodded. Crystal led Senora back to the throne room.

"Tell me what you've discovered," Katerina demanded.

"I fear this might be the final battle. One for one's very

soul. One that will span worlds. If we aren't careful more than just our world with fall," Crystal warned.

"He's growing in numbers. I'm not sure how many, and they're hidden in the shadows. But they're strong," Senora claimed.

"What do you think, Kat? Is this what we were told about in our childhood? The battle of Armageddon?" Crystal asked.

Katerina contemplated all their words carefully, but also considered her mother's old warnings: "'See that no one leads you astray. For many will come in my name, saying, I am the Christ, and they will lead many astray. And you will hear of wars and rumours of wars. See that you are not alarmed, for this must take place, but the end is not yet. For nation will rise against nation, and kingdom against kingdom, and there will be famines and earthquakes in various places. All these are but the beginning of the birth pains.'"[5] Katerina proclaimed, "This war will indeed cross worlds. I have already seen that. Not only will our world suffer, but that pain has already spilled over into your world, Nora."

"What're we to do?" Senora asked.

"Lucas and Drayvon fight with deception, fear, and lies. We need to fill our hearts with truth. I admit that I've been overwhelmed with guilt and grief," Katerina recalled.

"Let all bitterness and wrath and anger and clamour and slander be put away from you, along with all malice. Be kind to one another, tenderhearted, forgiving one another, as God in Christ forgave you."[6] Senora said, "When we give into the lies, we lose ourselves. We need to find strength in unity."

"I find it easier to forgive others, but I don't know if I can forgive myself," Katerina admitted.

"There is therefore now no condemnation for those who are in Christ Jesus. For the law of the Spirit of life has set you free in Christ Jesus from the law of sin and death."[7] Senora stated, "If we confess our sins, he is faithful and just to forgive us our sins and to cleanse us from all unrighteousness."[8]

"How can you forgive me? I almost killed you, and I might as well have injured Sam myself. I was the one who sent them to Shadow Dominion." Katerina hung her head in shame.

"Lucas is the king of deception. He knew you would do anything to save me. I probably would've done the same thing for you. Don't lose heart. You can't let him win," Crystal declared.

Katerina looked up at her with tears in her eyes. "Please leave me. I have to prepare for the Called Ones and finalize arrangements for the funeral procession. Go see how Sam and Bobbie are doing."

Senora opened her mouth to protest when Crystal raised her hand to stop her. Senora only bowed and left the throne room.

"Crystal, I don't think I can do this. I'm not Mother. She always seemed to have the answers," Katerina said.

"Guard your heart. You're not alone. The Saviour's with you and He'll give you the words to say," Crystal declared.

"How can you be so sure?"

"For where two or three are gathered in my name, there am I among them.[9] Let's pray together. The battle's unavoidable, but we need to surrender the outcome into God's hands. 'Trust in the Lord with all your heart, and do not lean on your own understanding. In all your ways acknowledge him, and he'll make straight your paths.'"[10]

"I'm full of fear, grief, doubt, and shame. How could the Saviour ask me to lead this group into battle? Isn't there someone more qualified? What about Sir Gervon?" Katerina asked.

"Let no one despise you for your youth, but set the believers an example in speech, in conduct, in love, in faith, in purity.[11] For nothing will be impossible with God."[12] Crystal stated, "Kat, pray with me. Let's surrender this battle into the Saviour's hands." The two girls knelt and prayed.

———〰〰〰———

$\mathcal{T}$he guard opened the door to a large bedroom. Robert cautiously walked toward the bed and placed Sam onto it. "Thank you, Bobbie," Sam replied.

"How're you doin? What did they do to you?" Robert asked.

"I-I'll be ok," Sam whispered as Senora entered the room. The guard left to return to his post. "Nora? How are you?" Senora touched her eagle pendant, "Scarlett's pendant, you still have it," Sam said as she pointed at the scar on Robert's arm. "How is it he carries the same symbol on his skin?"

"He got it when he saved my life." Senora smiled at Robert. "I think that's what brought him here."

"What do you mean?" Robert asked.

"There's so much I need to tell you, Bobbie. You're in danger, though," Senora warned.

"I don't have time for this. Lucas and Drayvon need to pay." Robert grumbled and clenched his fists. "No one deserves to be tortured like this."

"I know, but we need to trust God's plan," Senora said.

Pacing around the room, he punched his left fist into his right hand. Spitting each word as if it were poison in his mouth, and said, "God's plan? Was its God's plan for you to get caught in the fire? Was its God's plan for my dad to be tortured as a kid? Was its God's plan for my dad to beat my mom? Where was God when Trevor died?" Robert said each word with conviction and hatred in his eyes.

"As for *them*, *they* meant evil against *you*, but God meant it for good to bring it about that many people should be kept alive, as they are today. So do not fear; *God* will provide for you and your little ones.[13] Please find comfort in this truth. We may not understand these things, but we need to trust that God will work things out for good," Senora proclaimed.

"How can you be so sure?" Robert asked.

"Because God knows all things, and He has a plan. I've seen Him work in your life as well as mine. He won't abandon us now," Senora declared.

"I don't know. I need to think about all this," Robert replied. Senora approached him and placed her hand on his shoulder, but Robert pushed her away and left the room.

"I'm sorry you had to see that." Senora turned her attention to Sam.

"I understand. He's a mystery to me," Sam said.

"He has suffered a lot. Anger has been his wall of protection that kept others at a safe distance. He knows the Saviour, but he struggles with trusting Him."

Sam scooted herself up to rest her back against the headboard. As the room began to spin, she raised her hand to her temple. "We all carry lies from our past. I understand his doubts. One thing Drayvon revealed to me was an old memory from my childhood, one long since lost or forgotten. He meant the memory to destroy my belief in the Saviour, but instead of feeling forgotten, abandoned, and unworthy, I was reminded of my faith, adoption, forgiveness, and hope."

Fiddling with the corner of the blanket, Senora stared out the window. "God has never given up on us." She looked intently into Sam's eyes. "You taught me that. You're one of the strongest people I know." Waving her finger through the sun rays flowing in through the window, she got a far-off look. "Where there's light, darkness is forced to flee. We're more than conquerors."

Staring at the shadows Senora's hand formed on the floor, her thoughts drifted back to the memory of her mom. "You need to know that Sam is not my real name."

Suddenly dropping her hand in her lap, she turned in shock. "What do you mean?"

Sheepishly fiddling with the edge of her sheet, she swallowed a lump forming in her throat. Coughing to clear her voice, she said, "When Delores found me, I was a scared and lost child. The Silver Dragon killed my mother. When Drayvon revealed this memory to me, he revealed my old name. I was called Starstorm."

Curiously looking at the ceiling, Senora scratched her chin, deep in thought. "There are meanings behind names. Starstorm means 'my courage has just started to turn into freedom,' and Samantha means 'God heard.'" Senora jumped from the bed excitedly and clapped her hands. "So, your courage has been turned into freedom because God heard you. He has not forgotten you, but He has strengthened you in both your faith and your name. Hold onto both names, and God's strength will shine through your weakness." She began to skip around the room.

Unable to contain her laughter, Sam started laughing until it hurt and tears welled up in her eyes. "I never thought of it that way." She sadly shook her head and became somber. "But Drayvon has somehow blocked my dragon side. I can't transform anymore. I fear I'm stuck in this form forever. I may have lost part of myself, but I haven't lost who I am."

Stopping in her tracks, she looked around the room. Near the far wall sat an old rocking chair, and on it was a knitted blanket. Senora shuffled over to it, grabbed the blanket and returned to the bed. She placed the blanket over Sam, and said, "Regain your strength you're still a fighter. Just like Bobbie, you have that determination to prevail. I believe in both of you."

Sam took hold of her hand and gently squeezed it. "I don't know about Bobbie; he holds a lot of anger and doubt within him. But when I look into his eyes, I feel strangely drawn to him."

Trying to stifle a laugh, she snorted. "Bobbie? No, he's just a broken man who seeks to protect and serve his Saviour. He's on his own faith journey as we all are. But he's chosen by God."

As sleep began to take over, Sam snuggled down under the

blanket, resting her head on the pillow and yawning. "How do you know for sure?"

Tucking the blanket around Sam's body, she smiled. "I've seen his pain and turmoil. I've also seen his transformation from darkness into light. He understands he can do nothing without God."

Her eyes fluttered, and her words were but a whisper. "It's different with Bobbie. I felt safe with him but also fear his anger."

Backing slowly away, she turned toward the door. "Trust the Lord's guidance. Trust in the LORD with all your heart, and do not lean on your own understanding. In all your ways acknowledge him, and he will make straight your paths."[14]

"How did you get so smart?"

Resting her hand on the doorframe, she looked over her shoulder. "Ever since we first met, I've been praying for wisdom, and I've been getting to know God more by faithfully studying His Word."

"Nora, can I speak with Sam alone?" Katerina asked as she appeared in the bedroom doorway. Senora turned with a start, nodded, and left the room. "Sam, I'm sorry for my deception. Can you ever forgive me?"

Sam turned to face the wall. "We've all been deceived, and all have sinned, but we need to not lose heart. Our faith in God's plan will unify us. I'm tired; please let me rest for now." Sam sighed.

Katerina turned toward the door, but before she left the room, she looked over her shoulder and said, "Thank you."

Startled by Katerina's response, Sam stared at her. "For what?"

"Despite my betrayal, you still stand with me. I need your support; honestly, I'm barely holding myself together. Rest now. I want you at the funeral procession tomorrow." Katerina stepped out into the hallway. The head of the guard was waiting for her.

"Lady Kat, The Called have come, and their leaders are waiting for you in the war room. Are you ready to address them?" the guard asked.

"Tomorrow. I need to rest now. Show them to their accommodations. We'll gather after the crowd address and procession tomorrow," Katerina replied.

"As you wish." The guard bowed and retreated down the hallway.

Katerina headed to her room and closed the door.

15

FAREWELL

*T*he door creeped open, startling Katerina awake. Crystal jumped on her bed. "Come on, lazybones. Time to wake up." Crystal laughed and jumped so hard Katerina bounded out of bed and landed on the floor with a thud.

"I forgot how much of a morning person you are."

"I know this is a somber time. Today's the day we say goodbye. But with a little laughter to start the day, maybe you won't feel so weighed down and crushed." Crystal sat cross-legged on Katerina's bed. Katerina stood and walked over to her wardrobe. Crystal leaped to her feet and dashed ahead of her. She quickly pulled out a green hooded cloak, black dress, and a dark green top.

"Are you kidding me?" Katerina grabbed the black dress, tossed it into the wardrobe, and quickly pulled out a green pair of leggings.

Crystal rolled her eyes and giggled. "You never want to wear a dress, do you?" Crystal sighed as she left the room to get ready.

Once dressed, Katerina stepped out into the dimly lit hallway. The head guard met her. "Lady Kat, it's almost time," he said as he handed Katerina a locked golden chest.

"Is it in there?" Katerina whispered trying desperately to swallow her fear.

"Yes, Lady Kat. Queen Scarlett's heart is safely inside," the guard replied.

Cradling the small golden chest, she thought. *Such a small thing to hold something so precious.*

She focused her eyes as she made her way to the balcony. Overlooking the courtyard, she was surprised to see the large crowd below. Joined by Crystal and Sam, she raised the golden chest in the air. A wave of people raised their hands in honour of Queen Scarlett. "As the Saviour binds our hearts together in life, may we always be bound in death. Join the procession. We ride to the Forest of Truth. Scarlett's heart stood for truth. Today, we'll bind it with truth," Katerina declared. The crowd erupted with applause.

Crystal embraced Katerina and whispered in her ear, "It's ok to cry. Today we say goodbye, but remember our hearts are always bound together in love. You're not alone in this."

Thought she still felt a little weak, Sam raised her hand and placed it on Katerina's shoulder. "You start the procession." Katerina lowered the chest and held it close to her heart. *Now's the time to show strength. There'll be a time to shed tears, but today's not that day. At least not for me,* Katerina thought to herself. She turned on her heel and stormed toward the courtyard. Sam and Crystal were in tow. With her eyes fixed on her horse, she gently laid the golden chest in her saddlebag and mounted her horse. Sam and Crystal did the same and lined their horses to stand on either side of hers. She set her stone face on the horizon, turning to examine the others as they each, in turn, mounted their horses. Continuing down the line was Sir Gervon, followed by Donella and the elves, and two horse drawn wagons that carried Queen Scarlett and Princess Delores's bodies. Senora and Robert stood confidently on either side of the cart. Katerina's eyes scanned the sea of creatures and humans alike who had turned out to honour them, and the Muddlings were in the rear, where they always preferred. She nodded as they set out to empty the castle and made their journey to the Forest of Truth.

———❧❧❧———

"*T*hey've emptied Castle Calvarias. Treasure Kingdom's open for the taking," Drayvon reported to Lucas.

"Give them this day. Their destruction's at hand. Patience." Lucas sighed.

"It's much more fun to toy with their emotions. Their brokenness and grief will make them weak. We'll crush them but not in the Forest of Truth or on this day. We'll crush them, you'll feast. Don't worry about that."

"Worry? I don't worry."

"Patience." Lucas watched the procession marched on from his shadowy hiding place. He turned and made his way back toward Sheol Mountain. Drayvon growled in frustration but followed Lucas anyway.

———❧❧❧———

*A*s Katerina's horse reached the edge of the Forest of Truth, she dismounted and pulled the golden chest from her saddlebag. Crystal, Sam, and Sir Gervon dismounted too. Katerina turned and smiled at them. "I only want a small procession here. The forest must not be disturbed. Crystal, Sam, Sir Gervon, and Nora. Please join me?" Katerina called.

As all eyes fall on Senora, her eyes widened and cheeks went red. "Me? Why me?" she asked.

"You, although only here for a short time, brought my mother back to Crystal and I. You gave us a few more years with her. I see you as family. As I see Sir Gervon as a wise guide and protector," Katerina stated. The five left the large group at the border of the Forest of Truth as they walked to the center of the forest.

Senora hugged her shoulders. *This is nothing like any funeral I've ever been to.* Katerina turned to face the other four. The group of five formed a small circle as Katerina raised the golden chest in the air once more. She bent down and placed it on the mossy ground. While Crystal's cheeks flooded with tears, Katerina's eyes were dry and set. Sir Gervon discreetly brushed a tear away, hoping no one noticed, as Sam knelt beside the chest.

"Even though I walk through the valley of the shadow of death, I will fear no evil, for you are with me; your rod and your staff, they comfort me," Sam whispered.[1]

Crystal kneeled next to Sam, "Very truly I tell you, whoever hears my word and believed him who sent me has eternal life and will not be judged but has crossed over from death to life."[2]

Sir Gervon placed his hand on Crystal's shoulder and declared, "The people living in darkness have seen a great light; on those living in the land of the shadow of death a light has dawned."[3]

Suddenly, the Tall Bearded Man appeared and said, "Then I heard a voice from heaven say, 'Write this: Blessed are the dead who die in the Lord from now on. Yes, says the Spirit, they will rest from their labour, for their deeds will follow them.'"[4]

Katerina looked up with a start. "Father? Is that you?"

"Kat, Crystal, your mother and I are one. We're so proud of you," The Man stated as he disappeared again.

Katerina looked at the golden chest once again and kneeled. She placed her hand on the chest. "For if we've been united with him in death like this, we'll certainly also be united with him in a resurrection like this."[5] Katerina sighed.

Senora paced uncomfortably. *I feel like I'm intruding. Why am*

I here? Suddenly, she found herself face to face with her brother, Trevor.

"Then they cried to the Lord in their trouble, and he saved them from their distress. He brought them out of darkness, the utter darkness, and broke away their chains."[6] Senora stumbled backward, almost losing her balance.

"Trevor? Why're you? How're you here?" Senora asked.

"I'm here to remind you, but now that you have been set free from sin and have become slaves of God, the benefit you reap to holiness, and the result's eternal life. For the wages of sin is death, but the gift of God is eternal life in Christ Jesus our Lord," Trevor reminded her.[7]

"I thought I would never see you again. Are we bound in death now? Or through God's eternal life?" Senora asked.

"Just remember because of the tender mercy of our God, by which the rising sun will come to us from heaven to shine on those living in darkness and in the shadow of death, to guide our feet into the path of peace.[8] Your strength comes with truth. I'm with you. May you be a light in this dark time." Trevor replied and was gone as quickly as he had appeared. Senora turned her attention back to the group of four. She stepped close and kneeled next to Crystal.

"For the perishable must clothe itself with the imperishable, and the mortal with immortality. When the perishable has been clothed with immortality, then the saying that's written will come true: 'Death has been swallowed up in victory. Where, O death, is your victory? Where, O death, is your sting?'" Senora whispered.[9] Crystal hugged Senora and Katerina. Sir Gervon dug a deep hole as Katerina slowly lowered the chest in.

"Mother, I'll remember what you have taught me. As your heart's surrounded with truth, may your spirit be at peace," Katerina said as Gervon carefully buried the chest.

The four girls slowly rose and embraced. Katerina straightened and nodded to Sir Gervon to lead the way back to the larger group waiting for them at the edge of the forest. *This day's not over yet,* she thought to herself.

As the five emerged from the forest's edge a wave of whispers and mumbled prayers reached their ears. One by one they mounted their horses and turned west toward the Peaceful River. *The place where Mother and Delores's bodies will finally be at peace,* Katerina thought as she felt a wave of comfort wash over her.

As the group moved forward, the sound of humming began to grow. "What's that?" Senora asked.

"It's our song of mourning. They're bringing honour to Princess Delores and Queen Scarlett the best they know how," Sir Gervon replied.

Senora nodded and was mesmerized with the beautiful chorus that surrounded them. She rode on in silence. She could hear the slowly moving river ahead. *So much has happened since the last time I was here; I just hope Jo is safe.*

She watched as Katerina and Crystal dismounted their horses and walked to the wagons. Sam dismounted and followed. Senora watched as five other soldiers and guards carefully held each coffin with care as they gently placed each coffin side by side at the river's edge. She watched as Katerina, Crystal, Sam, and several archers made their way to the top of the bridge overlooking the Peaceful River. Sir Gervon lit a torch and walked behind each archer, igniting each of their arrows. As each arrow ignited one by one each archer stood aiming, standing ready to fire.

"Goodbye Princess Delores, you have taught me so much. Goodbye, Mother, I miss you deeply. I only wish to be as strong as both of you," Katerina whispered.

"Goodbye, Mother, you've always been my inspiration. You taught me to be true to myself. Goodbye, Delores, may your wisdom ring truth all the days of my life. You taught me to never give up. I miss you both every day," Crystal stated.

Katerina and Crystal released their flaming arrows,

followed by each archer releasing theirs in turn. Each arrow hit their intended mark. The coffins were engulfed with flames, and as they turned to ash, the wind carried the remains down river. The large group exploded in celebration and cheers. As they mounted their horses once more and returned to the castle, they all shared laughter and memories on their way back. Life lessons that both Scarlett and Delores had taught, never to be lost in death.

Robert rode a horse up next to Senora and Sam.

"I don't understand all that just happened, but I'm honoured to have been a part of some of it. How're you two doing?"

"Honestly, I'm at the most peace I've ever been in during these past three years." Senora sighed.

"I'm glad." Robert turned his attention to Sam, but she only looked forward and rode on in silence. When they re-entered the castle, Sam quickly dismounted and headed back up the stairs to her room to rest.

Robert stumbled off his horse and turned to follow, but Senora stopped him, "Give her some time. She's still pretty weak, and I think today took a lot out of her." With sadness, Robert nodded his agreement and led his and Sam's horses to the stables.

Katerina and Crystal dismounted their horses, handed the reins to some nearby soldiers and headed into the castle walls. "Gather the leaders. We'll begin our battle plans," Katerina ordered, heading to the war room. Pausing at the door, she turned suddenly and said, "Please, call Nora and Bobbie to join us. There's strength in numbers. This affects their world as well as ours." Katerina pushed the door open.

"Right away, my lady." The guard rushed to the courtyard to find Senora and Robert.

PART 7: FIGHTING THE DARKNESS

16

GREATEST STRENGTH

*S*enora walked toward the stables as the bright sunlight illuminated around her. N*ow, where did Bobbie go?* She looked around, suddenly startled by loud crashing sounds coming from the stables. She rushed over to investigate. When she peered inside, she saw Robert throwing things around, kicking hay bales, and grumbling under his breath.

"Bobbie? Why're you so angry?"

"Why will I never be good enough? I couldn't protect them."

"Protect who?"

"I couldn't protect my mother from my dad, I couldn't protect you from the fire or Kat's deceptions, I couldn't protect Sam from Lucas or Drayvon, and I feel like a weak, insignificant, useless, a waste of skin." Robert tossed a hammer on the tool bench. "I could never do anything right."

Senora walked toward Robert to calm him. "That isn't true. It isn't your job to protect us. That's God's job. You need to forgive yourself and ask God for guidance."

"How can you say that? I don't deserve forgiveness; you know what I've been through."

"Come now, let us reason together, says the LORD:

though your sins are like scarlet, they shall be as white as snow; though they are red like crimson, they shall become wool."[1]

"I always make the wrong choices. Why would they want me? I'm just a big mistake."

"As far as the east is from the west, so far does He remove our transgressions from us. As a father shows compassion to his children, so the LORD shows compassion to those who fear him."[2]

"I know God has forgiven me, but I don't deserve His forgiveness."

"For I will forgive their iniquity, and I will remember their sin no more.[3] God's forgiveness is greater than any sin we commit."

"It's easier to hate than to hurt."

"I know, but God's bigger than your hatred. For this is my blood of the covenant, which is poured out for many for the forgiveness of sins.[4] So, Christ took the sacrifice of death that your sins created, he has defeated death's hold on you. For freedom Christ has set us free; stand firm therefore, and do not submit again to a yoke of slavery."[5]

"I just wish I was stronger that I could keep everyone from getting hurt."

"But we learn through our pain. If I didn't hurt, I would never move forward. To deny my pain, is to deny my salvation," Senora said. Robert paced around the stable, kicking straw around. "Therefore, if anyone is in Christ, he is a new creation. The old has passed away; behold, the new has come."[6] Robert felt a wave of peace wash over him. He turned to say something to Senora when the head guard entered.

"Sorry to interrupt, but Lady Kat has requested both of you to attend the war meeting. Please follow me." Both Robert and Senora turned to follow.

When they left the courtyard and re-entered the castle,

Robert glanced at Senora. "You said you have lots to tell me. What did you mean by that?"

"Ask me again after the meeting. I promise I'll fill you in."

———

*T*he head guard opened the door to the war room with Robert and Senora following. "Oh, good! You're here. Now we can begin. You were saying, Donella?"

Robert scanned the room. His sight landed upon a lady dressed in a black pantsuit and a long black cloak. *Wow, she must be like ten feet tall.* Robert unknowingly stepped backward. She stood with long pointy ears, pale skin, and small narrow grey eyes. Her face was creased as though it had forgotten how to smile. She carried an uninviting demeanor. Raising her chin and narrowing her eyes, she set her stone-cold gaze on Katerina. "The Firedites are ready to fight with you, Lady Kat." Standing as still as a statue, allowing only her eyes to move, she scanned the room. "My concern was Lucas' deceptions. He's the king of lies and deceit. How could we guard ourselves from that sort of attack?" She shifted her feet ever so slightly. If someone had blinked, they would have missed it. "I mean, we could battle his armies, but if he plants a seed of doubt within us, we'll fall."

The silence hung in the air almost like ice daggers waiting to attack the next to speak.

A man in the corner covered in mud coughed, breaking the silence as all eyes shot to him. "Yes, but our armour's impenetrable. We Muddlings can withstand lies. Maybe we can train you to guard your thoughts." He stood only two-feet-tall but grinned from ear to ear.

Stomping her feet, causing the Muddling to fall to his side, Donella glared as she looked down her nose at him. "You Muddlings are all talk, but where's your action?"

Dirt and mud splattered on others standing nearby as the Mudding scurried to stand.

Raising her hands in defense, Katerina said, "Please, hear me. I may be the youngest one here, but my mother put me in charge. We need to unify and stay strong. Sam's still with us."

Shaking the very thresholds of the room, Donella stomped around, and stopping in front of Katerina, she crossed her arms and growled.

"Yes, but is the Red Dragon going to join the fight?" A small, gangly creature asked.

Donella shot him a dagger-like stare. Softening her expression, she smirked and scanned the room as she spoke. "That's a fair question. What about the Red Dragon? Why's she not in this meeting?"

Busying herself with the maps on the table, she stammered, not knowing what to say. "I'm sorry; her captivity with Drayvon has done a toll. She's resting now." She shook her head sadly without looking up from the maps.

"Will she be ready to fight when called?" the small creature asked as it scurried up the wall.

"Stop questioning the child. We'll bring strength to the table, but if the Saviour isn't with us, we've already lost." A tall, giant-like man spoke boldly from the back of the room. Senora noticed everyone jumped to attention when he spoke. "For *God* equipped me with strength for the battle; *He* made those who rise against me sink under me."[7] She stared at him as he sat still as a statue in the darkest corner of the room. If he hadn't spoke, Senora wouldn't have noticed he was there.

To get everyone's attention, Katerina slammed her hands on the table and let out a loud sigh. "Sir Geryon's right. We all have strength, and the Saviour's our guide. This isn't the final battle, but it will set things in motion and will affect not just our world. We make our stand at the Fiery Crossroads, where two worlds collide. Who'll stand with me and fight Lucas and

Drayvon?" Silence filled the room and weighed heavily on them all.

Eyes madly searched for what to do next as Sir Geryon rose to his feet. "I will fight by your side, Lady Kat." One by one, everyone followed his example. As the affirmations to follow and fight grew, the anticipation, fear, and excitement rushed through Robert's body.

———⧉———

*D*eep in the Sheol Mountains, hushed whispers echoed throughout the caves. "The Master has lost the Lord's prize,"

"The Lord called for revenge," one beast said.

"Master was weak?" another replied.

"No, Master was strong. Lord deceived us all," a third declared.

"Who do we follow, Master or Lord?" The echoes spread like wildfire.

Far into the deep, Drayvon and Lucas communed. "What do you mean they escaped? This dark kingdom's impenetrable," Lucas said. "No one can get in or out without permission, you said."

"The Shadow Knights are patrolling. We'll find the breach, I guarantee you. But I was able to block the Red Dragon's fight. Sam will be grounded," Drayvon answered.

"Not good enough. Who was on patrol that night?"

"The Misfits. You know, Chester, I believe his name is."

"Bring him in."

Chester slunk into the dark room and bowed toward Lucas and Drayvon. "You called for me Master and Lord? Remember, I didn't do it, unless it's good." Chester said, followed by nervous hyena laughter.

"Silence. How did they get past your patrol?" Lucas asked.

Chester swallowed his nervous laughter. "They must

have found a secret breach. Those stinky creatures. Funny-looking things." Chester chuckled. Lucas kicked Chester in the stomach. He wheezed and fell on his back. "I serve the Master. Let me go. I learn fast. I'm a good deceiver."

"I'm listening. What do you propose? I'll see through lies," Lucas said.

"I can deceive like the best of them. Deception's what keeps us alive. Master taught me that. I can take a small scouting party into their kingdom," Chester said with a sly smirk on his face.

"Go! Report what you find," Drayvon ordered. Chester crawled away with his hyena laughter following him.

He crawled into the shadows right out of sight, listening in to learn more details. *I love rabbit trail conversations. They take you on a journey you don't know where you'll end up.*[8] *If I listen, I might learn something useful.*

"I should have devoured him," Lucas declared.

In any moment of decision, the best thing you can do is the right thing, the next best thing is the wrong thing, and the worst thing you can do is nothing, Chester thought from his hiding place.[9]

"He may still be of use," Drayvon declared. "Now, what were you saying about your plan? What was this about another world?"

"I've already begun my attack upon them. My specialty: hatred, lies, deception, division, and death," Lucas conveyed.

"Yes, but why choose such a low-populated place? There must be more population," Drayvon said.

"Oh, there is, but in a low population, the attack goes unnoticed until it has spread like a plague upon an unsuspecting world."

"Is the pending war here?"

"All connected. In time, both worlds will burn," Lucas declared. "If we cut the snake's head off, Deadened Valley will only be the beginning."

"So, where does the Red Dragon fall in with this plan of yours?" Drayvon asked.

"It began with the dragons going into hiding. The dark powers will rise. Before the end of this day, blood will be spilt and you'll have your feast," Lucas revealed, "I've divided them; they just don't know it yet. I have my eyes within their ranks; they'll fall defeated once more. There'll be no light this time. Darkness will prevail."

"I'm nothing but mischief. I'll show them. Doing the wrong thing is like getting shot by an arrow. It's usually a long-lasting pain that doesn't go away. I'm smarter than they think. I can thwart plans. Misfits unite. The Master will see our strength now." Chester chuckled as he vanished into the darkness, leaving only a faint hyena chuckle behind.

———

"This battle will determine our destination, a battle that would either bring unity or division. We need to put aside our differences now. Only together can we stand firm," Katerina declared. "Who's willing to stand?"

The room fell silent; uneasiness started to build. "Haven't you all lost someone? Haven't we all fallen to Lucas's lies and deceptions?" Senora asked.

"Who're you to question us? You're but a stranger in these parts." Donella glared at Senora and stepped closer to her with her fists clenched.

"Be still, Donella," Gervon declared. Donella shrunk back into her corner as all eyes turned to Gervon.

"Why does everyone seem afraid of Sir Gervon?" Senora asked.

"What? Afraid? Why do you say that? Sir Gervon's strong and wise. But he also is cunning and tactful. He's the title-holder, combatant, and guardian," the Muddling revealed.

"What's he the guardian of?" Senora asked.

"You must live under a rock," the Muddling said, laughing at her.

"I don't understand," Senora said.

"Obviously," the Muddling replied sarcastically.

"Now, Lady Kat called us here. Let us hear her out," Gervon demanded. All eyes shifted back to Katerina.

——∞∞——

*T*wo guards leaned against the castle gate. "It's so eerie quiet," a guard stated.

"Oh, you're just sour that you weren't invited to the war room. Am I right?" the other guard replied.

"What? No. We can't leave the castle unguarded," the first guard said. A strange, small, hairy creature approached. "Halt. Castle Calvarias isn't open for visitors. We're in lock-down. Identify yourself."

The creature paused, looked briefly over his shoulder, motioned to a dozen Misfit Shadow Knights hiding right out of sight for them to wait for his signal, and continued forward. "We're warning you: stop and identify yourself," the second guard called. The creature stopped, looked up at them, and pulled his hood off. "Halt, we need you to stop. You're out of your dominion. Why're you here, Shadow Knight?" the first guard asked.

The creature raised his hands in surrender and chuckled nervously like a hyena. The two guards cautiously approached the creature. "Stop that infuriating laughter. Will you?" The first guard punched the creature in the side.

The creature stumbled but chuckled even louder. "I bring news for Lady Sam." The first guard clenched his fist. The creature winced and prepared to receive another hit, when the second guard stepped in and grabbed the first guard's arm to stop him.

"Wait. Let's hear him out," the second guard said.

"But he's a Shadow Knight. They're at war with us. We don't want to bring the enemy in. We might as well raise the white flag now," the first guard stated.

"I'll go to the cell block; Sam can meet me there. The difference between genius and stupidity is, genius has its limits." the creature offered.

"What did you say to me? Are you calling me stupid?" the first guard asked pushing himself into Chester's face.

"Stupid is as stupid does," Chester replied.[10]

"Move." The first guard shoved Chester forward. Chester moved willingly with a smirk forming on his face. Calling out to a group of nearby soldiers training in the courtyard, the first guard snapped. "Nate! Allistair! Watch the gate, while we take this thing to the cell block. Make sure his friends behave."

Two young soldiers lowered their weapons, nodded, and ran toward the gate. "Yes, sir!" they responded.

The guards moved him into the cell block. "You go inform Sam; I'll return to the gate. Someone needs to be guarding it. And you, creature, be silent." The first guard stormed back to his post.

"Don't mind him," the second guard said as he left the cell block and headed for Sam's room. Chester paced his prison cell and chuckled.

—◦◦◦—

S am rested in bed when the door flew open. She jumped in fear and nearly fell off the bed. "Sorry to disturb you, Lady Sam," the guard stated.

"What is it?" Sam asked.

"A creature no, an enemy no, a visitor."

"Well, what is it? A creature, an enemy, or a visitor?"

"Yes."

"You aren't making sense."

"Sorry, this whole thing doesn't make sense. Can you stand? Walk? Follow me."

Sam staggered to her feet. "I think so. Where're we going?"

"The cell blocks."

"Wait! Did I do something wrong? Is Lady Kat sending me to the cell block? Is that young lady losing her mind?"

"No, someone's in the cell block. Asking for you."

"Asking for me? What sort of visitor?"

"I can't explain. Just follow me, please." The guard led Sam down to the cell block, and she followed, feeling a little uneasy about this mysterious visitor.

Sam froze in her tracks when she caught sight of the dark creature pacing in his cell. The creature raised his hands, pleading, "Wait and hear me out." He chuckled nervously. Sam walked close to the cell door.

"Ok, talk."

"Master defeated you. Yes?" Sam reached through the cell bars and grabbed a handful of the creature's fur and pulled him into the bars, banging his head. "Ouch! I mean no disrespect. This meeting isn't going well."

Sam released his fur and relaxed again. "Speak but guard your words carefully."

"I knew your mother." Sam staggered back a few steps.

"What did you say?"

"You heard me, Starstorm. I was the one who warned her. Don't be sad, because sad backwards is das, and das not good. You know it takes patience to listen: it takes skill to pretend you're listening.[11] But she didn't listen. No one ever listens to poor Chester. Misfit to the end, I guess."

"How do you know that name?"

"Master wanted you to think you were unlovable. But your mother chose to give her life to save yours. That's courage. I may not understand love, but I know courage. I learned that courage was not the absence of fear, but the triumph over it.

The brave man isn't he who does not feel afraid but he who conquers that fear.[12] Fear is like poison, it will keep harming you until you find the antidote. Dragons are strong. I'm close to Master. Learned to deceive. I deceive to survive."

"That's just it: deception is the way of the dark one. Lucas is the king of deception. Why should I trust you?"

The creature looked up into Sam's eyes. "Courage is resistance to fear, mastery of fear, not absence of fear.[13] You have your mother's eyes. Your mother trusted me."

"And she's dead."

"May be dead, but you live. Lord Lucas's plan was thwarted before. I'm already doomed, but I can still deceive. 'Above all, be the heroine of your life, not the victim.'[14] I clumsy Misfit Shadow Knight, burden, but I can get close to Master."

"You haven't said anything that makes me trust you."

"I know you're wise to guard your heart. But when you don't trust, you stand alone. Divided and easily defeated."

"What do you have in mind?"

"The lord and master will gather at the Fiery Crossroads. The fires will ignite. The battle will cross over. No stopping that."

"You aren't sounding helpful." Sam crossed her arms.

"I get close to Master. I use his plan against him. He divided you spy in your ranks." Sam jumped at the cell door again. Chester shrunk back.

"Spy? What do you mean spy?"

"I know not who. I just know there is one. Get me in the war room meeting. I join the fight."

"Yes, but whose side would you be fighting on?"

"I got you out, didn't I? I showed that girl where you were. Me! No one else. I fight both. But Master believes I fight only for him. Deception, see?"

"No, I don't see. I'm not allowing the enemy into that meeting."

"Enemy? I helped you. Does no one listen around here? No wonder Master captured you so easily last time. Why were you in Shadow Dominion was beyond me."

"You're not doing a very good job of convincing me."

"The Dragon Kingdom is now in hiding. Your mother gave her life for you so you could stand against him at the right time. With you still alive, the Dragon Kingdom still survived. Lord's failure the Silver Dragon's deceit. He wanted you to be no more. You mustn't surrender. No matter what. Guard your heart. Don't allow anyone close. The spy could be anyone. You know I'm not spy. Get me in the meeting. I provide intel?"

Sam walked over to the cell block entrance, grabbed the key, and unlocked the cell door. "Don't make me regret this." Chester wobbled toward the entrance "What do they call you anyways?"

Chester paused before leaving the cell block. "You mean besides Misfit? They call me Chester." He bolted up the cell room stairs and out of sight, leaving a lingering hyena chuckle in the air. Sam staggered and leaned against the wall to wait for the room to stop spinning. *Father, please; I hope I didn't do the wrong thing. Please reveal the spy before it's too late. In Jesus name, amen*, Sam prayed as she slowly made her way toward the war room.

———※※※———

Soon, a strange laughter permeated from outside the war room door. All eyes shift toward the door as it flew open. "I hear you're plotting to stand against the master and lord." Senora's eyes grow wide as she stared at Chester. "I may be a Misfit, but I know the master. Master Drayvon will attack at the Fiery Crosswords. This war will cross over. I can help. My misfits and I know the gaps in his perimeter."

"You and what misfits?" Katerina asked

"There are more of us. I have a small following just outside your gates."

"More Shadow Knights?" Katerina questioned.

"No, Misfits, silly. I'm the head guide to Misfits within the Shadow Knights. Try to keep up, will ya? I offer our help to you, Lady Kat. Will you accept? My misfits hide just beyond your gates, waiting for my signal."

Katerina feared these creatures. *They're Shadow Knights.* "You serve Drayvon. Why would we trust you?"

"It's ok if you don't like me. Not everyone has good taste."

"Wait. May I speak?" Senora asked. All eyes shifted from Chester to Kat and now to Senora.

"Speak then," Katerina ordered.

"I know he's a Shadow Knight, but he risked his life to free Sam and Bobbie. He helped us escape. He could have killed us or turned us back to Drayvon and Lucas, but he didn't," Senora said.

"Can you promise me that he won't turn on us?" Donella asked.

"I…" Senora looked from Donella to Chester, back to Donella to Katerina, then from Katerina to Robert, "I…" Soon the door creaked from behind Chester.

All eyes looked to the door. "I believe in him. He risked everything, even though he knew it was a death sentence for him. He won't turn on us," Sam declared with such authority behind each word.

"Lady Sam, we were told you were resting," Donella stated.

"It's true; I'm weak. But the Lord's strength shines through my weakness. Both worlds depend on us. We need to put aside our differences and trust the Saviour's leadership," Sam replied. Everyone nodded in agreement.

"Well said. Now we need to gather around and discuss our battle strategies," Katerina declared.

"One question for Lady Sam," Donella interrupted.

"What is it, Donella?" Sam asked.

"The Red Dragon. Will she fight?" Donella asked.

"Drayvon has blocked that side. But I'll fight. I've been trained in combat by both Queen Scarlett and Princess Delores," Sam declared. "I fight for freedom and for family. Family isn't just blood. The ultimate King and my Saviour is eternal and unchanging. He's the one true God and King."

"You say that with such authority. By whose authority do you speak?" Donella asked.

"Therefore, I am a chosen one of God. We need to stand firm in His truth and leading. Unify as the true body of the King. I speak with the authority of the Saviour," Sam said.

"A child of the Saviour, ok. If you speak with the Saviour's authority, how do we know you're true? You just were a captive of Drayvon. Were you not?" Donella asked.

"Leave her be, Donella," Gervon commanded. Donella leaned back against the wall as if struck silent by Gervon's words. "Unity is what we need now, not division. Let's hear Lady Kat out. Donella, you can just be silent."

Everyone turned their attention toward Katerina and the battle map before her. Robert walked over to Sam. She leaned on him for support as Katerina laid out a battle strategy. Senora was amazed at the calming connection Sam had with Robert.

17

CROSSWORDS OF FIRE

$\mathcal{A}$ s the battle meeting came to a close, Robert turned his face toward Sam. "Are you sure you're strong enough to fight?" he asked.

Sam looked up at him, pushed him away, and stormed out of the room. She looked over her shoulder and said, "'Even youths shall faint and be weary, and young men shall fall exhausted; but they who wait for the LORD shall renew their strength; they shall mount up with wings like eagles; they shall run and not be weary; they shall walk and not faint.'[1] This is my fight more than yours. I'll be fine."

Robert scratched the back of his head in confusion. "What did I say?"

Senora approached Robert and placed her hand on his shoulder. "Give her some time."

Robert glared at Senora and shrugged her hand off, "From the sound of it, time is what we don't have." Robert stormed out of the room and headed to the courtyard. As he slowly made his way down the staircase his thoughts started to convict him. *Why did I snap at Nora? I know she's here to help. But when I look in her eyes, I'm reminded of how I have failed her. It's my time to prove myself worthy. I need to do this, not just for Nora, but for myself too.* Robert secretly made a promise to himself. Senora was left staring at the open door, confused by Robert's actions and questioning what she should do next.

Katerina walked up behind her and said, "How can you still trust me after what I did to you?"

Senora turned her attention toward Katerina. "Oh, Kat, you've suffered so much at the hand of Lucas. We all make mistakes, but you've learned from yours. I trust you." Senora held her hand out toward Katerina. Katerina hesitantly shook it.

"Are you up for this battle? How much combat experience do you have?" Katerina asked.

"I...well...um...none, I guess," Senora sighed.

Katerina jumped in surprise. "What? Come with me." Katerina ordered as she grabbed Senora's arm and dragged her from the war room. The two emerged into the courtyard; Katerina dragged her toward the barn and shoved her forward. Senora turned to look at Katerina in confusion. Katerina tossed a sword at her feet. "Pick it up."

"What? Why?" Senora asked.

"Pick it up fight me. You learn by doing. Pick it up."

Senora hesitated. *I don't want to fight. Katerina is half my size.* In her hesitation, Katerina kicked the sword away, sending dust flying at her face. "The enemy will attack even if you hesitate. Lucas is relentless. You cannot afford to hesitate. Fight me." As Senora staggered and brushed dirt from her eyes, Katerina lunged toward her. Her sword came down, and the clang of metal frightened Senora. She looked up through her tear-filled eyes and saw Robert standing over her, holding the sword Katerina had thrown at her. Both swords were connected right above her body. She quickly crawled out of the way.

"Leave her alone. What's wrong with you, kid?" Robert asked.

"Nothing. We need to be our best. Lucas must fall. If we

aren't good enough, why're we here?" Katerina stated as she swung her sword at Robert. He swung his sword and blocked her attack. "I see you've some sword experience."

"A little. I used to sword fight with Trevor, when we were young. Sam taught me some things too. But I've more experience with a rifle." Robert dodged another swing of Katerina's sword. He closed his eyes and saw Trevor's bloody body at the bottom of his basement stairs. Instantly grief invaded his thoughts. He opened his eyes to Senora glaring at him.

Staggering backward, Senora wiped a tear from her eyes. "Trevor taught me stuff too. I can fight my own battles. Stop hindering me." Senora folded her hands in front of her and stomped her foot.

Robert quickly shoved Senora aside while Katerina's foot kicked him in the face, knocking him to his knees. Robert spat blood on the ground.

"What are you doing, Bobbie? I said, I can fight my own battles."

Ignoring Senora's words, Robert leapt to his feet. "Don't worry, Nora. I got this."

Senora stood and stared Robert down. "The horse is made ready for the day of battle, but the victory belongs to the Lord."[2] Senora heard shuffling from behind her when Robert shoved her out of the way once again. Katerina's sword clanged with Roberts once more. Senora watched frozen as Katerina spun and kicked Robert in the side of the head, knocking him to the ground.

"Stop it, both of you!" Senora shouted. Robert pushed Senora away and stood.

"Again, you may have caught me off guard, but I'm not broken," Robert said, lunging at Katerina. Katerina staggered backward and kicked dirt at Robert's face. Seeing her attack coming, he swiftly placed his arm up to protect his eyes and swung his sword downward, knocking Katerina to the ground. He held the sword in front of Katerina's face. "Do you yield?"

"You're a good fighter. But mercy isn't a luxury that Lucas or Drayvon will ever offer." Katerina tossed her sword aside. She stood, nodded at Robert and returned to the castle.

Senora approached Robert.

"What was that?" Senora asked.

Robert's anger subsided, and he turned to face Senora, sighing. "I just don't know, Nora."

"Hey, you say that we need to be focused, and yet you mention Trevor. Trevor has nothing to do with this battle. His strength is always with us, but he is gone. He is not coming back. It is not your job to protect me. 'But the Lord is faithful, and he will strengthen you and protect you from the evil one.'"[3]

"I can't focus and protect you all the time."

"So? You are not God in this situation. God will protect me. You don't have to. Who ever said it was your job to protect me?"

"You know what I mean. You know. Since…"

"Since what?"

"Trevor. I mean, I think." The sound of police sirens rang softly in her ears flashes of her mom dropping the phone, the sounds of the car tires squeaked, as they rushed to the scene. Pushing the thoughts aside, she reached for the sword at her feet.

"What? I told you, Trevor is not here. I am. Stop trying to be him." She raised the sword and aimed it at Robert.

Robert rolled his eyes and sighed. "You're just getting in the way here. Go home."

"Ummm, I have been here before. Besides, 'For where two or three are gathered in my name, there am I among them.'[4] God is with me. He directs my heart in His love and Christ's perseverance. I have a reason for being here. Do you? Allow me to show you."

"Show me what? We are at the eve of battle. We need to train, not argue. Mind your own business." He spat the words at her. "Why're you even here? Go home. Before you get hurt." Robert scanned the crowd standing around staring at them. "What're you all lookin' at? You need to be ready too." Robert threw his sword to the ground. *What can I say to make her leave? I don't mean to be rude, but I want her to be safe. I know she cares. At least she understands me,* Robert walked over to a stack of rifles leaning against the stable wall. He selected a 303 rifle with a scope and strap, draped it over his shoulder, grabbed a small box of cartridges, and walked toward a targeting range. Senora's sword slipped from her fingers as she stared at Robert's back.

———

Sam watched the whole scene play out from a high window in the castle. Both admiration and fear lingered within her. She understood the pain of loss Katerina faced right now, but Robert, his anger was so great, yet he held such compassion too. Torn by the wave of confusion lying beneath the surface, she watched as Robert fired at the target shot after unrelenting shot. She looked at Senora, who picked up the sword and clumsily swung it around in the air. Sam turned to head down to the courtyard when Katerina stopped her. Staggering back a little, Sam reached for the wall to stabilize herself. "You're still weak," Katerina declared.

Sam stared at her. "This is my fight."

"Yes, but I've got a quest for you."

"Another quest? How dare you! Are you sending me to my death this time? Have you forgotten me completely?"

"Forgotten you? No, never. I know what I did, and I'm paying the price. But this is different." Katerina walked past Sam and looked out the window at Robert. "He's strong, but Lucas knows anger. He feeds on it." Katerina looked at Sam with concern. "He's torn between two worlds. This battle will be at the Fiery Crossroads. You'll need to be ready."

"Ready for what?" Katerina pulled a red gem from her pocket and handed it to Sam. "What's this?"

"It's how I crossed over before. If the battle crosses worlds, you'll need to find the strength and wisdom to unite Bobbie."

"I don't understand." Sam stared at the strange red gem.

"You will. If you see smoke rising, think of Bobbie, and the gem will take you to him."

"On the battlefield? But you said I was too weak. You're not making sense."

"No, not the battlefield."

"But you said he was a good fighter. Why would you hold him back?"

"No, he'll fight, but he'll need to fight in his world too. He'll need you. Just think about Bobbie, and the gem will do the rest."

"I don't understand."

"Your quest will be to unite Bobbie. He must be whole to fight the battle both within and the battle that'll invade his world. He'll need Nora too. That's why I'm hard on her. She needs to survive."

Sam nodded in agreement, still with some uncertainty of what Katerina had told her. "Let me at least train her. I know her strengths. It's not with a sword. But she holds the words of the Saviour. Let me go."

"Find the strength to train, but you also need to rest recover so you can fight the real battle of the soul and mind." Katerina walked out of Sam's room again. Sam walked toward the window and looked back and forth between Robert and Senora. She saw Crystal approach Senora.

———

Senora looked over her shoulder at Crystal, quickly wiping away tears. "I understand. Here, let me try. I sometimes have a softer touch than Kat does."

Senora nodded as she picked up her sword again.

"Good. First, you need to adjust your grip. If you hold it that way, you leave yourself vulnerable to attack." Crystal tapped Senora's left side, and Robert shifted his stance and stared at the two out of the corner of his eye.

Senora moved both hands side by side aligning the handle of the sword with more comfort and ease. "Good, first work on blocking. If I step this way, you mirror my actions." Crystal stepped to the right and, swung her sword toward Senora's arm as Senora stepped left and collided her sword with Crystals. "Now, the fight is more like a dance. Just observe and anticipate. Crystal jumped into action swinging her sword close to Senora's chin, and Senora reacted by dodging and raising her sword upward, knocking Crystal off balance. Senora lowered her sword right away when Crystal kicked her side.

Senora staggered and gasped to catch her breath. "You forgot to mirror. But you are getting the idea."

Robert chuckled despite himself. *Ok maybe there is some hope for Nora.*

"No weapon forged against you will prevail, and you will refute every tongue that accuses you. This is the heritage of the servants of the Lord, and this is their vindication form me, declares the Lord."[5] The Tall Bearded Man appeared beside Robert. Jumping, he staggered to his feet.

"How can talking defeat anything?"

"Do not be deceived, my beloved brother. Every good gift and every perfect gift is from above, coming down from the Father of lights, with whom there is no variation or shadow due to change."[6]

"Yes, but…" Robert looked over his shoulder at Senora and Crystal. "Nora has no battle experience. She doesn't know anger like I do."

"The Lord will strengthen you and Nora. He will uphold you both with His righteous right hand. Trust in the Lord; let

Him deliver you. Let Him rescue both of you, for He delights in you both."

"Trust is hard. But I know your ways are greater than my own. I will try to give her a chance." Robert turned toward the Man, but he was gone.

———✦———

"The sword isn't your strength," Crystal declared. Senora slumped her shoulders, feeling defeated. The sword slipped from her fingers and fell to the ground. "Follow me. You see?" Crystal pointed at each different group of creature and men alike. "We all have different strengths. Look at the Grassland folk: their strength is stealth. That's why they'll be in charge of sneak attacks. Look at Donella and her group: they're strong warriors. They attack head-on and with great force. That's why they're the first formation. I see your friend, Bobbie. He's a sniper. He hit the bullseye every time. He's accurate and concise. Me? I'm more of an archer like my sister Kat. We're short-range, but also accurate and concise. Kat's always training if not physically, then mentally. She's stronger than most people think and always has a plan in motion before I can even say boo. And then, there's Sir Gervon."

"Yeah, what's with that guy? When he speaks, everyone jumps to attention. Who is he?" Senora asked.

"He's a mystery, that one. He's like Sam."

"What do you mean like Sam? Is he also a transformed dragon?"

"What, dragon? No, that's silly. Sam's the last of her kind. We haven't seen others for quite some time. The other dragons are in hiding somewhere. No, Gervon's the last of his kind."

"What kind is that?"

"He is the last of the Giant Royal line."

"So, that's why his words hold such authority. What's the deal with Donella?"

"Donella's also a mystery. Gervon's last of the royal line, yes, but there're still giants. Donella's both giant and elf. You see her father was a giant, Gervon's brother, but her mother was an elf. She leads the warrior clan."

"Does she ever smile?"

"Never." Crystal chuckled. "She's focused on her end goal, and I'm not always clear what that is."

"That's good, but I can't do any of that. Maybe Bobbie's right. Why am I even here? I can't do anything right." Senora sighed.

"That's a lie. You, you hold the words of the Saviour. That's your strength." Crystal declared. "Don't be deceived. There's great power in words."

"The battle will be loud. How'll they hear?" Senora asked.

"The Fiery Crossroads connects worlds. When you speak there, your word will be carried as far as the east is from the west. The Saviour is with you," Crystal declared.

"She's right. It's your courage and your boldness that has brought me here," Chester replied, sending both girls jumping.

"What do you mean by my courage? I'm not courageous at all," Senora claimed.

Chester chuckled nervously like a hyena. "Lies and deception. You braved entering the Shadow Dominion, knowing full well it could destroy you. Your light shines through their darkness. I'm already doomed. My days are numbered, I'm a Misfit Shadow Knight, but I've seen that darkness is forced to flee in the presence of light. I know not of any Saviour, but I know that Lord Lucas wants to rule over the ultimate Creator. Envy drives him, but he knows the ultimate end will be his defeat. I made the wrong choice: once and was cast out. I chose to follow Lord Lucas when he fell from the Heavenly Realms. He promised power and wisdom. He's a great deceiver. I made my choice now I have to live with that. My end will be doing the right thing. You showed me that," Chester said. "Fear is what keeps me going. That's why I have you around. Fear of going against both Lord Lucas and Master Dravyon. It's terrifying." He bowed and stared at Senora. "A word of advice?"

"What's that?" Senora asked.

"The next time a stranger talks to you when you're alone, just look at them shocked and whisper, 'You can see me?' Trust me gets them every time," Chester replied with a wink as he slunk away.

"Um, what do I say to that? He's a strange one, that's for sure," Senora said.

"Never mind him. You need to focus now. See, the Saviour brings truth and life through you. Jesus's sacrifice gave you life abundantly and a boldness to tell others. Never lose that, Nora," Crystal warned.

"How do you know that the battle will be at the Fiery Crosswords?" Senora asked.

"Lucas's forces are gathering there. The gate will be opened for a short time. This only happens when the stars align. That's when your world will become more vulnerable. We'll be all that stands in the way." Crystal reached for a quiver of arrows and a bow. "I should do some training myself." Crystal nodded and headed to the targeting range where Robert was still shooting.

Robert paused to watch Crystal as she reached in her quiver for an arrow. She aimed her bow and released it. Direct hit in the middle. "Beginners luck," Robert mocked. Crystal pulled another arrow out, aimed and shot, splitting the first arrow in two, directly in the center. Crystal turned and smiled at Robert. He blushed and nervously ran his fingers through his hair. "Ok, you're good."

"I've been holding a bow since before I could walk. Mother's rules were to always be training and prepared for anything. Kat and I can hit a target every time. Mother raised us to be strong. We trained every waking second of the day. The only times we had downtime was on our weekly outing with Princess Delores. Even when Lucas took us captive, Kat was training mentally, always trying to think up a new way of escape. That's why Lucas moved us around the castle so often. He kept us guessing on our location and destination constantly. Kat's the strong one: she's far more mature than I'll ever be. We may be twins, but Kat was born first. She surpassed me in many ways. She even holds leadership when it comes to martial arts fighting. No one can combat her, not even an adult," Crystal said, "Kat's thoughts of escape always held a full plan, whereas my idea of escape was to make as much noise as I could in hopes someone would find us. Like Nora and Jo did. I find archery is mine and Kat's greatest competition." Crystal inspected the target Robert had been shooting at. Her eyes widened in shock as the center of the target was gone. Every shot had been on target, both short-range and long-range. "How did you learn to shoot like that?"

"I guess that was one thing I learned from my dad prob-ably the only thing." Robert placed his rifle down and kicked some dirt off his shoe.

Senora approached Robert.

"Bobbie, are you alright? Can we talk, please?"

"I don't know why you're still here. I can't protect you here," Robert snapped. *I fear for Nora's life. What can I say or do to convince her to leave? War's no place for her; she's just too soft.*

"I don't need your protection; I've just as much right to be here as you do. But the battle belongs to the Saviour. I was brought here for a reason."

"I admit you do have some skill."

"God has a plan for you. Some things you can hold onto are…You're never alone; when the enemy reminds you of your past mistakes, remind him of his future. He has already lost; the Saviour has paid the cost for your sin. For to pay for sin only death will suffice, Christ's death on the cross paid that price. So, he has already lost. He's just trying his hardest to bring down as many to his prison with him as he can. Stand firm and hold to the truth."

"I understand. It has taken me a long time, but I finally understand that God's healing love and power are stronger than holding onto pain, hatred, and unforgiveness. Nora, I've found a way to forgive my dad for what he has done to both my mom and I."

Senora hugged Robert despite herself. She quickly pulled away and tried to compose herself.

"That's such a blessing, Bobbie."

"Is that all you wanted to talk about? If so, I should get back to training."

"No, there's one more thing. It's the reason I came."

Ok, here it comes. Maybe this'll be something I can use to convince her to go, Robert pondered.

"What do you mean? You never told me how you got here. I don't even understand how I got here."

Senora touched Robert's scar on his arm, and he flinched and pulled away. "You see…" Senora pulled the eagle pendant out from under her shirt. "The pendant, I believe, acts as a gateway. But I don't know how it works exactly. But with you, it's different."

"Different? How?"

"You never left our world." Senora looked at the ground.

"What do you mean? I never left? I'm here, aren't I?"

"Yes, but you're there too. I don't understand it myself. But you sleep in a coma in our world."

Robert staggered backward at Senora's words, confusion boiling to the surface. "You lie. I don't know why you're trying to distract me just before battle, but I need to focus. Why don't you just leave me alone? I am willing to give you the benefit of a doubt. I only ask you to give me the same curtesy." Robert stormed back to where he left his rifle, grabbed another box of cartridges, and stomped back to the target range. *Why does she want to distract me? Does she see me as a failure too? I wish I knew how to tell her. I'm glad to see her, but I fear if she stays, I can't keep her safe. Maybe if I push her away, she'll leave. I just don't want her to get hurt. I need to focus and train. If I can't convince her to leave, it'll take all my strength to make sure nothing happens to her.*

"But," Senora said, hanging her head in discouragement, "if we all give into our fears and the lies, we have believed, then what's the point?"

"The LORD reigns, let the earth rejoice; let the many coastlands be glad! Clouds and thick darkness are all around him; righteousness and justice are the foundation of his throne. Fire goes before him and burns up his adversaries all around. His lightning light up the world; the earth sees and trembles. The mountains melt like wax before the LORD, before the Lord of all the earth. The heavens proclaim his righteousness, and all the peoples see his glory," The Tall Bearded Man said from behind Senora.[7] She jumped.

"Give me wisdom now. What should I do?" Senora asked.

"Pray. 'Yet regard to the prayer of your servant and to his plea, O LORD my God, listening to the cry and the prayer that your servant prays before you this day, that your eyes may be open night and day toward this house, the places of which you have said, 'My name shall be there,' that you may listen to the prayer that your servant offers toward this place. [8]The Saviour is with you. You hold all that you need. Stand where it has already burnt, and be refined in the truth. Trust in Him, and He'll guide you." The Man disappeared just as quickly as he appeared. Senora was left pondering this truth in her heart.

She looked over her shoulder toward Robert as he aimed at the target once again. "Lord, please protect Bobbie, unify this mismatched group, strengthen our faith, and go with us, in Jesus name, amen." Senora's prayer seemed to hang in the air as she was filled with courage and hope, moving her to action.

18

TWO WORLDS COLLIDE

Senora turned on her heel and stomped into the castle, up the winding staircase, and straight into Sam's room. Sam jumped as the door opened behind her with a bang. She turned from the window to see Senora standing there. "Nora? You scared me. What's troubling you?"

"Bobbie. What happened to you two in the Shadow Dominion? His anger seemed to be even more heightened than normal." Senora said.

Sam stared out the window again, lost in thought as she looked down toward Robert. "I'm not sure what they did to Bobbie, but I could share that while I was there, it was horrible. Drayvon had a way of bringing your worst internal fears to the surface and igniting them with fire." Sam staggered. Senora ran to her to stop her from falling, guiding her back to the bed. Once Sam safely lay down again, she continued. "You see, he uses old memories, ones that you might have blocked out or buried from long ago. He filled those memories with lies in a way that they appeared as truth. He showed me my mother."

Sitting on the side of the bed, Senora asked, "Your mother? Who's she?"

Glancing at Senora and quickly back at the window, she said. "She was kind, strong, and brave. Oh Nora, she gave her life to protect me."

Placing her arm around Sam's shoulders, she turned her ear to listen. "Protect you from what?"

"The Silver Dragon. He also showed me my real name. It is all my fault." Staggering to her feet, she cradled her head in frustration.

Standing in shock, she reached to steady Sam. "What's your fault?"

"My mother died because of me. Drayvon did something to me. I can't access my dragon self anymore." Sam stared toward the window.

"That's a lie, Sam. Listen to me." Senora turned her to face toward her and shook her shoulders. "God has 'made *you* a little lower than the heavenly beings and crowned *you* with glory and honor.'[1] So, if you were worthless why would God say, 'greater love has no one than this, that one lay down his life for his friends, or that 'God demonstrated His own love toward us, in that while we were yet sinners, Christ died for us.[2] So, you're loved, you have value, and Christ has chosen you. You need to rebuke these lies that Drayvon has filled in your head and used to cloud your mind." She stomped her foot to make her point.

Sam hung her head, "You're right, Nora. The scars are deep. The lies are embedded in my wounds, but I know that truth is stronger. Bobbie holds great bitterness. His wounds seem unending. I've seen his forgiving heart, but I've seen what torments him just under the surface too. He passed the test, but Lucas is the Father of Lies. How do you know he has not succumbed to his deceptions?" Sam looked up with such burning conviction.

"Look inside your heart. What do you see when you look at Bobbie?" Senora closed her eyes and whispered, "I know the trauma and the turmoil he battles daily, but I also know

God has chosen him." Opening her eyes, she looked intently at Sam. "He longed to understand God's love, but after knowing such torture all his life, he has a hard time believing he's loved. Sometimes, he runs from love."

Turning away, Sam fell back on the bed, she took a deep breath and sighed. "I understand. When you love someone you make yourself vulnerable. In times of war, vulnerability is dangerous."

Pinning her hands behind her head, she paced around the room. "That's just it. When you embrace love and open your heart and mind to understand what true love really is, nothing else matters." Allowing her hands to fall at her sides, she smiled. "You may feel vulnerable, but in that vulnerability, God's strength ignites. Sam, Bobbie's the strongest person I know. Don't give up on him yet."

Sitting up and crossing her legs on the bed, she rolled her eyes and giggled. "I couldn't give up on him, even if I tried." Fiddling with the corner of the blanket, she looked up at Senora. "I don't understand him, but I feel connected to him somehow. I'm sorry, I won't be well enough to go into battle with you this time. But my prayers go with you. I know the Saviour is with you."

Senora hugged Sam and left the room without saying a word as she heard the battle trumpet sound. Sam carefully stared out the window to see Senora run out into the court-yard. She watched as Robert strapped a belt full of bullet casings around his waist and slung the rifle strap over his shoulder. Senora ran up to Katerina and Crystal, and they helped her mount a tall brown horse. Katerina mounted her large black horse and led the way through the main gate. Robert fell in line with some of the Grassland people, followed by a mix of different creatures that scratched and pawed the ground. At the rear, Donella and her giant-like people stomped up the dirt around their feet. Just before the last of the giants left the castle, Donella looked up toward Sam and smirked. *What was that all about?* Sam shook in confusion. Once the last of the group left, Sam shivered at the silence that fell upon her.

—◦◦◦—

*R*obert's eyes widened as a large pillar of fire came into sight. Seeing his surprise Crystal rode up beside him. "This is the center pillar. It has begun, and the crossroads have already been lit. The Fiery Crossroads are there." Crystal pointed toward the pillar of fire. The ground beneath them started to shake. The horses' reared up and started to pace in fear. Katerina, Crystal, Senora, and others quickly dismounted their horses as the horses ran away.

"Now what?" Senora asked.

"We're close. Lucas knows we're here," Crystal proclaimed. Soon, Crystal's words were drowned out by the thunderous laughter and snarls as waves of shadows appeared beyond the fiery pillar. Senora looked around at each one in their group. Some were already wide-eyed with fear, and others focused on destruction. Chester and his Misfits slunk out of sight. Suddenly, everything went deathly silent. Senora held her breath and wished for the ground to swallow her up. Robert ran to the highest viewpoint he could find and dove on the ground. He braced himself as he looked through his scope. The silence became maddening. Almost in unison, the masses of shadows built in a thunderous cry.

Katerina armed her bow and aimed at the closest shadow. "Stand ready. Make them act first."

Within half a breath, the Shadows fell like waves upon the fearful army. Robert watched the scene play out as he scanned the horde of colliding creatures and people. He saw Senora. Four Shadow Knights surrounded her. He took aim, shooting each one as they came close to her. Senora looked in the direction of Robert and nodded. She grabbed a sword and swung at a nearby Shadow. The Shadow dodged, and something cut into her left hip. She screamed and fell forward as Robert shot again. The Shadow landed on Senora's back.

Robert panned the masses and saw Katerina as she and Crystal stood back-to-back, shooting down any Shadow that came close, one arrow at a time. He soon caught a glimpse of Drayvon and Lucas standing at the back of the Shadows. Drayvon sent orders to each Shadow in unison. Robert took aim, but Lucas hid behind a tree branch. He turned his focus toward Drayvon. The Misfits came closer to Drayvon from behind. Chester lunged first, but Drayvon spun and caught him mid-air by the throat. He shrieked as the rest of the Misfits scattered in fright. "You betray me?" Drayvon threatened.

"I learn from the best. I may be a Misfit, but I die doing what's right. My level of sarcasm has gotten to the point where I don't even know if I'm kidding or not," Chester claimed, gasping for breath.

Drayvon pulled Chester close and said, "Doing what's right? You're damned and will always belong to me." Chester gasped for breath as Drayvon threw him against a large stone. Robert armed his rifle and took aim. Drayvon looked straight at him. He sent waves of pictures flashing before Robert's mind: his dad on the prison cell floor, lying lifeless, Trevor lying at the bottom of his basement stairs in a pool of blood; his mom crying in a hospital waiting room. Robert closed his eyes and hesitated for a split second. When he opened his eyes again, Drayvon and Lucas had disappeared. He quickly panned the wave of chaos below and saw Crystal push the lifeless shadow creature off Senora.

———⁓∿∾⁓———

*S*am stared out the castle window, scanning the horizon. She looked down at the red gem in her hand. *What do I do with this?*

Soon the Tall Bearded Man appeared behind her, "There are two halves of one whole," the Man proclaimed.

Sam turned to face him. "I don't understand. Michael, is that you?"

"I'm only in the image of Michael. I'm here to remind you of the truth and of who you are. When you find your other half, you're bound together for life. You're complete and whole."

"But I feel so broken. What truth are you here to remind me of, and who do you think I am?"

"You're chosen, forgiven, loved, and adopted. Know the truth, and the truth will set you free."

"You speak in riddles. I've lost everyone I've ever cared about."

"Not everyone."

"Who do you speak of?"

"In time, you'll understand. For now, 'Trust in the LORD with all your heart and lean not on your own understanding; in all your ways submit to him, and he'll make your path straight.'[3] Sam looked back toward the empty horizon.

——⟨∅∅⟩——

"*F*ollow me," Crystal ordered Senora as the two girls ran toward the pillar of fire. "Use your strength. Speak the Saviour's truth." Three Shadow Knights surrounded them. Shots sent each one falling to the ground.

Senora wavered with crippling fear as the chaos unfolded around her. *God, please give me the words. I need you now,* she prayed. *Stand where it is already burnt, face your fears, and refine your courage.*

A faint whisper almost carried on the wind surrounded Senora. "Remember my affliction and my wanderings, the wormwood and the gall! My soul continually remembers it and is bowed down within me. But this I call to mind, and therefore I have hope."[4]

The Shadow Knights turned their attention like a flood toward Crystal and Senora.

"Don't stop; don't allow them to silence you," Crystal said as she aimed her bow and shot arrow after arrow, sending each Shadow Knight falling at her feet.

Senora looked around at the sea of Shadow Knights converging on them. She felt like they were surrounded in a sheet of darkness. The Pillar of Fire at her back, illuminated her surroundings. "Taste and see that the LORD is good; blessed is the one who takes refuge in Him."[5] Senora declared boldly. The Shadow Knights shrunk back and moved around to the other side of the two. Crystal continued to aim and shoot her arrows. Robert continued to pick off the Shadow Knights from behind. Soon, Katerina pushed her way through the knights, grabbed a nearby sword and sliced a knight in the side as she stood firmly on the other side of Senora.

"A friend loves at all times, and a brother is born for a time of adversity."[6] Katerina swung again, knocking another knight to the ground.

"For I am convinced that neither death nor life, neither angels nor demons, neither the present nor the future, nor any powers, neither height nor depth, nor anything else in all creation, will be able to separate us from God that is in Christ Jesus our Lord."[7] Senora declared as five Shadow Knights stormed against Katerina. She swung her sword knocking two knights to the ground, but they dodged around her.

"Hey, why not take me on?" The two knights turned abruptly toward Gervon. Each leaped in unison. Gervon nodded at Katerina as he punched the two knights to the ground. One of the knights rolled and dug his claws into Gervon's left heel. Gervon kicked the knight away and grabbed the second knight by the scruff of the neck. Katerina nodded toward Gervon and stabbed her sword into another knight at her right.

Ten knights surrounded Gervon. He adjusted his stance and beckoned them to challenge him. The knights stood frozen for a split second. "Stand true to yourselves. A day may come when darkness prevails, but today we are united. Stand firm, stay true, and hold nothing back," Gervon commanded. Soon the ground quivered and broke apart beneath the Shadow Knight's feet. They struggled to stand. Senora watched as Muddling's jumped out of the ground pulling knights into the deep. Three Elf-like men leaped off the mountainside and landed firmly by Gervon's side.

"We're with you, Sir Gervon," an elf declared. Gervon nodded and swiftly spun and swung his sword at a Shadow Knight behind him. Then, he spun around again and dove under another knight raising his sword up and cutting the inside of his leg. The knight fell. Gervon leapt up and stepped toward Crystal and Senora, using each Knight's head to guide his next step forward. Right before Gervon reached the girls, a Shadow Knight came up behind Crystal. It raised its claws to penetrate her back, when a knife flew past Gervon's ear and plunged into the knight's eyes. Crystal turned and kicked the knight away from the pillar. Gervon turned to see who threw the knife. A skinny, spiky creature waved a handful of knives his way, nodded, and threw five more knives, each one hitting their intended marks. Katerina shoved another knight away from Senora, spun and sliced another one's head off. Then she kicked a third to the ground, and moved her sword upward slicing off another one's arm. Katerina turned when Drayvon stepped in front of her. He ripped the sword from her fingers and slammed his head into her forehead. She staggered backward. Robert aimed his rifle and focused on Dravyon's face. Crystal leapt to her feet, spun, and kicked Drayvon in the stomach. He bent over, clutched his stomach, and reached for Katerina's hair. He pulled her up by the hair as she kicked and screamed. He drew her close to his mouth.

"Have you ever heard of a shower? You stink!" Katerina gasped and coughed as Drayvon turned and reached for Senora. Robert fired. Drayvon fell to one knee as the bullet penetrated his hand. Still holding Katerina, he turned to put Katerina between Robert and himself, using her as a human shield.

"I can't get a shot!" Robert screamed.

A voice reached his ears, "Judge not, that you be not judged."[8] Robert's thoughts began to race, and he struggled to focus.

"Not now!" He stood and slid down the hill to get a different angle.

"Let her go!" Senora demanded as she kicked the back of Drayvon's knee. Drayvon turned and hit Katerina's body into Senora, rose to his feet with Katerina still firm in his grasp, madly kicking at his side. Crystal ran along the Pillar of Fire, and kicked Drayvon in the face. As he stumbled, Katerina pulled free. Gervon leapt off a rock platform and rammed his knee into Drayvon's back. He stumbled forward and growled. Katerina kicked his side again, Gervon punched Drayvon's back, and Senora stood frozen, unwilling to step aside.

"We got this," Katerina said. Gervon caught sight of Lucas. "Go after him." Gervon lunged toward Lucas. Drayvon grabbed Katerina by the back of her neck and held her up. Katerina kicked her foot downward toward Drayvon's knee, shattering his kneecap and falling to the ground. She bent back as a claw flew by her face. Flashes of Senora lying in a sea of fire and smoke invaded her thoughts. Katerina shifted her feet as a wave of guilt stabbed at her heart.

Drayvon spun and leaned close to her ear. "Remember

your betrayal?" Katerina saw that young soldier's last breath as his hand went limp in her arms. She fell to her knees.

"Make it stop!" Katerina screamed.

"For the word of God is alive and active. Sharper than any double-edged sword, it penetrates even to dividing soul and spirit, joints and marrow; it judges the thoughts and attitudes of the heart."[9] Senora's words reached Katerina's ears. As Drayvon raised his hand to sink his claws into her back, she raised her sword and stabbed his arm. He screamed in pain and kicked Katerina over. Drayvon stumbled backward as Crystal jumped between Katerina and Drayvon. In an effort to eliminate his enemies he lunged forward, embedding his sharp claws into Crystal's chest. He raised Crystal above his head and tossed her like a rag doll into Katerina, knocking both girls to the ground.

Senora tried to run to Katerina, but she froze in place when she heard Crystal whisper softly. "If you move, all is lost. You can't leave the gate unguarded."

"What gate? I don't understand." Senora looked in horror as three knights drew near to her. Crystal desperately shot one knight with her arrow, and she reached for another. A knight scratched Senora's left arm, and she stumbled to one knee. Looking up, she expected the worst when a bullet penetrated both knights, and they fell.

"You must stand firm," Crystal ordered. Hearing Crystal's words, Senora found the strength to rise.

"For God alone my soul waits in silence; from him comes my salvation."[10] Senora gasped as she pulled herself up on one knee. Drayven turned his full attention on Senora. "He alone is my rock and my salvation, my fortress."[11] She pulled herself up and stared confidently in Drayven's eyes. Drayvan staggered and slunk away slightly, feeling disoriented. "I SHALL NOT BE SHAKEN!" she yelled.[12]

—⚬⚬⚬—

*R*obert shot and reloaded as quickly as he could as one by one, the Shadow Knights fell at Senora's feet. He scanned the sea of Shadows below and paused when he caught sight of Drayvon getting closer to Senora once again. He took aim and fired. To his surprise, the Shadow Knights scattered in confusion as Drayvon fell. He panned the chaos to look for Lucas. He saw Lucas briefly before he disappeared in the sea of shadows. Panic filled him as he saw Lucas again even closer to the Fiery Crossroads. He aimed, but Lucas avoided his sights again. The next time Lucas came into view, he appeared from behind Senora. He aimed but before he could shoot, Lucas pulled Senora around in front of him. Katerina searched the ground for a weapon, grabbing a sword she turned to face Lucas. "It's over. You've lost," Katerina declared. "Let her go."

"Look around you, Kat. You tell me who has lost," Lucas replied. Robert observed the horrible scene before him; a mix of dead bodies both Shadow and other. Only a few were left standing.

"Kat, look at me. If he reminds you of your past, just remind him of his future;" Senora said as she stomped on Lucas's foot and elbowed him in the side. He staggered back, and Robert re-adjusted his aim. He shot. But when Senora turned to see, Lucas had left. "Where did he go?"

"I don't know. Stay on your guard. He could be hiding somewhere," Katerina declared. Robert searched the sea of bodies for movement. He saw only a few random soldiers stand and move toward Katerina and Senora. The rest of the Shadow Knights retreated. Chester opened his eyes and staggered toward Senora.

"The battle's over for now. But the war's far from done. Sorry I was not more help," Chester stated.

"Yeah, what were you doing?" Katerina teased.

"I guess I took a much-needed nap," Chester said, laughing nervously.

Robert stood and slung his rifle over his shoulder. "Did we win?" Robert asked. Katerina and Senora looked around for any sign of Lucas. Robert turned toward a grassy ridge to make his way to Senora, losing sight of them for a short time. A tree branch hit his face. He staggered and touched his nose, feeling the blood oozing. As his eyes adjusted, Donella came into view. "Donella? What're you doing?"

"You think you have won?"

"Wait! But you were fighting with us."

"That's what I wanted you to believe. You know as well as I do, Lucas holds the true power." Donella tossed the tree branch aside. "Join us. I know your greatest strength is your anger. I can help you get revenge."

"Donella, have you lost your mind? Lucas is deceiving you with his lies." He knelt as Donella swung her leg at his face.

"If you won't join us, I know someone who will." Donella smirked. Robert looked up in surprise. He swung his fists, connecting to her left shoulder. She jumped up and, kicked him in the stomach, knocking the wind out of him. As he fell to his knees, Donella grabbed him by the scruff of his shirt, lifted him up off the ground and pulled him close. "I release you. There's no more protection for you or your family."

"Wait! What does my family have to do with this?"

"Just know this: you may think you have won, but Lucas is still out there." Donella spun in a circle and released Robert. She sent him flying into the rock face, all went black, and he fell to the ground. Donella dragged him over to a bush and tossed his rifle out of sight. Leaning over Robert, she whispered in his ear, "Tony will be an easier target. Nothing will get in my way." She stood and quickly found a horse, turned, and rode away, returning to Castle Calvarias.

Katerina spun around with her sword in hand, but she couldn't see any movement. Soon, she lowered her sword and ran to her sister's side. "Crystal, stay with me." Crystal screamed in pain as Katerina pushed hard on her sister's wound. "You just have to be ok."

"Kat, I can't feel my legs." Tears streamed down Katerina's cheeks."

"Crystal, you are strong. We are together. Together we can get through anything. Remember?"

"We had a good run. But I have nothing left. Stay strong. I'll always be with you. You're never alone. Mom and Delores are calling me home. Kat, you still have things to do. We will be together again." Crystal gasped as she breathed her last.

"I'm sorry, Kat. She was a strong girl," Senora said.

A wave of uncontrollable tears soaked the ground. Katerina gasped for breath as a lump formed in her throat. Drawing Crystal's lifeless body close to her own, she whispered, "Bring her back."

"What? I can't." Senora fell to her knees with a blank stare, searching her thoughts for words to comfort her.

"Bring her back!" Katerina shrieked.

"How?" Tears stung Senora's eyes as she allowed them to flow freely down her cheeks.

Katerina gently lay her sister on the ground, stood, spun around abruptly, and aimed her sword at Senora. Anger flared in her eyes, as she screamed, "BRING HER BACK! USE THE PENDANT! LIKE YOU BROUGHT HER BACK BEFORE."

Sonora rose her hands in defeat. "It doesn't work that way. She's gone. I'm sorry." Senora cautiously approached Katerina. She stood just inches from Katerina's sword and looked into her eyes. Katerina lowered her sword and fell to her knees as if she were punched by a wave of despair. "I know. She always said I was the strong one. But she didn't fall prey to Lucas's deception. That was me. What am I going to do, Nora?" Katerina asked.

Senora knelt beside Katerina and embraced her. "I know

251

it hurts." Katerina punched the ground, surrounding them in a cloud of dust.

"I can't leave her!" Katerina yelled.

"Here, let me help you," Senora whispered. Soldiers approached the two girls with cloth and rope. Senora watched as one soldier carefully wrapped Crystal's body, while others made a pull cart so they could lie her body upon it.

"We'll take turns pulling. Lady Crystal won't be abandoned. I promise you, my lady," one soldier said.

Katerina peered through the strands of Senora's hair at the soldier. "Thank you, Allistair." She gave Senora a tight squeeze before standing.

"We need to regroup. Lucas is still out there," Senora declared.

"You need to protect your world as I need to protect mine. This Crossroad will bring you and Bobbie home," Katerina revealed as she motioned for Robert to come down to them. "Wait. Where's Bobbie?"

"I-I don't know. He was just here. Bobbie?" Senora yelled over the masses.

"Time's running out. I'll look for him, but you need to go through while the gate's still open," Katerina declared. "This is the gateway that bridges worlds. You need to step through the Pillar of Fire. Don't be concerned. The fire doesn't burn. It cleanses and purifies," Katerina declared. "I know I'll see you again." Katerina shook Senora's hand.

"Thanks, but I can't leave without Bobbie," Senora stated.

———⟨ฅ/ฅ/ฅ⟩———

*S*am looked down as Donella rode into the courtyard. A small group of guards met her as she dismounted. "Secure my horse. I won't be here long," Donella ordered as she ran up the stairs to Sam's room.

She jumped as the door banged open. "Donella? Did you

flee the battle? What has happened? Report on the progress of the battle. Where are Lady Kat, Lady Crystal, and Nora? What has happened to Bobbie?" She staggered as she felt her lungs burn as if a sledgehammer had just slammed into her. A lump formed in her throat as her thoughts wandered.

Donella approached Sam. "Lady Kat has fallen. Soon, all of Scarlett's reign will fall."

"What? What do you mean? Scarlett's reign will fall? Tell me what happened."

"Annihilation's at hand. The destruction of two worlds collide." Donella moved toward Sam and pulled out a small knife. Sam's thoughts turned to Robert and Senora. She looked up as Donella swung the knife at her chest. Sam's hair glowed crimson, her eyes igniting with fire. Donella wasted no time. "Just as Lady Crystal fell, Kat will find her end, and you'll fall too." She kicked Sam in the chest, knocking the wind out of her. Sam leaned against the windowsill.

Thoughts of Robert raced through her mind, and she looked down at the red gem as it glowed and ignited the room in a blinding red light.

Donella lunged toward her, determined to fulfill her mission. Sam looked straight into her eyes as the knife appeared to penetrate her heart. The red gem expanded energy from within, sending Donella flying backward and crashing into the wall. Sam struggled to maintain her balance as Donella leapt to her feet once more.

"I won't be defeated that easily. You've no idea what you hold. It'll be mine, and Lord Lucas will finally have his victory." Donella ran at Sam.

"You don't know my strength," Sam said.

"Your thoughts are divided. They betray you. He'll fall forever."

Sam worried for Robert and Senora. With one last blast of red light, Donella vanished, and Sam fell to the floor, the red gem slipping from her hand and rolling under the bed. *No matter how far apart you are, your lives and hearts are intertwined.*

—◦◦◦—

A wave of sorrow washed over Robert as his eyes re-adjusted to the leaves hanging above him. He turned and stared toward Castle Calvarias. "Something's wrong." Robert's thoughts turned to Sam as he crawled out from under the branches. The ground spun as he fell to one side. He reached for his ear as it pounded in agony. He looked down as his hand lowered from his ear, a pool of blood forming. He turned to his right when he heard footsteps quickly approaching. He rolled to his feet and saw Lucas standing in front of him. "Face it, Lucas. You have lost," Robert warned.

Lucas punched Robert in the stomach. Robert spit out blood. Lucas raised his knee to connect with Robert's bloody nose, but Robert pushed his back. Lucas staggered to get his footing again and said, "You understand pain. You said yourself, how could someone let pain happen to their own child? Tony is not worth your time."

"You leave my dad out of this. Your fight is with me."

"Fight? No, your fight is over. Mine has just begun. You have only scratched the surface of what I can really do."

"For your obedience is known to all, so that I rejoice over you, but I want you to be wise as to what is good and innocent as to what is evil."[13] The Tall Bearded Man's voice whispered in Robert's ear. Filling with courage and a new understanding Robert boldly stood in front of Lucas.

Lucas rushed toward him and pulled him close. "Remember, I have spies everywhere. You will not defeat me."

Robert locked eyes with Lucas full of determination and conviction. He boldly stated, "The God of peace will soon crush Satan under your feet. The grace of our Lord Jesus Christ be with you."[14]

Lucas smashed his head into Robert's forehead as his world fell into darkness once more. "We will see who gets crushed." Lucas turned and disappeared into the valley below.

Suddenly, Senora was pulled into the Fiery Pillar and disappeared. Katerina spun around in search of Robert. *I won't let Nora and Bobbie down. I know I'm not Crystal, but they're counting on me. Now their world's in as much danger as mine.* Katerina searched the sea of bodies for any sign of Robert.

———

*S*enora opened her eyes to find herself lying on the floor in the hospital chapel. She stood and looked around. "Bobbie," She called as she ran to Robert's hospital room. She slowed her steps as she walked up to his bedside. "Bobbie?"

Robert's mom looked up at Senora with sadness in her eyes, and said, "Sorry, Nora, no change."

"No! That can't be! He has to wake up, Sarah! We've fought so hard! He has fought so hard!" Senora screamed.

Sarah stood and pulled Senora out of Robert's room. "What're you talking about?"

"He just has to wake up!"

"I'm sorry, young lady, but I have to ask you to leave. You're disturbing the other patients," a tall nurse said as she approached Senora from behind.

———

*A*s Robert lays in darkness, he could barely make out Senora's voice, "He just has to wake up!"

Tony will be an easier targe..."What did Donella mean? Lucas and Donella can't win. I can't protect them. Oh, please, God, show me the way. You're the great protector. You can do this better than me. You hold all authority. Show me where to stand." *But you sleep in a coma in our world.* Senora's words flooded his mind.

"Stand where it has already been burnt." Robert heard the Man's voice at a distance.

—◦◦◦—

"She's right, Nora. You're hysterical and making no sense. This isn't helping Bobbie," Sarah stated with concern in her voice.

"But you don't understand!" Senora ordered.

"You're right, I don't understand. Just leave," Sarah ordered as she folded her arms in front of her and impatiently tapped her foot on the floor. Senora hung her head as the tall nurse led Sarah back to Robert's room.

"I'm sorry, nurse. I don't know what has gotten into her," Sarah replied as she stared over her shoulder at Senora. The nurse turned to stare at Robert. His eye lids fluttered, and the nurse frowned and walked over to his IV. Adjusting his vision, he suddenly spoke, "Mom?" Sarah turned when she heard Robert's voice. She ran to Robert's bed and held his hand. Robert turned his eyes to look at his mom.

"Bobbie! Oh, thank God. You are awake."

"Mom, can you…" His eyes rolled back and his eye lids fluttered. The nurse adjusted the IV drip more.

"Bobbie, can I what? Bobbie, speak to me. I am here!" Sarah screamed.

"I need to talk to dad." Robert whispered.

"He's here! Just out in the waiting area. Stay with me, I will call him." Sarah quickly hugged Robert and dashed out of the room. The nurse raised the IV drip yet again when Robert locked eyes with her. "Wait, Don"

"Shhhhhh." The nurse smirked. She leaned close to his bed briefly, "He will win. Tony's an easier target." The nurse stood right before, Tony and Sarah entered Robert's room.

The code blue alarms sounded and Robert started to convulse. Senora rushed to the door as doctors pushed Sarah and Tony out of the door. The tall nurse closed the door behind them, and Senora looked up. The nurse glared at her, followed by a strange smirk. *Wait, there's something strangely familiar about that nurse.*

———

*A*s the sun set upon the gruesome sight, Katerina found a lonely horse walking the perimeter of the battle-field. She desperately reached for its reigns and led the horse over to the soldiers dragging the makeshift cart that held Crystal's body. Without saying a word, she attached the handles of the cart to the back of the horse and mounted. "I will be the one to bring my sister home." Katerina tried desperately to push her anger, sadness, and fears down. *I will be strong. For Mother and Crystal,* she reminded herself as she briefly looked over her shoulder at Crystal's body. She squared her shoulders. Before leaving, she panned the sea of bodies one last time. "It's getting dark harder to see. I must return to Castle Calvarias for now, but I won't give up my search for you, Bobbie. I'll find you! I promise!" Katerina shouted as she returned home with her sister in tow, Chester, some staggering Misfits, and the rest of the surviving soldiers.

Katerina arrived, dismounted her horse in the courtyard, handed the reins to a stable boy, and turned to look one last time at her sister. "Take care of this horse and prepare my sister's body. I need to commune with Sam." Katerina raced up the stairs. When she entered Sam's room, she found her unconscious on the floor. She ordered a guard to place her in the bed. "Lucas's still out there, somewhere." She looked around Sam's room at the overturned nightstand, the night candle broken in two, and a large crack in the wall next to the door. "What happened here?" Katerina asked as she held

Sam's hand. "It looks like you had a battle of your own. I won't stop my search for answers until I've woken Sam and understand what happened to Bobbie." As Katerina stood, Chester entered the room. He stood next to her and placed his wounded hand on her shoulder.

"You defeated the Master. Only time will tell. Rest now; fight later." Chester chuckled.

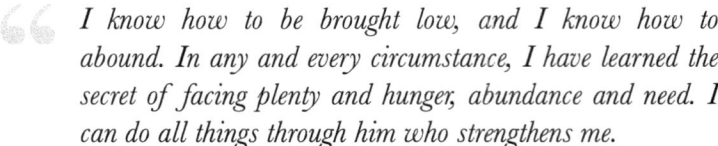

I know how to be brought low, and I know how to abound. In any and every circumstance, I have learned the secret of facing plenty and hunger, abundance and need. I can do all things through him who strengthens me.

— *Phil. 4:12–13*

NOTES

1. Deception Arises

1. Sudfeld, Pastor Dan, *The Fellowship of the Saints,* Wetaskiwin Mission Church. January 5, 2020 http://wetaskiwinmissionchurch.org/media/494841-2004455-2290236/the-fellowship-of-the-saint.
2. Phil. 2:15b
3. Sudfeld, Pastor Dan, *The Fellowship of the Saints.*
4. Sudfeld, Pastor Dan, *The Fellowship of the Saints.*
5. Ibid
6. Ibid
7. Phil. 3:14

2. Divide and Conflict

1. Ezekiel 28:12
2. John 8:44b
3. John 8:44c
4. 2 Cor 4:4a
5. 2 Cor 11:14–15
6. 1 Peter 5:8–9
7. Eph 6:11–13

5. The Rescue

1. Proverbs 21:31
2. Phil. 4:13
3. Jer. 16:19a
4. 2 Cor. 1:9–10

7. Cave of Exploration

1. Gen 22:14
2. John 15:16
3. Eph. 4:32
4. Luke 7:47
5. Deut. 7:6

8. Broken Bonds

1. Deut. 32:39
2. Job 5:18
3. Ecc. 3:3
4. Mark 2:17

9. Sheol Mountain

1. Psalm 9:9
2. Rom. 8:37
3. Ezekiel 28:13
4. Ezekiel 28:14
5. Ezekiel 28:15
6. Ezekiel 28:17–18
7. Isaiah 14:12
8. Isaiah 14:12–14

10. Deception Ignited

1. Matt. 10:16
2. Matt. 26:41
3. John 8:31b–32
4. Job 34:12
5. Psalm 15:2, 5b
6. Prov. 21:31

11. Storms of Deceit

1. Exodus 15:2–3
2. Exodus 14:14
3. Heb. 13:8
4. James 4:12

12. Lost to Unforgiveness

1. Elbert Hubbard
2. Rev. 12:7a
3. Rev. 12:7b
4. Rev. 12:8–9
5. Rev. 12:12
6. Matt. 24:22
7. George F. Will

8. 2 Peter 1:3–4
9. Luke 1:30b
10. John 1:12; Rom 5:1; Rom 8:1; 1 Cor. 2:16; 2 Cor. 5:21; Eph. 1:3
11. Psalm 103:13-14; 2 Cor. 4:7; Deut. 14:2
12. Jer. 31:3b
13. Eph. 1:4–5
14. Matt. 10:30–31
15. Mark 10:27
16. 2 Cor. 12:9
17. Is. 49:15–16; Matt. 28:20; Heb. 13:5
18. 1 John 3:1
19. John 1:12
20. Eph. 1:4–5
21. 1 John 5:4
22. 1 Cor. 15:57
23. Phil. 4:19
24. 1 Cor. 10:13
25. Heb. 4:15
26. Eph. 4:32
27. Eph 2:8–9
28. Phil. 1:6
29. John 15:16
30. Prov. 3:5–6
31. 1 Peter 5:7
32. Psalm 139:13
33. Psalm 139:15–17
34. Jer. 29:11–12

13. Forgotten Secrets Revealed

1. Ellen Degeneres
2. Yogi Berra
3. Rom. 8:26
4. 1Cor. 15:43b
5. Joel 3:9
6. Zach. 10:5
7. Rev. 16:16
8. Eph 6:10

14. The Called

1. Eph 4:26–28
2. Joel 2:21
3. Matt. 10:28
4. Heb. 13:6
5. Matt. 24:4–8

6. Eph. 4:31–32
7. Rom. 8:1–2
8. 1 John 1:9
9. Matt. 18:20
10. Prov. 3:5–6
11. 1 Tim. 4:12
12. Luke 1:37
13. Gen 50:20–21a
14. Prov. 3:5–6

15. Farewell

1. Psalm 23:4
2. John 5:24
3. Matt. 4:16
4. Rev. 14:13
5. Rom. 6:5
6. Psalm 107:13–14
7. Rom. 6:22–23
8. Luke 1:78–79
9. 1 Cor. 15:53–55

16. Greatest Strength

1. Is. 1:18
2. Psalm 103:12–13
3. Jer. 31:34
4. Matt. 26:28
5. Gal. 5:1
6. 2 Cor. 5:17
7. Psalm 18:39
8. Heather Congo
9. Theodore Roosevelt
10. Zemeckis, Robert, dir. *Forest Gump.* Hollywood, CA: Paramount Picture, 1994.
11. Marmon Okinyo, motivational speaker.
12. Nelson Mandela
13. Twain, Mark, *The tragedy of Puddi'nhead Wilson.* New York: Charles L. Webster & Company, 1894.
14. Nora Ephron

17. Crosswords of Fire

1. Isaiah 40:30–31
2. Prov 21:31
3. 2 Thess 3:3
4. Matthew 18:20
5. Isaiah 54:17
6. James 1:16
7. Psalm 97:1–6
8. 1 Kings 8:28–29

18. Two Worlds Collide

1. Psalm 8:5
2. John 15:13; Rom. 5:8
3. Prov. 3:5–6
4. Lam. 3:19–21
5. Psalm 34:8
6. Prov. 17:17
7. Rom 8:38–39
8. Matt 7:1
9. Heb. 4:12
10. Psalm 62:1
11. Psalm 62:2a
12. Psalm 62:2b
13. Rom. 16:19
14. Rom. 16:20

Are You Ready To Discover Your True Identity?

F.I.G.H.T.

40 Day Kingdom Identity Program

- FOCUS, You are not worthless
- IDENTIFY, You have a purpose
- GROWTH, You can FIGHT
- HONOR, For moving from feeling invisible to becoming inspirational
- TRIUMPH, Become a Kingdom Definer

https://www.authorloriegurnett.com/

Is Fear holding you in Bondage?

F.L.A.M.E

Fan The Flames & Snuff Out The Fear

- FEAR: Do you feel crippled by fear?
- LIES: Do lies invade your thoughts?
- ACTION: Take action, fight for yourself
- MAGNIFY: Magnify your strength
- ENCOURAGE: Encourage others to unity

https://www.authorloriegurnett.com/

ABOUT THE AUTHOR

Lorie Gurnett is an award-winning author, coach, and speaker who helps individuals and families move from feeling invisible to inspirational so they can overcome the lies and fears created by childhood trauma with the truth of who God created them to be.

As a young lady, Lorie doubted herself at every turn, and she felt invisible and worthless. She even contemplated suicide. Today with newfound knowledge, Lorie strives for the value of the human heart. She believes everyone has value, and nobody is invisible.

She is the founder of Kingdom Definers, which serves young adults who struggle with their identity and value. She and her husband, Merv, are blessed with two encouraging children and live in Wetaskiwin, Alberta, Canada.

Connect at authorloriegurnett.com.

facebook.com/Author-Lorie-Gurnett-100375455075312

instagram.com/authorloriegurnett

linkedin.com/in/lorie-gurnett-17aa0770

ALSO BY LORIE GURNETT

Treasure Kingdom

Lightning Source UK Ltd.
Milton Keynes UK
UKHW021857010321
379622UK00012B/1175/J